Born in Salford, DAVID CONSTANTINE has published several volumes of poetry, and two novels (most recently *The Life-Writer*) as well as four previous short story collections: *Back at the Spike* (1994), the highly acclaimed *Under the Dam* (2005), *The Shieling* (2009) and *Tea at the Midland* (2012), which won the Frank O'Connor International Short Story Award in 2013. David's story 'Tea at the Midland' won the 2010 BBC National Short Story Award, and his story 'In Another Country' was adapted into *45 Years* – an Oscar-nominated film, directed by Andrew Haigh and starring Tom Courtenay and Charlotte Rampling. With his wife Helen, David edited *Modern Poetry in Translation* for many years. He is also translator of Hölderlin, Brecht, Goethe, Kleist, Michaux and Jaccottet. He lives in Oxford.

'*The Dressing-Up Box* does the deepest work of fiction – it tells us strange, hard, beautiful truths for our time. Constantine offers a quietly furious and moving collection packed with undefended children and lost adults, personalities grown eccentric under stress and raging for mercy. Nightmares shift, blood flows in rivers and humanity responds with strange mercy, humour and a desperate appetite for love.'
– A. L. Kennedy, author of *The Little Snake*

'Precise in their intensity, unsettling, suddenly and unexpectedly luminous, these stories will stay with you and unfurl within you.' – Lucy Caldwell, author of *Multitudes*

'David Constantine's fifth collection of stories is a fierce and tender meditation on our struggle to live – a lyrical and plainspoken portrait of humanity at its pernicious worst and its suffering, creative, resilient best.' – Carys Davies, author of *West*

'This fifth book of superb short fiction confirms an extraordinary talent' – *The Times*

'Inventive... incredibly moving' – *The Daily Mail*

'Subtlety marks every tale in this intelligent, unshowy and often moving collection.' - Ian Sansom, *The Guardian*

'Dramatic, daring and dark... There's enormous tension to the stories, but there is often a small but powerful moment of hope.' – Saturday Review, BBC Radio 4

'Profoundly a book for our time, full of despair, sorrow, terror, hope and tenderness... *The Dressing-Up Box* confirms what Constantine's readers have suspected for a long time: that he may be the greatest living English short story writer.' – Gregory Norminton, author of *The Devil's Highway*

'A beautifully crafted tender, evocative collection. Full of wisdom and light.' – Irenosen Okojie, author of *Speak Gigantular*

'David Constantine is fearless. His work is dark and daring while, at turns, also humorous and tender.' – Paul McVeigh, author of *The Good Son*

'One of the short story-writers who matter, poetic, passionate and humane.' – Maggie Gee, author of *The White Family*

'Constantine's writing is addictive. Every sentence is another shot of beauty, of mystery and mastery.' – Lara Pawson, author of *This is the Place to Be*

THE DRESSING-UP BOX

And Other Stories

DAVID CONSTANTINE

Also by the same author

First published in Great Britain in 2019 by Comma Press.
This edition published in 2020 by Comma Press.
www.commapress.co.uk

'The Diver'and 'bREcCiA' were first published in *The Reader* (67, 2017; and 70,
2018) 'Rivers of Blood' in *Protest* (Comma Press, 2017); 'La rue de la Vieille-
Lanterne' in *Paris Street Tales* (OUP, 2016); 'What we are now' by Guillemot Press/
The Word Factory (2018); 'Ashton and Elaine' in *The Red Room* (Unthank Books,
2013); and 'Autumn Ladies Tresses' was broadcast on BBC Radio 4,
4 November 2016.

A CIP catalogue record of this book is available from the British Library.

ISBN-10 1912697300
ISBN-13 9781912697304

The publisher gratefully acknowledges the support of Arts Council England

Supported by
**ARTS COUNCIL
ENGLAND**

Printed and bound in England by Clays Ltd, Elcograf S.p.A

For the children and their children, in hope…

Contents

The Dressing-Up Box   1
Midwinter Reading   29
Siding with the Weeds   35
The Diver   49
Rivers of Blood   55
Seeking Refuge   69
bREcCiA   75
Autumn Lady's Tresses   99
When I Was a Child   107
A Retired Librarian   137
Rue de la Vieille-Lanterne   153
Neighbourhood Watch   173
The Phone Call   183
What We Are Now   193
Wrestling with the Devil in the Run-up to Christmas   213
Ashton and Elaine   223

The Dressing-Up Box

1

THAT EVENING ELSA WAS front sentry. They sat her on the bottom stair. Keep watch, they said. Run up and tell us if anything happens. Elsa folded her arms, sat very still, fixed her eyes on the letter box. Early January, already dark outside, but the light in the hall wasn't bad, she could see well enough. She watched. Nothing happened. She fell asleep.

The younger children were always tired and could fall asleep even in uncomfortable places. They slept, they dreamed, bad things, strange kinds of happiness. Still, Elsa was not the worst sentry in the world. She woke when the letter box rattled. Something was happening. A hand came through, a small right hand, not clean but not especially dirty. Elsa watched it. Its fingers moved as though they were exercising or signing, very quickly, very slowly, then halted, open, showing the palm, then began again, all manner of clever movements, fast and slow, with stops and starts. Elsa took a pace towards the door. Stay there! she shouted. And ran upstairs to tell one of the bigger children. They were all busy, they sent her back down with a command: Show me your eyes! The hand withdrew, then its forefinger reappeared and with it the forefinger of the left hand, together holding open the metal flap, showing a pair of eyes. Stay there! Elsa shouted, and ran upstairs, to report. It's got blue-grey eyes, she said. It's not fierce. Ask it its name, said a big

1

girl getting a toddler into his pyjamas. Elsa ran down again. They said ask, What's your name?

The flap fell shut. Silence. Elsa sat on the bottom stair, watching the letter box. Nothing. So sleepy. Her eyes were closing again. But suddenly there was action. A soft brown head with big ears shoved through into the light, quite a squeeze, quite an effort, then two paws, and after that, with a gasp, a face, a monkey's face, it lifted up and smiled very cheerfully at Elsa. The head waggled, the arms waved, the paws even managed to clap. Elsa was entranced. She sat quite still on the bottom stair, elbows on knees, her chin in her hands. It was the happiest thing she had seen in a long while. The arms and paws seemed to be conducting a band. She could almost – but not quite – hear the music. The head nodded in time but the eyes and the smile concentrated on Elsa.

Abruptly the performance ceased. The head drooped, the arms flopped and a sort of struggle seemed to be taking place. Monkey was trying to get back through the letterbox. Now Elsa was as distressed as, two minutes before, she had been delighted. She felt the creature's panic. And then the worst thing happened. Monkey got quite stuck, the wriggling hand could not withdraw nor even hold him. He fell headfirst on to the doormat where the post had lain in a damp heap when the children moved in. And there he lay, on the horrible doormat, crumpled. Bare tips of fingers still showed, feeling around hopelessly. They vanished, and the metal flap fell shut. Elsa went to the door and, not looking at Monkey lying lifeless between her feet, she put her ear to the letterbox, and listened. Fast as she could then she ran back upstairs. Its monkey fell on the mat, she said. It's crying.

Nadeen, the oldest girl, and Ahmed and Billy, two boys big for their age, came downstairs with Elsa to sort the matter out. Ahmed held Elsa by the hand. You're OK, he said. Nadeen listened at the letterbox. Still there, she said. Still crying. We'll have a look. They slid back all three bolts, turned the key in both deadlocks and, leaving the chains on, opened the heavy door a hand's breadth. The child, not more than six or seven and very bizarrely dressed, stood in the slit of light, shivering and crying. Friend or foe? Billy asked through the crack. But the boy only shivered and cried. Billy said again, Friend or foe? And added: You're one or the other, mate. But still the little stranger made no answer, only nodded and shook his head and with his small right hand, that he could not hold steady, pointed downwards through the gap. And then he put his hands together, closed his eyes and raised his weeping face to the highest of the faces there in the warmth and shelter where he wished to be. He wants his monkey, said Elsa. That's why he's crying. Please, Nadeen, can I give him his monkey? Nadeen nodded. Elsa lifted up the crumpled creature from the doormat and with the greatest care held it out through the narrow opening into the cold.

Fast as a lizard's tongue, the small boy grabbed the monkey. Hugged it against his heart, then gloved his right hand with it. He stopped crying, the tears glazing his cheeks like ice. Then, stepping close, he lifted up the monkey's gleeful face between the chains into the light and warmth indoors. Clear as an icicle striking a wind-chime, a voice said: Friend. Enter, said Nadeen. The both of you, said Billy, taking off the bottom chain and hooking the top two back to their maximum, plenty wide enough for the monkey-puppet and his little minder to slip through sideways.

Ahmed and Billy locked and bolted the door. Then all stepped back and contemplated the newcomer who stood there in silence on the doormat while the monkey smiled and bowed and raised his paws, showing their pale open palms. You look like an ostrich, mate, said Billy. Well, the top half of you does, said Ahmed. Except your head's like a bull. The bottom half of you, I don't know what it's like. Dustman, said Billy. Down-and-out butler, said Nadeen. Prince, said Elsa. And he has come through fire and flood. What's your name, kid? Billy asked. Monkey, said the small clear voice. That's him, said Billy. Who are you? Monkey, said the same small voice. Elsa took the child's left hand. They're freezing cold, she said. Please, Nadeen, can we go upstairs now where it's warm? Nadeen nodded. You do sentry down here, Ahmed? Just for an hour. OK, boss, said Ahmed. Elsa led Monkey by the cold left hand. Nadeen and Billy followed behind them.

That, then, was the arrival of Monkey in the Big Safe House on an evening early in January as the cold deepened. After Monkey nobody else knocked at their door. There was a silence and a stillness, almost as though a cessation, or at least an exhausted pause, had been agreed. Those in a safe place stayed put and thanked their lucky stars.

2

The Big Safe House stood in its own grounds. The children posted four sentries. Front door, where Elsa had met Monkey. The back door, opening into a large walled garden and orchard, needed somebody who would stay awake and not be too easily frightened. A third sentry, called the Rover, must go from room to room on the top floor, checking through the windows, parkside, townside and neighbours, whether anything was stirring down there, good or bad. Cellar was best done by one of the older children and nobody liked it. The sentry sat on the top step. Below, the light was feeble and yellowish. The cold came up. You heard things slithering and scratching. Deep down, a door opened inwards, from nothing but darkness. The children feared that door as a possible way in and had barricaded it with old furniture.

Every morning, before it was light, the two Foragers went out. They rode a tandem, towing a cart. Nadeen at an upstairs window watched them leave, and stood watching till she saw them coming home. Then she alerted the back-door sentry, who ran down the garden and let them in at the gate in the wall. Quite close by they had found a food bank in an abandoned church and day by day they brought in tins and jars and packets, all the cart would hold. They were stocking up.

The streets around the Big Safe House were mostly deserted. Only once, and not too close, there was gunfire. Every now and then, usually during the night, some vehicle or other hurtled by along the parkside avenue. And the Park itself, a vast dark space, most nights flickered sparsely with campfires. Helicopters, and those seldom, were the only air-traffic. In the north-east, the worst quarter, a dense black smoke sagged and heaved in the sky. Large flecks of it drifted over, touched the windows, lay like poisoned butterflies on the sills.

In the second week of the children's occupation, somebody had shouted through the letter box that if they didn't get out the enforcers would be round with sledgehammers and alsations. But nothing happened. One morning a note dropped on the mat. The handwriting looked to be that of an old lady. If you are in need of help, it read, do, please, telephone this number. Nadeen kept the note in a safe place but did not phone. They were lying low. There was fuel and food in the house. Water, gas and electricity were still connected. It was the dwelling of a very rich man, who by certain signs – a half-eaten sandwich on the billiard table, clothes and a half-packed suitcase on one of the beds, for example – seemed to have left in a hurry. The children cleared such evidence away and, fearful but hoping for the best, made themselves at home in the uninhabited spaces.

Many of the children had phones of one sort or another. Nadeen said they should be switched off and left with her. The less we're traceable, the better, she thought. The landline was dead. All television had ceased abruptly soon after they moved in. There were radios in various rooms, the stations came and went, and gave no comfort.

Every morning at nine all the children gathered in the big sitting-room. They sat cross-legged on the floor, facing the low platform that filled the whole space of the large curving bay window. On stage, as it were, on a circular blue carpet patterned with a labyrinth, Nadeen sat with her lieutenants and chaired the meeting. But anybody could speak, you only had to put your hand up. The day's sentries were appointed. All day and all night, changing as agreed, they watched the four quarters of the outside world and the door that opened inwards from the cold damp cellar. The day's tasks were decided and allocated to the three tribes and within the tribes then to pairs or trios of children. Of course, much of every day was taken up minding and amusing the very smallest, preparing meals, keeping the place tidy (or ready for any sudden danger). And each day, after the urgent tasks, there were lessons. Whatever their subjects, they made a continuation, out of the past, out of what had once been normality. Nobody said as much, but that sense of the teaching and the learning, that idea of its value, was there most of the time in all but the youngest.

3

The last arrival in the Big Safe House would answer only to the name of 'Monkey', and only through that creature on his right hand would he address or reply to his fellow human beings. At least, it was only through Monkey that any *words* issued from him. But he said a lot just by his body in its outlandish dress, by all his gestures and by his face. He seemed always to be watching for an audience. Or, you might say, when in a gap between tasks or lessons, and especially in the afternoons when the dark was already coming in and the children's fears began to possess them, Monkey appeared, stood still, saying nothing, waiting for them to become what they wanted to be, an audience, *his* audience. In the youngest and oldest equally a yearning to be entertained arose. Monkey stood still, very faintly smiling at them and at himself. In the silence, in the stillness, the children having a focus for all their pairs of eyes, the sweet springs of mirth welled up in them. He stood, very slightly shaking his head, as though it never ceased to amaze him how easy it was, how willing they were, how much they wanted what he had to give them: laughter. Small pale face, blue-grey eyes which – as Elsa had reported – were not in the least fierce, and on his head the crooked horns, some remnant of old Viking gear or relic of the bellowing minotaur enchanted out of the dark into the life of a childhood pet. At arm's length, the puppet-monkey turned his head from audience to performer, back and forth, with an expression and with gestures of his paws that said, Not bad, not bad at all, you are doing pretty well.

The usual ventriloquist speaks through his dummy with no visible moving of his lips. It was as though Monkey knew that and had perfected a technique of his own, for a better effect. His lips moved, you could see them moving, and the patter – it might be quick questions and answers – issued sideways and hovered like Tinkerbell somewhere midway between his mouth and the puppet's. His face meanwhile, always towards the audience, scarcely bothered itself with that conversation but looked instead to be trying on the thousand expressions of a quite different show. Abruptly then, with a shrug, the whole performance ended. Pressing his hands on the seams of his baggy butler-trousers, the puppet motionless and upside down, the impresario bowed and in a vague musing manner ambled away.

4

The snow came towards the end of January, silently, all night falling and not a breath of wind. The weird flickering light of it showed at the big windows next morning. Such a hush, such silence, no sight nor sound of any humans, brief flights of small dark birds in the back garden, brief flurries and showers of snow from the leafless orchard trees. All in their own ways, according to age and their memories of previous circumstances, the children thrilled with an excitement laced with fear. The very youngest, held up to the windows and having no premise for such whiteness, softening, silencing, stared at it as though it were a thirst which with their wide-open eyes they must quench.

The Foragers could not go out. It was debated at the Morning Meeting whether the helpless wish for some fun in the snow should be granted or not. Surely the Big Safe House was safer than ever now that the sky had fallen? They could build a snowman in the orchard and have a regular snowball battle? Nadeen kept quiet, let anyone who wanted, speak. She and the half dozen others of her age were already thinking, What if it lasts for weeks? We'll starve. The Big Safe House will be a mausoleum. At last she said she thought they mustn't break their routine for a snowfall. So: tasks and lessons all morning. Then make up our minds. In the event, the issue was decided for them. By late morning it was snowing again, thick flakes, in a steady haste, in absolute silence, a whole higher level of the heavens intent on burying the earth.

They were in the big sitting room on the third floor. The classes from other rooms had come in to be all together. Nobody spoke. They sat on the floor watching the dark hurrying of snow at the big window. The mood was beginning to be fearful.

As though from nowhere, Monkey passed slowly and silently through the children, through the rows and clusters of them, to the front. Climbed the three steps on to the hemisphere in the great bay window, and quickly, on tip-toe, making no wrong moves, threaded the labyrinth of the night-blue carpet to its very centre. There he turned to face the audience, and stood still. Over his ostrich feathers and his dustman's trousers he wore a red silk cloak and on his head a stained and crumpled Tilley hat. His right hand was gloved as always, but in his left he gripped a staff like one a scoutmaster might carry as a sign of office and authority. I told you he was a prince, said Elsa in a loud voice. The glove-creature sniggered.

Having behind him the silent tumult of the snow, Monkey stood mute, watching his audience. They were rapt, on the brink of mirth or tears. The puppet, at arm's length, watched for a sign from his master, who himself seemed undecided whether to laugh or cry. The firmament was in shreds and tatters, falling, falling at a stupendous speed, countless millions of flakes, all different, but seeming in their entirety to have only one purpose: the burial of the earth in a deep white silence.

Then sideways to the right, crystal clear, came three words in the queerly disembodied voice: Monkey knows something. The puppet hid its eyes, as though bashful. Three times the child struck downwards with his staff at the floor between his feet. How it boomed! The monkey uncovered his eyes, threw wide open his furry arms, and silently chortled. The child rapped again. Boom! Boom! Boom! Down there, he said in his Tinkerbell voice. Monkey found it. Monkey knows.

Speechless, the audience watched him. He smiled at them as though he were himself almost as deeply entranced. Very faintly could be heard the kisses of the snow at the big window. Raising his staff and his glove-accomplice, fixing his audience as though it were from them that he got his power, Monkey stepped slowly backwards as far as the sill. Then, in a hurry, he threw down the staff, fell to his knees, and with the bare hand and the gloved began to roll up the circle of the night-blue labyrinth rug. At the midpoint, where he had stood, he halted, sprang to his feet, rapidly fetched his staff and, staring hard at the enchanted children and muttering sideways and inaudibly to the monkey, again he struck downwards, at the uncovered boards. Louder, with more reverberation: Boom! Boom! Boom! He capered once anti-clockwise, once clockwise, around this mystery, then knelt, looking quite exhausted, and with his bare left hand tugged up a silver ring embedded flat in the floor. He showed it, raised up, and beckoned then like any worn-out child to Nadeen and her lieutenants.

The trap-door, a perfect circle, was hinged on the audience-side. Nadeen, stooping by Monkey, grasped the silver ring and began to lift. Then Louis and Ahmed, to left and right of her, got their fingers into the gap. The hinges were oiled, easily the two boys raised the lid, and when it was vertical they held it there, showing the audience the whole disc, like an ancient shield or a bare *mappa mundi*. Monkey and Nadeen, kneeling side by side and hidden now behind the uplifted trap, peered down into the opened pit. There it is, said Monkey in his slant little voice. Just where Monkey said it was. The dressing-up box.

The boys laid the heavy disc of floorboards flat on the stage and sat back on their heels. Monkey, kneeling on the edge, facing the audience, felt with his gloved hand for the switch on the joist. The pit filled instantly with light. There below stood a large square wicker basket overflowing with bright materials. From the joist a wooden ladder slanted down to it. Monkey waved, and vanished.

The floor of the pit was a good deal lower than that of the sitting room. Standing there, Monkey on tiptoe in his soiled Tilley hat still did not reach to the rim of the box. He climbed back up a couple of steps and surveyed the illuminated hoard. Over all four sides, in the colours of the cloths of heaven, of humming bird and firebird, of opal, Blue John and amethyst, the contents of the dressing-up box overflowed. They were watery, of lakes and seas in every weather, and earthly, of hills and meadows and valleys of both hemispheres in every season, they were air and fire, the blue, the crystal clear, the burning dawns and sunsets, the ever in shape and colour changing clouds. And they were not just cloths – they were *clothes*: outfits, costumes of all the humans in every land and in every age. And not just of humans: snakeskins and sealskins were in that box, shaggy bear-pelts, hawk and kingfisher plumage, dragon and mackerel scales, shells of snail and nautilus, and the outward appearances of the inbetween creatures – mermaid, centaur, minotaur, angel – they were in there too. A wicker box is a familiar thing, you'll say, by its depth and by its width you could calculate its capacity. But this particular box on the secret floor under the sitting room in the Big Safe House, this dressing-up box discovered by Monkey, seemed more like the opening, the upsurging and overflowing, of a source that would always replenish and never never end.

Monkey leaned from the ladder and with his gloved right hand swiftly chose himself an outfit, dropping the items of it to the floor. Down there, he took off his Tilley, his cloak, his ostrich-top, his butler-dustman trousers, his wellington boots (one red, one black), tossed them up into the box, and changed. Climbing out, the puppet drew his attention to the strange fact that his old togs had vanished, the box had taken them under into the heaving welter of its endless stock.

Monkey appeared on stage. He signalled to Ahmed and Louis to lower the trap-door and roll the night-blue carpet back over it. That done, he took up his staff, stepped forward to the heart of the labyrinth and stood still, for the children to gaze at him. He wore flip-flops, sulphur-yellow leggings, a grass skirt, pink chain-mail, a red necktie and a battered stove-pipe hat. All stared, nobody spoke, he stood before them as the living proof that under his feet, under the labyrinth carpet and the trap, were all the makings of never-ending metamorphosis. The snow whirled and flitted at the window behind him. He stood, half-smiling in the silence. Then, watched quizically by the monkey on his right hand, he bowed, stepped down from the stage and through the groups and rows of children ambled away.

All that night it snowed. Daybreak came early, the children woke and peeped through the curtains into the snowlight. There was no sight or sound of any human activity, no campfire smoke in the Park, no clatter of black machines through the pristine air. In the Big Safe House the children moved about quietly, speaking in whispers, in a wonder touched with fear at the vast depth, stillness, silence of the completed fall of snow.

At the Morning Meeting it was soon decided that every late afternoon, till a thaw began, the three tribes of children should take whatever clothes and props they liked from the dressing-up box and the shelves and racks in the pit under the stage, and put on an entertainment of one sort or another, each tribe in turn, for an audience of the other two. But first Nadeen, with Louis and his particular friend Frieda, went down to have a closer look at the treasure trove under the labyrinth carpet. Good job, we did, she said to herself, having opened a large black portfolio that lay with nothing else on a trestle table under a shelf of theatrical paraphernalia. On the left were five rows of photographs of children dressed, as you would suppose, in clothes taken from the wicker basket. These children, boys and girls, some only toddlers, others about the same age as Nadeen, were all of different races and all wore the costumes of their native lands. Hard to tell with traditional dress and the photographs all black and white, whether these were children of now or of many years ago. But what troubled Nadeen and why she decided at once that nobody but she and Frieda and Louis should see them, were the faces. Not one child was smiling. All had their eyes fixed on something or somebody commanding their total attention. Nadeen called the others, less for their opinion than for her own comfort. They're petrified, said Frieda.

On the facing page stood the same children each in the same place on the rows, so that it was easy to glance across and see the transformation of each and every child. All differences in dress had been expunged; all, boys and girls, wore the same

12

black smock and loose black trousers; all were bare-foot; all bare-headed, their hair cropped uniformly short. And whatever had held their gaze in the first photograph held it still, and more so, in the second. Every child's face stared out at what commanded it, all those pairs of eyes were fixed upon some thing or person they did not for a split second dare to leave.

Nadeen turned the page, so that again the images left and right lay open to be seen. Almost at once Louis leaned over and closed the portfolio. Hide it, he said. We've seen enough of that sort of stuff. He carried the heavy volume to the farthest corner, laid it flat on the floor, covered it with a rag rug, and on to that, helped by the girls, dragged an old safe whose doors were missing. Conscientiously then, they checked all the shelves and racks of props. Nothing too bad there. The guns were plastic, the swords and daggers were silver-painted wood. And a small black cooking pot with six inches of red string coming through its lid and BOMB! written across its belly in big white letters, they thought more comical than terrible. The masks of werewolves, vampires, zombies and the like aroused in them more nostalgia than dread. Still one of us should stand down here, said Nadeen, and keep an eye on what they choose.

The performances began that afternoon. Three at a time the children came down the ladder and by Louis, Ahmed or Billy, were helped onto an upturned packing case, to see over the rim of the great wicker basket. Some reached in, others climbed or dived in, all from the multitude of flamboyant possibilities made their costumes. Then, having selected a few items from the store of props, they climbed back on stage and in a breathless haste transformed themselves, while three more of their tribe descended behind them into the pit.

The entertainments staged by the three tribes had much in common. Nothing was carried through to any conclusion, everything swung this way or that with no apparent rhyme or reason. It was beginnings, like chaos. There was no dialogue as such, certainly no plot. Now and then an idea arose, which some of the actors, each as he or she pleased, made occasional flurries at. The smallest, in a magical daze, wandered to and fro among the larger creatures, copying for a while, until a vagueness overcame them and they passed to the borders of the mêlée and there lay down and fell fast asleep. There was a good deal of music, especially brass and percussion in a sort of combat. But also, at times, in one or other of the older children, the gift and the hours of practice suddenly surfaced and from a flute or a fiddle sang out through the general din.

Really, the dressing-up was an end in itself. Every child wondered at the creature and character he or she had chosen to become. And in the medley they all astonished one another by their metamorphoses.

Monkey, changing three times (once for each performance), stood on stage to one side, and in his piping, disembodied, Tinkerbell voice conducted a commentary between himself and his gloved right hand. Sometimes the action swirled over him, he was taken up, carried along and cast out again somewhere else, gasping like a shipwrecked mariner. Nadeen, dressed as Isis, Goddess of Motherhood and Magic, stood in the audience, at the very back, alone, arms folded, wholly absorbed in the spectacle. Often, viewing it through tears, the ceaseless jostling on stage appeared to her like a festival of the sea.

Every late afternoon, nightfall never quite dimming the brightness of the snow, the Big Safe House did indeed gather towards another festival. The children woke in excitement, saw by their beds the costumes they had worn for the performance the day before, and the memory of that and anticipation of the next, flowed to and fro in them like competing currents. All day, every day, at mealtimes, at the Morning Meeting, at the tasks and lessons, everyone was in costume. Some were complete and particular. You saw Thomas as Lord Ganesha stand up and recite his twelve-times table, Dvora as Greensleeves stood at the sink drying dishes passed to her by Mahmoud the Hippocamp. But most wore whatever bits and pieces had taken their fancy: a head-dress from the Plains, a golden torque from Avalon, dinner jacket and Bermuda shorts, sandals from Rome, kilt, silk trousers, flapper dress, bowler, hijab, sash of the garter, policeman's helmet, turban, sequins, mantilla, leopard-skin pillbox, eye of Horus, pentagram, amber necklace, all manner of charms. And although this mix appeared every day, still no one got used to it. You could say that wonder and admiration rose again every morning at first light. What any child put on, excited amazement – and emulation – in the beholders. So invention called to invention all the waking day long and in the rapids, the calms and the depths of dreams.

One strange thing, scarcely noticed in so much strangeness, was that the ordinary clothes the children had worn before the dressing-up began, had vanished. Who had removed them? And where to? Monkey, perhaps? To the marvellous box under the night-blue carpet of the labyrinth? That seemed possible, to anyone who gave the mystery a second thought. For when, every afternoon, the children tore off their costumes and flung them up over the high rim of the great wicker basket and climbed then or were hoisted on to the upturned packing case and pondered what new outfit they should appear in now – of the old there was no trace! Those clothes were never seen again, or never in any form a previous borrower of them would have recognised. The box was so deep, its contents so abundant and various, no wonder things flung in there did a disappearing act. Standing on the upturned packing case, mulling over the possibilities for the day's performance, every child had the feeling that the materials, in their changing colours, could not keep still. It was like a seething, it frothed and swirled like a maelstrom. And yet you could stand barefoot in there, in the middle of it, fish around in it, haul out what pleased you best, and somehow the whole boiling bore you up, you were only ever waist-deep and buoyant amid millennia of clothing, plumage, skin, hide and hair covering, in every variation of show and camouflage.

Most of the children gave only joyous thought to the morrow. There would always be fuel and food, the sanctuary of the snow would last for ever. And every late afternoon there would be a festival.

5

A week had passed. No sign of a thaw. Stocks of even essential foods were running low, and more logs would have to be fetched – dug from under the snow – very soon. Nadeen, Billy and Frieda, all in costume, stood at an upstairs window looking out over the white deserted Park. Still no traffic on the drifted roads and none through the cold bright air. I've been thinking, said Billy. We should try the cellar door. See where it leads. We might need a back exit. Agreed, said Nadeen. She had kohled her eyes, deepening the dark rings of tiredness around them, to fit her appearance as the Goddess Isis. You two go. Tell the sentry but nobody else. Go this afternoon. Torch, compass, notebook – get the distance and the line of it exactly.

As it happened, the sentry on that watch was Monkey. He had transformed himself into a very lifelike mole and sat there two steps down with a lantern between his feet, conversing as usual with the furry puppet who, on the mole-master's paw, looked more bizarre than ever. Billy wore a civil defence coat over his Hannibal outfit; Frieda said she would be warm enough in her Inuit furs. Monkey fell silent. They heaved the barricade aside. The three bolts slid back, the key turned in the deadlock, the door opened inwards – easily, almost soundlessly. Billy raised his eyebrows. Why so well maintained, why so smooth? Switching on their torches, they could see some way down a clean white-washed and vaulted tunnel. They hesitated. But then, another surprise, suddenly in a dead straight line the way was lit, sixty yards or so, to a second door. Monkey, standing behind them, had flicked a switch. Monkey wants to come, he said. You can't, said Frieda. You're sentry. Monkey frowned, and brought the puppet to his ear. He says what do you need a sentry for when we can see all the way and nobody's here but us and there's another door? OK, said Billy. Just so long as we can get back in. Pull the door shut. If we can't open it this side, we'll bang. The door opened with ease. Monkey went ahead, swinging the lantern and muttering to the puppet. Wait, said Frieda. She read the compass, the line was east-south-east. Billy, you stride and count. He did so. At the second door they halted. He made a careful note. Again, three bolts and a deadlock, all easy. Monkey let them through, stayed behind the closing door till it was certain they could get back in. Now the tunnel, wide enough to walk three abreast, ran north-east. The lights lit a hundred strides, then another hundred strides, then a dead end. But there, at that wall, a fixed iron ladder climbed to a flat ceiling, in which was a square trapdoor, hinged at the far side, bolted midway along each of the other three. Frieda went up, and holding a rung in her right hand, with her left slid the bolts. At her touch then, gently the trap tilted upwards. Climbing two rungs higher, she leaned in the opening, and shone her torch. Then quickly down again, bolting the entrance. Guess what, she said. We're under that church. Under the vestry. And someone's filled up the food bank.

That same afternoon, the Foragers (Frieda and Louis) and a couple of the other big children, manhandled the tandem and its cart down the cellar steps and parked them ready just the other side of the first door. Monkey made himself almost invisible on the top step against the wall and in a rapid burbling, more like a starling than a man-child, explained to his astonished puppet exactly what was happening. When he changed for the entertainment he retained the smooth black head and the snout of a mole, in the rest of his costume becoming more Luke Skywalker. Thereafter, in all of his transformations, something molish remained. And he never again took up the scoutmaster's staff, but always the lantern, a fireman's torch, a light sabre. Nadeen looked wonderingly at him. Lux in tenebris, she said. Light in the tunnel, light in our darkness. The glove-monkey chortled, Oh my word, oh my stars and garters, oh my giddy aunt, whatever next?

Early next morning the Foragers went out. Nadeen sat with Monkey on the bottom step, watching down the tunnel to where, at the second door, it kinked northerly, out of sight. She was silent. Soon, like a stream exhausting its underground springs, Monkey and his piping ceased. He laid his soft mole-head in her lap, she stroked it, he slept. The next he heard was, They're coming, Monkey! The Foragers are back. He sat up, watchful as a March hare, and saw the tandem and cart halted at the second door which Frieda was locking and bolting behind them. Then they pedalled in, laden and jubilant. Fetch some big kids, said Nadeen. We'll unload at once.

6

It began to thaw, but very slowly, freezing hard again at night. The younger children had an hour in the garden, building a snowman. The snow had softened and was good for it. They rolled three great snowballs and called the oldest boys, who were keeping watch, to come and pile them one on top of another. For a fourth, to make the head, they needed steps. Zephania went to fetch a pair from the garden shed. Turning with it, viewing the children at a distance, he felt very certain that his brief childhood was over. And that theirs would be soon. But he fixed the head in place and their glee raised his spirits. He faces this way! he shouted. Away from the Big Safe House. He's the guardian. How will you dress him? They ran to the dressing-up box and came back with an azure cloak, a crimson cummerband, an antique helmet, a two-handed sword, a spear, and a ginger handlebar moustache. Eyes and nose, said Monkey. And from a pouch he took two red billiard balls and a small horn of plenty.

Nadeen paced out the line and the distance of the tunnel. As she had calculated, the second door must be immediately below the right-hand garden wall, in the far corner. And from that point it was two hundred strides to the church. How long will the food bank last? What provisions can we carry with us if we move? Where, if we move, shall we go? Where is there any other sanctuary?

At midday, with no warning, the gas gave out. The cooks had barely begun. Save it till evening, said Frieda. We'll get the Aga going by then. There's plenty of wood. But slowly the rooms, the halls, the stairways cooled. One small work party brought in more logs and the rest of the coal; another, with bow-saw and axe, began making firewood of the rich man's furniture and stockpiling it in all the rooms where there was a hearth or a wood-burning stove. The Aga did well. The cooks served a giant pillau. The two big tables were loud and very cheerful. We shan't freeze! We shan't go hungry! By firelight, clutching rugs, costumed as Eskimos, polar bears, woolly mammoths, the children's bedtime was a great adventure. They lay in the dark, watching the dances of the flames. Long before the fuel was ash and the air too cold, they slept.

Now in the daytime there was more to do: more foraging, more preparation. Every morning the grates needed cleaning, the ash taking out, the new fires laying in. The dressing-up box donated woollen trousers, scarves, buffs, bobble-hats, gloves and an abundance of warm coats and jackets. It was like a show of all humankind's inventiveness against the cold. Elsa found something not unlike Monkey's ostrich top and, wearing it, ran to show herself to him. Oh that, he said, and added, These days Monkey is more mole than ostrich. Elsa was indignant. It's swan's down, she said. Can't you see I'm a swan? Not a bit like an ostrich.

The Morning Meeting was largely a matter of deciding the work parties and the sentry duties. Lessons continued, but all in one room, for some warmth. Games were organised, things hidden to be found, a string-trail through the whole chilly house. Nadeen conferred with the oldest children. They sat together and tried hard to subdue anxiety by weighing the possibilities and by planning. The cold was bad, they feared for the very youngest, but a greater fear still was of what the thaw, the opening of the streets, the revival of the business of adults, would bring.

The afternoon's entertainment changed. After a week standing on the side-lines or being suddenly taken into the maelstrom and spewed out again, Monkey became the Director. He never said so. He never said, You do as Monkey tells you from now on. And perhaps no one even noticed? Or if they did notice, they didn't mind. Whatever the case, wearing a trilby, Monkey took charge.

The biggest innovation was that all three tribes were on stage together. This new state of affairs needed to be managed since the old sweet anarchy, if allowed to continue, would now surely, among so many, have ended in tears. So there they stood, front stage left, front stage right, upper stage centre, distinct. The costumes too, inventive and various as ever, distinguished the tribes, whose mix, as to origins, shape, size and spirit, was of course undiminished. If anything, the separation for art's sake brought the plurality home.

To whom? The only audience now was Nadeen, standing, arms folded, and Monkey, sitting cross-legged with a large papier mâché glow-worm by his side and the puppet at arm's length or close to his right ear. They watched, how they watched! But differently. The three tribes themselves were all actors, not spectators.

At the start of the first of Monkey's productions two tribes stood front stage facing the audience shoulder to shoulder in one continuous line in total silence. Every child was a drummer, the sticks held ready. Their costumes, left, were of every shade and degree of blue; right, of green. Still silent, the two tribes shuffled apart and through the gap, facing, the third was shown, in various reds. The action was simple. Tribes left and right, abruptly and all together turned about, and the costumes they showed now were uniform and black. Facing the red tribe, they began to drum, in unison, louder and louder. They closed ranks, very slowly, in step, with a heavy tread, they advanced. All one then, all uniform, they halted but continued drumming loudly and loudly marching on the spot. The drumming ceased, the drummers shuffled apart, and now through the gaps there was no sign of the reds. The black line at a marching pace advanced across the whole width of the empty stage and, splitting into their two separate tribes, exited.

Nadeen went and sat by Monkey and put her arm around him. Choreographer, she said. For a moment he looked at her with the blankest terror on his face. Then the puppet-monkey tittered, Cripes, oh cripes, Monkey's a choreographer! Whatever next?

In a rush the stage filled again. Over the black every child had cast a multi-coloured cloak. Now the drumming was wild and as they pleased. The reds returned with flutes, horns, fiddles. The motley became general and yet with a sort of purpose. There were continuous currents through it, like threading. You saw and heard the beginnings of patterns of movement and sound. But never a completion. Coming into a shape, the makers abandoned it and began sketching another.

For the next entertainment there was no separation of the three tribes. They were abolished and became instead one crowd of children. And on this occasion, the last as it turned out, the dressing-up box gave more than ever before. The cast appeared to be not just of all shapes and sizes, colours and characters, but also of all ages. They were a small sample of the human race, from the new-born to their great-grandparents.

The action – so far as it proceeded – lasted less than ten minutes. As soon as it began, Monkey glanced round to locate Nadeen. Seeing his look, she again came and sat cross-legged on the floor beside him. That settled him. The puppet, the little boy and the young woman gave their full attention to the spectacle.

Entering left, very slowly, a troop of people advanced along the edge of the stage. You heard the shuffling of feet, the tapping of sticks, the squeaking of wheels. You saw children, as bearded old men, as bent old women in black, also young and upright, three girls carried babies, an older boy had a toddler on his shoulders. They wore stylish clothes, football strips or tracksuits, or remnants of such, with sacks, blankets, a tarpaulin over their shoulders. They were shod for the office, the beach, the dance-floor or the sports hall, some were limping, a couple were on crutches. In single file they passed slowly along the arc of the stage, one by one showing themselves, stooped under burdens, pushing a pram, a wheelbarrow, a handcart, in which were infants, a grandmother, rolls of bedding, food and water, and turned and bore away again, passing out of sight behind those still arriving, and appeared again, as those in their turn passed out of sight, on and on, in a loop, round and round, getting nowhere. Then came a change. The leaders, far right, halted, and one by one, bunching close, those following also halted. All now, facing out, raised a hand to their eyes as though to see better against the glare of the snow or the sun how far they must trek, would the road never bring them to where they wanted to be? One minute, in silence, they stood there, a handful of humans, looking ahead. They saw nothing for their comfort. They turned, they were about to begin their circling again. It seemed they must do this for ever, trek in a loop, line up along a frontier, look across, see no help, begin again. But at exactly that moment, when all were still touching, when all knew their neighbour's despair at having to set off yet again, the lights in the big sitting room went out.

In the first pitch-darkness the children screamed. Nadeen leapt to her feet. Stay where you are! she shouted. Hold on to one another! Don't move! And through the darkness and panic Monkey, standing by her, cried in a voice that was louder and more piercing than any he had used before, That's not the end! That's not how it ends! Then a little light, the fire and its reflection in the big mirror, asserted itself. Ahmed, Billy and Frieda hurried to fetch candles and torches from the stockpile near the door. Logs went on the fire, the room became friendly.

The children came down from the stage – leaving their props and some of the costumes strewn over the boards and the carpet like the debris of a shipwreck – and packed close together around the hearth. Nadeen said they should eat supper there, it would be cosier. The cooks went off with torches. Give us half an hour, they said. Something simple. Nadeen turned to Monkey. While we're waiting, she said, why don't you tell us how it really ended? Monkey stood up, his back to the fire, and through the puppet, in his midway disembodied clear-as-crystal small voice, very rapidly he answered: The third time they come to the edge, it's the sea, they've reached the shore, they can't do it all again, they're too tired, they're falling asleep, but they look out – he shielded his eyes and looked out in an arc from left to right across his audience – and they see a ship, coming in, nearer and nearer, and it has seven sails, one in each colour of the rainbow, and the people are so tired they can hardly even wave, they can hardly raise their voices, and the big ship comes in closer and drops anchor. The people watch. And this is what they see: seven longboats, one for each sail, are lowered into the water and four strong oarsmen row each boat through the surf and a fifth man in the bows leaps ashore with a line as they beach. And they are glad to see us safe there on the shore. And those of us who can, wade in. And the strong men carry those who can't through the surf, the babies, the little ones, the old, the crippled, the sick, those who are too tired to move. And when we come alongside the rainbow ship, the captain and crew lean over the rail and shout, Welcome aboard! They haul up the anchor, a breeze fills the sails and in no time at all the bad place has sunk out of sight behind us and is gone for ever. And that, said Monkey, is how it really ends.

Nadeen stood in the bay window peering out between the heavy curtains. It was raining hard. Ahmed, Billy, Frieda and Louis shone their way with torches through the debris of the final performance and joined her there. Behind them, like an aviary, the children sat noisily over their firelight supper. Nadeen said, This rain, the snow will be gone by morning. The rest – that the grown-up world would be back to business as usual – she did not need to say. I'm thinking of phoning that lady. Shall I? They nodded. Billy, come with me, will you. Let's do it now.

They went by torchlight to the rich man's study which she had used as a sort of office. All the phones were there, and the Lady's note: If you are in need of help, telephone this number. Their mistrust of adults ran deep. Her hand was shaking as she put down the note and reached for her phone. But one day, one night, they'll be back with sledgehammers and alsatians. Billy nodded. Phone her, Nadeen.

She answered at once, crisp and posh. Yes. Who is it? We're in the Big House, said Nadeen. You wrote us a note. We're thinking we do need help. Ah, said the voice. Nadeen's blood ran cold. There was a silence, during which, shaking as though in a fever, she believed she had made a mortal error. Oh, Billy, she whispered. All those children. Billy patted her shoulder. OK, Nadeen. It's OK. Then, very crisp and clear, the Lady said:

My dear, I have been praying you would ring. You are in the nick of time. You must leave tomorrow. I gather you have discovered the tunnel to the vestry? That will be your escape route. How many are you? Thirty-three, said Nadeen, and six of them can't walk far, they're too little or not well. We can manage thirty-three, said the Lady. Now give me five minutes. I will phone you back with exact instructions. Really, this is the eleventh hour.

Nadeen and Billy sat at the rich man's desk. She didn't sound like a butcher, said Nadeen. Anyway, it's too late now. We're at her mercy. They waited. The phone rang again. 3.30, said the Lady, outside the church, use the tunnel, come in through the vestry. It will be the school bus, red and white, the driver's name is Tommy. You'll be heading west, the bad things are in the north and east. Only one bag each. Warm clothes, boots or stout shoes. Food will be provided. Tommy is a good man, he will look after you. 3.30 tomorrow. After that it will be too late. Bon voyage and God speed, my dears. I should come to see you off but, alas, I am confined indoors. Nadeen put the phone down. We're moving, Billy, she said. I trust her.

Back at the fire they conferred quickly with the other older children. Then Nadeen clapped her hands. All those faces in the firelight, so many hues of complexion, and all eyes, one fierce focussing of attention, on her, for her announcement. Good news, she said. We're leaving tomorrow afternoon on the red and white school bus. The driver's name is Tommy. In the morning you must pack your bags, only one each. Monkey stood up. Monkey wants to know do we have to wear school uniform? Nadeen stared at him. Why on earth would that child ask about uniform? Of course not, she answered. Wear what you like, the barmier the better. But it must be warm and your footwear must be good. She turned to her lieutenants. Two night sentries, I'd say. Both roving. Two hours each. I'll sort it, boss, said Ahmed.

For the sleepers – in just two rooms, the fires burning – the night passed quietly enough. The sentries reported flares and perhaps firing quite far off, north and north-east. Early morning, though, the first black helicopter rattled low over the empty park. Worse, along the Avenue, through the dirty slush, a pick-up truck went by, very slowly. You'd have said the driver was looking for something and might halt at any minute. From a first-floor window, keeping out of sight, Louis saw a pair of Kalashnikovs in the back of the truck. Also, that the tarpaulin there had been carelessly drawn over a mound of something. He reported the pick-up, but kept the details to himself.

That morning Elsa was front sentry again. She sat on the bottom stair, watching the letter box and thinking of Monkey who had mistaken her swan's down for his ostrich top. That thought made her giggle. She planned, as soon as her watch was finished, to go looking for a pair of white-feathery (but warm) trousers in the dressing-up box. Monkey would help her.

The letter box rattled, a pair of eyes showed through. Then, instead of the eyes, a red and whiskery mouth, out of which came a voice, Well, you're a rum one, sweetheart, and no mistake. Elsa stood up. Friend or foe? she said. Oh, friend, friend, friend, very friendly, said the voice. Wait, said Elsa. I'll go and ask. Do that, said the voice. Ask your big sister. Ask your nice big sister to come down and have a chat through the letter box. Will you do that, darling?

Elsa ran fast upstairs. There's a thing at the door, she said. Its eyes are horrible, its mouth is wet and its voice is very creepy. It said to fetch my big sister. I'll go, said Billy. Elsa, stay here. He saw the eyes, they disappeared and the red mouth took their place. I said big sister, it said. She doesn't have a big sister, said Billy. She has nine big brothers and I'm the littlest. But come back this time tomorrow by all means, if you'd like to make our acquaintance.

The caller made them nervous. The sentries, but not just the sentries, peered frequently through the drawn curtains. Even from the Park most of the snow had gone. The grass looked dirty, the trees looked dead. Black smoke rose at a distance into a sky that was clearing. The older children checked all the rooms. The house was to be left safe, no candles, or fires still burning except, for now, in the sitting room. They cleared the office, only Nadeen and her lieutenants kept their phones, the rest went in a bag, for later.

They were ready, with time to spare. They sat on the floor, facing the stage, their packed bags next to them; firelight, torches and candles were all their lighting. Nobody spoke. They were in a fearful solemnity, at the peril and wonder of their enterprise. Their costumes for the departure were as outlandish as any they had worn for the entertainments. Several were more bird or beast than human, some were between-creatures whose element might have been earth, sea or air or even fire. Some carried musical instruments, which Nadeen had said wouldn't count as baggage.

Four sentries now, all Rovers, lingering longest at the back door and the cellar door.

Nadeen, in a mortal terror of leaving any child behind, took the register. Lucy? Here. Ishmael? Here. Beatrice, Carys, Little Ahmed, Piotr, Misuko, Fred… Here, Nadeen, here. How she loved their names! Sam, Zeno, Felicity, Farrough and Lizzie, Eleni and Benjamin, their solemn voices, each matching with its person. Those wearing masks answered so peculiarly, that Nadeen, in her anxiety, asked would they show their faces, to make assurance double sure.

From nowhere, so it seemed, Monkey appeared on stage and stood before his audience, saying nothing. He raised his left hand, as if for silence, though nobody was even whispering. He wore the Director's trilby, tilted back. The monkey-glove, at arm's length, contemplated him. He nodded to the audience, removed the trilby, and skimmed it down into the darkness of the pit. You need headgear, said the puppet. Can't go out in the big wide world bare-headed. No fear of that, said the small voice that came out sideways from his mouth. Just a moment, please. Arms out, as though on a tight rope, he walked clockwise, anti-clockwise and clockwise again, around the rim of the pit. Halted, waited, and with a jump vanished.

Silence, an eerie silence, edging towards terror. Nadeen took a step forward. But at that moment Monkey, or some of him, reappeared. On his head he wore a sleek grey skull cap, around it a head torch, below that a pair of sunglasses. He climbed fully out: a smart navy-blue pea jacket with golden galleons on the buttons; a scarlet scarf; thick emerald breeks; grey worsted knee-stockings; pink sea boots. His emblem now, held under his arm, was a globe about the size of a football which, when the puppet struck it with a small wooden mallet, flashed like lightning and sang with the music of the spheres.

Nadeen looked at her watch. Monkey set down his globe. Stooping, he and his glove-creature felt under the lid of the pit, heaved it upright, and showed to all the gazing children the bare disc, the shield, the empty *mappa mundi*. Next lowered it slowly by the silver ring as long as they had strength to, then let it fall, with a clack that visibly shocked him. He knelt, and rolled the night-blue labyrinth carpet back over the lid, the pit, the fabulous dressing-up box. Retrieved his globe, and without a single wrong step, this way and that, along curves, sudden kinks, short freeways, winding detours, danced to the very centre, and there, first smiling upwards to the angels and sideways to the puppet, he bowed, smiling, to his audience. That's it then? said the puppet. That's it then, said the Tinkerbell voice of the child. That's it but for the tunnel and the red and white school bus.

Midwinter Reading

To FINISH, SHE SAID, closing the book and clasping it, with her glasses, in both hands against her dress, I'll tell you a story, a true story. It is all in my head and around my heart and I will tell it as it comes back into its words and sentences in me. And best, if you don't mind, if I close my eyes.

How disclosed she looked standing unseeing before an audience whose eyes, by closing her own, she had licensed to contemplate her. She stood in silence for perhaps a minute – longer it seemed – collecting herself, attending. White hair, a pale face, the roses on her book's cover very bright against her black dress. Several in that room remembered with a shock the ancient childhood faith that if you close your eyes you yourself along with everything and everybody else will be invisible.

She sighed deeply, and smiled. Towards the end of my life, she said, I came to give a reading at a house on a Barratt estate somewhere in Birmingham. It was midwinter, I disliked driving in the dark and the rain and had set off early, fearing I wouldn't find my way. But the organiser's instructions were exact, and only at the last, having turned into a cul-de-sac, did I become doubtful, and was glad to see a man walking his dog whom I could ask. That house there, lady, he said.

The porch was lit with winking fairy lights. I rang the bell. I hadn't heard a ring like that for many years: three ding-dongs, a pause after the first and the second two coming together rapidly. She tilted up her face and uttered them: Ding-dong.

29

(Pause.) Ding-dong-ding-dong. Then she said, The house door opened and Robert appeared. I suppose everybody is astounded by their first sight of him. Bare hairy arms, bald crown, lanks of black hair, a paler walrus moustache, a heavy silver crucifix. Reaching for the outside door he entirely filled the porch. Hell's Angel, I thought, as I guess most newcomers do. He stepped back, beckoned me in, took my shopping-bag, shook my hand, mumbled a welcome.

Curious to witness her − quite a small woman − reliving the big man's welcome. Her hands, clutching her book and her glasses, lifted in a gesture of acknowledgement, and across her face the faint shadows of past courtesies flitted.

Nobody here yet, he muttered. But, as you see, we're all set up.

In the living room, below a picture of Jesus in Gethsemane, under that wall on three or four tables pushed together and covered with a spotless cloth, Robert had laid out the refreshments: heaped plates of small triangular sandwiches with their crusts cut off, crab-paste, cucumber, lettuce and tomato, Kraft cheese slices, corn beef... All under cling-film. And quarters of Eccles cakes and of thinly sliced Dundee and halves of Battenberg and Kunzel. I stared at his big hands, she said. That in them should be such delicacy, patience and attention brought tears to my eyes. Hours of work. And before those hours the forethought, the shopping. There was a cut-glass bowl of tinned peaches, a jug of evaporated milk, a jar of pickled onions and another of piccalilli and a fork leaning in each. At one end a tea-urn, at the other the coffee, and milk and sugar for both. Two jugs of squash, and all the necessary cutlery and paper cups and plates and serviettes.

She stood, eyes closed, shaking her head in wonder at the supper he had laid on. Then she said, Just as affecting (the faith of it!) were the rows of all shapes and sizes of chairs. Between the back row and the laden tables he had left a narrow aisle.

After that, row upon row extended almost to the far wall on which hung a portrait of the Queen at her coronation. And it was below her, in a narrow gap, by a stool for books and papers, that the visiting reader stood.

Robert gestured me towards the stairs. Toilet's up there, he muttered. Still no audience when I came down. I'll get myself ready, I said. He nodded. I squeezed through to the far end with my shopping-bag.

Robert stood in the small space between the porch and the refreshments. He held a saucepan in his right hand. I am not famous, she said. I never had much of a following. Quite often I've journeyed many miles and read to two or three people. Once nobody at all turned up. The organiser was in tears. We had a nice meal together, only after half a bottle of wine would she stop saying sorry. So I felt for Robert! He looked like a man who had wilfully made himself dependent on a miracle. The reader, the rows of empty chairs, the love feast… Such a bid of faith, a sort of defiance. I do what I must do, recklessly and abundantly. Come now, miracle! From late autumn till early spring, on the first Friday of every month, witnessed by the reader, Jesus and the Queen, he stood waiting for the miracle to materialise, person by person, out of the dark.

She paused. She seemed seized again, for him, by the fear of unbearable disappointment. It was as though she herself must become the spectacle of trial and martyrdom. She seemed, eyes closed, to be attending, listening, hoping, praying out into that cul-de-sac and the night.

Then she smiled and said, Ding–dong. Ding–dong–ding–dong.

Announced by chimes, the faithful were arriving. Robert opened the outer door and let them in from the damp and the cold in ones and twos. They greeted him cheerfully, he was solemn, said nothing, but proffered the saucepan and into it they dropped, chink, chink, chink, three one-pound coins, one for each chime, the fee. Between these entrances there were pauses of silence, waiting, expectation. An old love of ceremony, of custom, ritual, proper form, took hold of me, she said. On the first Friday of the month, as the days shortened and turned again to lengthening, on a housing estate somewhere in Birmingham there was this cheerful solemnity, the biker as doorman, presider and prime mover, the takings heavier and heavier in the saucepan in his grip, an unsmiling man, gravely courteous, as the circle of the friends of poetry, a few young, most elderly or old, came in on chimes and a breath of the cold. And all, however skinny, pressed against his belly in the cramped antechamber amid the winking fairy lights. It was cumbersome and shambling, no room for poise or grace of movement was given them. After the porch, largely filled with Robert, they entered the straits between the refreshments and the back row of chairs and bore sharp right then into the narrows along the left-hand wall, to take their seats. Many had come on foot and were bulked up in overcoats and waterproofs. Divesting, they must crouch and push their belongings back between their legs under the chairs.

Slowly, with a courteous patience, chime after chime the living-room filled, she said. And last, quite without embarrassment, the front row. Though I stood as far back as I could, my dress touched the trousers of a large man looking up at me with an extraordinary candour. Nobody minded. That was what I had to learn. I am usually quite nervous on such occasions. Often I can't keep my hands from shaking as I hold the book; and always more or less close is the fear that my voice will desert me. But in Robert's semi-detached, the young Queen behind me and Christ in the torment of doubt on the far wall before me, I felt entirely at ease. I felt a great affection for everybody present and all were strangers. When I thought of the poems I would read, it comforted me to know for certain that I was their maker but not their owner, they came from me but did not belong to me. They were to be offered. And I felt a friendly sympathy for them, indulgence, pity, but also glad of them, almost proud of them, they were the best that could be hoped for from the person I am. I felt the kindness of the audience. And I said to myself, After all I will do. These poems will do, they will not last, but here and now they will do.

Robert waited five minutes after the last chimes, she said. For anyone hindered on the journey and arriving late. The pause became a thoughtful silence. Then the compere, the selflessly officiating Hell's Angel, squeezed sideways along the wall, halted half way, nodded to me, and addressing the audience, who all turned to listen, mumbled a few sentences on the subject of my achievements to date. Shrugged then, nodded again to me, and edged crabwise back to his post between the door and the refreshments. Thank you, I said. All of you. I am grateful to be here.

And that, friends, was my story. So saying, she made her little gesture of thanks and acknowledgement with her clasped hands. And opened her eyes.

She was not surprised, only sad, at the revelation of her remoteness. She heard applause, but only as on a small island one hears from over the hill the Atlantic surf on the western shore. The faces looked kind and appreciative, but she saw them as if through a mist or with very impoverished eyesight. She was tired, but had nowhere to sit. She looked beyond the rows of chairs to where Robert must be, but could make out only that he was bending over the tables, away from her. He's taking the cling-film off the little sandwiches, she said to herself. He's seeing to the coffee and the tea. How sad that I can't eat or drink. How sad that I cannot partake.

Siding with the Weeds

TWO YEARS LATER BERT phoned. It's me, he said. You doing anything Thursday? Not that I know of, said Joe. Wednesday, all being well, it's Help the Aged, and Friday I'm seeing the quack, but Thursday's a blank. Why? Thought you might come over for a spot of lunch, said Bert. And Thursday's as good a day as any, from my point of view. And come on the train, then we can have a drink. Oh I'm a great one for public transport, said Joe. Bus pass, railcard, what more does a man need? I never drive anywhere if I can help it. I can't think when I'm driving. Very good, said Bert. Don't ring at the front. Come round the side, I'll leave the gate open. I'll be in the shed. I'm mostly in the shed nowadays. See you Thursday. Mind how you go.

Late summer, many weeks of drought. Heading south on the 9.01, Joe of course noted the parched fields and the early dead leaves; but the carriage was quiet, he had a window seat, he'd be glad to see Bert again, and when you speed through and note the signs of a process you can do nothing about, who will blame you if you say to yourself, Oh well, enjoy what's left while it lasts? As he had said to Bert, he couldn't think on a motorway, not even in the slow lane, but in the train he could, he sat back and looked at the scenery and thought, I'm glad the old bugger phoned.

The way came back to him. Briskly he walked the mile from the station to Bert's estate, a cul-de-sac with a narrow entrance into a ring of semi-detached Sunshine Houses, all with key-hole porches, around a green. Bert lived at the far end, dead-straight ahead as you entered the close. You can't miss it, it's painted red and the only one with solar panels. Joe crossed the green which was threadbare, dirty yellow and as hard as concrete.

As instructed, Joe let himself in round the side and stood then looking down the garden– or gardens, to be exact: 77 and 76 ran with a broken fence between them, narrowing, to a common point. Neither was a credit to the neighbourhood and that could not be blamed on the drought. 76 had at least gone to ruin, and the remains – sundial, birdbath, headless nymph, etc. – were sort of picturesque; but in 77, Bert's, also let go, the struggle between nature and culture was still in progress and Joe, though without strong preference for either, felt uneasy. However, seeing the shed, Bert's new pride and joy, built towards the apex of the two gardens across the width of both, he cheered up and muttered, Well, I'll be damned – a land-grab! And behind that new thing the trees were still doing well, the three immense black poplars, the two out-soaring-them lombardies, and the sycamore Bert himself had planted thirty-five years ago, all far too big now, quite out of place, not baleful but very self-confident.

The long grass with its dandelions, poppies, cow parsley, was mostly dead. Joe followed the path that Bert had trampled through it and peered in at the large front window of the handsome shed. He saw books, maps, stones, minerals, a microscope, a laptop, a simple table and chair, sunlight streaming through a velux in the roof, white walls on which were charts, more maps and half a dozen scripts in red and gold lettering of which the most prominent, behind the back of whoever sat at the desk, was, GLORY BE TO GOD FOR THINGS THAT ROT.

But the room had no occupant. The sun shone brightly in upon a very particular kind of collection. Joe saw there was an idea in it. Yes, bringing things together like that was the work of his old friend; but peering through glass at it, Joe couldn't quite see what was going on. Again he felt the uneasiness he had felt at the first sight of the liberated garden. What's the man up to now? he wondered, with a twinge of something like bad conscience.

The shed door, to the right of that window, was half open. Joe pushed at it and entered a decently floored corridor with another door at the far end, closed and a darker light showing through its glass. A bench was fitted along the righthand wall and it, and the shelves above it, were crammed with the paraphernalia of odd jobs and gardening. Not a sound. Joe advanced almost fearfully, past the room he had viewed through the window, to a second, whose door was ajar. And there, breathing deeply, instead of knocking with the knuckle of his right index finger, he raised all five to the door and gently, very gently, pushed. Inside, in a black captain's chair, at a large black mahogany desk, facing a sunless window, sat Bert, slumped, chin on his chest, unshaven, dribbling slightly, faintly muttering, his eyes shut.

They were old friends, very fond of one another in an unspoken, evasive, rather shifty fashion, and Joe's first thought, like many of his thoughts said softly aloud, was, What's he doing this to me for? Yes, invited, summoned almost, Joe, seeing that his friend wasn't dead, felt he had a right to be quite vexed and he said to himself, *sotto voce,* Not made much of an effort, have we? The flip–flops, dirty shorts, stained tee shirt, grizzle. In the affront there was also an indecency, and some shame, that touched him too, and a thrill of fear. He was backing away, when Bert, not raising his head, opened one eye and perfectly audibly in his familiar doleful tone of voice asked, You been there long? And felt with his right hand for Joe's and gripped it tight. The old friendship, or needing help getting up?

On his feet, spacing his bowly legs, Bert looked livelier. He had big ears, dense curls of dirty grey hair, a sharp nose, a grin, most of his teeth. If you need a Jimmy Riddle, he said: out the back, any one of the compost heaps, there's logs to stand on, aim through the bars, or over if you prefer and can, don't fall off, and mind the wasps. Wash and brush up in that sink there. Champagne on the Pay-She-Owe soon as you're ready.

Returning, Joe found everything set up full in the sun on the brick circle, pleasing as a marble threshing floor, that Bert called the Pay-She-Owe. All from over the wall, he said, one or two at a time, in my knapsack. Be seated, friend. Dead centre in the brick ring stood a small round wooden table, either side of it two wooden slatted chairs and on it, at the midpoint, two glasses and a very dusty bottle of champagne. With his left hand he gripped the neck and with his right, delicately as a bomb-disposal officer, untwisted and removed the wire. Joe noticed that all his nails, some broken, were rimmed with black. Watch this, said Bert. The cork, as it were suspiciously, with a slowness Joe found hard to bear, eased itself out of a terrible constraint towards release. Bert gripped the neck and in silence both men concentrated their vision on the event. The explosion, though expected, was a shock. The cork flew up dead straight to a sky-lark height, and with great coolness, disregarding the white overspill, Bert got to his feet, and as the cork's ascent wavered, paused and was reversed, watching, watching, he positioned himself exactly and caught it obeying gravity plumb in the middle of his uplifted M & S sunhat. You've done that before, said Joe. Have indeed, said Bert. But never with an audience. Once I invited Freddy from next door but he was bad that day and wouldn't leave his bed. Easy when there's no wind.

Bert poured out. Here's to the endgame, he said. May it be as long as it is painless. You made any plans yet? Thought I'd wait till tomorrow, said Joe. Bert refilled their glasses. Already Joe felt what his Aunty Ev would have called tiddly. Good stuff this, he said. Won it in the Branch raffle, I suppose? Bert wiped the dust off the label with the brim of his hat. Veuve Clicquot 1998. Out the back, he said, over that wall, behind the big trees, two or three years ago they began demolishing Paradise Square but went bust before they could finish and put a hoarding round the site and buggered off. Some roofless walls still standing, much of the rubble never trucked away.

First there was the absence of noise, which only very slowly became the presence of silence. And then one night, said Bert, it sounded like somebody whispering, Take up your life again. No thanks, I said. I'm well off without it. No you're not, she said. You're neither use nor ornament without it. Whispering. I was already sleeping down here by then, on a camp bed in the back, where the noise had been worst and where the silence settling in was most persuasive. That whispering. It was two summers ago and I woke very early one morning hearing the owls. It was just getting light and a voice – my own as like as not – said, Now or never. So I dressed and went out and climbed over Freddy's fence to an old door in the wall he'd shown me once where he and his big sister had gone scrumping apples when they were kids. Through that door and through a gap smashed in the hoarding, I entered the ruins of Paradise Square.

I was a latecomer. The children were in first, lighting fires and making dens, and after them the drunks and the druggies, and lovers in the orchards and a desperate camp or two, men and women with nowhere else to lay their heads. But it's a roomy zone, I have my hours and my own interests, and any encounters with my fellow humans are courteous enough and brief. We have equal rights, we're all trespassers. I found the cellar that first morning, when I was looking for nothing. Standing there, spellbound by the birdsong and the flora in the flickering light, I saw a way underground through a thicket of buddleia. That's where the bubbly came from, and much else besides, and plenty left. But if you stayed the night, at daybreak I'd conduct you through the ruins and what I'd show you would be the weeds, the ragwort and the willow herb, buttercups, comfrey, chickweed, thistles, toadflax, doing well despite the drought, thirty-seven species I've identified, and I'm no botanist, not yet, but enough of one to tell you what it will be like in there when the rain comes as it surely will one day, to us, the undeserving. And what those flowery ruins are now and what they will be after a deluge of forgiving rain, you'd have it in your mind's eye till your dying day and all in the glorious downpour of the dawn chorus. I'm on the 17.33, said Joe. Or I have to pay again. Take your glass in there, old son, said Bert. Sit quiet among my curiosities for a quarter of an hour. We eat in the back where you found me drowsing.

The front room was entirely lit with sun. Joe took off his boater and with a spotless white handkerchief mopped his pink crown. He wore a pale linen jacket, a red shirt, light baggy trousers, sandals, red socks. He sat down at Bert's desk and gazed over the wildering garden at the family home which he got the feeling Bert had more or less vacated. Rum bloke, our Bert. The champagne had hushed all Joe's anxieties so that he grinned and shook his dapper little head in wonder at the life and habitation of his funny friend. On the window ledge before him were fossils, glistening minerals, the neat white skull of a gannet. In a little pot on the desk, lifting the lid, he saw shark's teeth, a flint arrowhead and an army button from the First World War. Pens and good paper for more calligraphy; an unfinished script: DON'T YOU FIND IT A BEAUTIFUL CLEAN THOUGHT… Half turning, he glanced along the shelves: so many maps of Britain, its modern appearance, its geology, and, on the shelf below, handbooks of flowers, trees, mammals, birds, fish, insects, fossils, a colourful run that ended in a black box-file labelled in neat red capitals EXTINCTION. Joe smiled, laid down his head and dozed. And at once he was back in an ancient nightmare from his years as a traveller, mostly through the Midlands, in self-help books and ladies' underwear. He moaned and pleaded, the terror always exceeded his memory of it, and feeling a firm right hand on his left shoulder he sat up with a terrible shout. Lunch is served, Mr Winterbottom, said Bert. Oh thank God it's you, said Joe. Give me a minute I'll be right as rain.

Leaving, he motioned to the back wall and its inscriptions. Lovely work, he said. Especially the 'Glory be…' And at the door he halted, to study a photograph blue-tacked above a display of fossil shells emergent, as it seemed, out of the dull limestone. In the photo a president's son stood grinning by the corpse of an elephant he had shot, holding in one hand his knife and in the other the creature's severed tail. Important picture for me that, said Bert. Not a Damascus Road Experience – I was on the right road anyway – but a powerful corroboration all the same. Come and eat and drink.

They moved next door, to the room facing north, not cold but many degrees darker than the room of the curiosities. Now Joe saw clearly that it was fitted out to be lived in: wood-burner, camp bed, sink, camping gaz, all the necessaries. The desk was laid as their table. Bert motioned Joe into the captain's chair and seated himself on an upturned packing-case that had once held tea from Assam. Only couscous, he said. Too hot for anything else. But to be honest, couscous is what I mostly eat. Very variable, I find. And it doesn't spoil the claret. He poured two glasses from a bottle draped in cobwebs. Tuck in, he said.

For a while they ate in silence, with a pensive appetite, Bert topping up the drink. Then Joe dabbed at his mouth and thin moustache with a square of kitchen paper, and said, That bastard and the poor elephant, how exactly did they advance your thinking? It made me admit a very shocking thing, Bert replied, turning to look his old friend in the eyes. I suddenly knew beyond a doubt that in my philosophy the elephant had more value than his killer, my fellow human. If I could have saved the life of only one of them I would have saved the elephant – as being more beautiful, more intelligent, more *intact*, more useful to his kind, and to Mother Earth herself far – oh far! – less harmful. And admitting that, my mind ran to other comparisons, quite a list I had in no time of well-known humans whom I thought less valuable than an elephant or, if I'm honest, than a dolphin, a kingfisher or a certain visiting black cat. Slippery slope, I said to myself. And I've never told a living soul till you. I don't want to end up a misanthrope. Joe sipped his wine and pondered a while. Then he asked, What was the beautiful clean thought you began writing in the other room? I think I shan't finish it, Bert replied. Or if I do I won't put it on the wall. It's not my thought anyway, but when I saw the photograph it came back to me, from many years ago, and I wondered. Well? said Joe. It's this, Bert said: 'Don't you find it a beautiful clean thought, a world empty of people, just uninterrupted grass, and a hare sitting up?' Let's change the subject, shall we? Have a plum. Our victoria has made its last effort, the blossom was a wonder and then more fruit than ever and none of it wormy. Made a good end, that tree did, a very good end.

So you're mostly down here, said Joe. Don't blame you. Peace and quiet and you can get on with your thinking. Like you, old chap, I've got the place to myself and sometimes, as my Uncle Horace used to say, I sits and thinks and sometimes I just sits. Just sitting's best, said Bert, if you can do it. Yes, every two or three days I have an hour or so in the house. Check emails, see if there's any post, phone if I have to, order books or another water butt, do my bit of washing. That sort of thing. But I'm easier down here, in the mornings at least, evenings are bad sometimes and there's generally a passage in the night I can hardly bear. Early mornings are best, among my curiosities. That cat I mentioned, now and then she comes to the window, I let her in, she lies quiet on the desk, very close, under the lamp, and she sleeps or sometimes she just bides still and watches my writing hand and in her own fashion thinks. I never know will she come or not. I like that. When she does, it's a blessing. This shed – in case you're wondering – I had it built with the insurance money. First death, you know. I was always sure that would be me. I asked Freddy could I buy the end of his garden. Take the bloody lot, he said. But I only wanted the end bit, with the door in the wall. He didn't want any money, but I insisted and got a lawyer and did it all properly. I want to leave things in good order. All signed and sealed. And the weeds thriving.

Joe thought he felt another slumping of his friend's spirits and that again a change of subject might be called for. What's that contraption out the back? he asked. Like a scaffold or something. Bert brightened. That, he said, is the beginnings of my Tower of Silence. *Was*, I should say – the council told me I'd need planning permission and I'd never get it. So what you saw there is the ruin of my big idea. I'm not sure I know what a Tower of Silence is, said Joe, pleased to see Bert almost jolly. They're very popular in Iran, said Bert, and in India too, so I hear, at least among the Zoroastrians. I really can't see why I shouldn't build one behind my own shed but the law's the law and I don't want the enforcers round. So you climb up and be silent? said Joe. In a manner of speaking, yes, said Bert. Except you don't climb, you're dead, somebody else has to winch you up and lay you out. I was going to ask you would you do me that favour but now I'm prohibited from proceeding so you are spared. I see, said Joe. And, after a pause, So you lie up there dead, in silence of course. And then what? The birds eat you, said Bert. As I told the council woman, cremation is bad for the environment, birds are the way forward. You may be right, she said, but you'll never get planning permission. Birds? said Joe. Not blue tits and such, surely? No, no, said Bert. You'd be there for ever if you left it to the blue tits. Abroad, it's vultures – where there's any left, that is – in India they've poisoned most of them – but here, if the idea catches on, it will be kites, red kites, they're about the only thing doing well in these desperate times. Approaching London in the good old days, you'd see the sky black with them. But then the tide turned and they came to the brink of extinction. Now they're back again, in force – marvellous what a bit of attentive love will do – and over this suburban garden, very often. My wish, though I'm no Zoroastrian, was to be eaten by red kites and leave nothing behind but a few bits of bone and gristle that would soon rot. And you elected me to winch you up and lay you out, said Joe. I'm very touched. The woman in the council office said my next best option would be a woodland burial, said Bert. It's getting very popular with people like you, she said. So if you outlive me, and I sincerely hope you will, I'll have your name down for a bit of help with that.

Silence, friendly, drifting towards melancholy. Finish it, shall we? said Bert, pouring. I could get a taste for this, said Joe, holding up the dark light. Plenty more in the darkness under the earth in the ruins of Paradise Square, said Bert. Come out the back, will you? I've no one else to explain myself to. Freddy's close to calling it a day, and besides it was never his cup of tea. Again Joe was touched, though he couldn't honestly say feeding yourself to the crows was his cup of tea either. Something to tell Alice. Fridays I have lunch with my lady-friend, he said. You won't mind me telling her, will you? She's very interested in the human race and what's to be done with it. She'll ask me what the quack said and after that she'll say, Well, Joe, what else have you got for me? You won't mind if I tell Alice about my visit? Not at all, said Bert. Two heads are better than one when you're trying to make sense of things.

Out the back Bert pointed first to the compost heaps, three of them, open to the air, built of sturdy uprights and well-spaced horizontal battens along the still-standing ivy-draped breeze blocks of Freddy's bunker. I scavenged the timber, needless to say, he said. Any amount of it going begging over there. I treasure my compost heaps. I love to think of the rotting, and all the microbial life in them, he said. You can't see it, of course, but it's in there, multiplying. I sit down on that box some evenings and watch what I can't see. I wonder do you have dark thoughts this side and light thoughts in the room at the front? Joe asked. Both in both places, said Bert, and always more dark than light. But I do also have ecstasies, which are neither one nor the other.

Joe strolled to the left-hand corner, past the abandoned beginnings of the Tower of Silence, to a large black plastic dustbin, and took the lid off. Whistled appreciatively, threw the lid aside and with both hands dug into the bin. Fine soil, he said, raising it up, squeezing it, sniffing it. Haven't seen the like since I was a kid. My father was nuts about it. Riddling soil was practically all he did when he came back from the War, so my poor mother said. Grow anything in soil like that. Too rich for the weeds, said Bert. It does for my few vegetables. But that's not why I spend so many hours over it. I can't stop seeing that x-ray photo of the baby albatross its loving mother stuffed to death with bits of plastic. Freddy's bunker had a polystyrene roof on once and it blew off and shattered and much of it's in little pieces in the body of this earth. Plastic, crumbs of old cladding, broken glass: it dances on the riddle when the soil's gone through. True, there's a flint now and then or a length, or even a bowl, of an old clay pipe and they go to heaven in my sunny front room. But it's Gehenna for the rest, via the council landfill bin.

There's Freddy's door, said Bert, nodding beyond the compost heaps. I like to think of him and his big sister sneaking through it for the apples. He's such a big man now. I don't think he appeared last time I visited, said Joe. I've no memory of him, to be honest. He's been a recluse for years, said Bert. He'd come out at night sometimes and if it was a night when I couldn't sleep I might see him in his ruined garden. He wore his trilby and his greatcoat, for all the world as if he were going travelling, which he never was. I'd stand in the dark in the back bedroom, watching him. I never saw a man so good at standing still. He'd have his hands in his pockets and he'd stand there looking at

God knows what, and thinking. He wouldn't let me in to sign the contract for his bit of land, he wouldn't even read it, just signed his name over the fence and said, Good riddance to it and good luck to you, neighbour. He's big, not corpulent, and when I was building my tower I couldn't help thinking of the weight of him. Cheerful neighbours might do you good, I'd say, said Joe. A young couple with a couple of kids, looking on the bright side, making a go of it. And now I must be making tracks. I haven't shown you the triumph of the life of weeds in the ruins of Paradise Square, said Bert. Next time, said Joe. Bert shook his head. Well, I'll imagine it, said Joe. Do you recall the bombsites? said Bert. And the old army camp where they practised what they'd need to be able to do in the war? The Camp and the bombsites where we used to do as we liked from dawn till dusk and nobody thinking we'd get carried off by evil strangers? All the weeds, the willow herb especially, that everybody said came in with the bombs, that surge of it, so tall and delicate, the soft pink purple red and the billions upon billions of seeds they released to rise and drift and occupy elsewhere? Truth is, the seeds are in there waiting, Joe, biding their time, they've got all the time in the world, one day the fire will come again, one day there'll come the colossal ruin and the plough of some disaster will break through the concrete and find the good earth deep down that is full of far more seeds than all the galaxies in the universe are full of stars. Paradise lost, the garden enclosed, where the bombs hit and young men trained with bayonets, guns and grenades. Remember that late afternoon we sat in a circle in gasmasks for a lark, in a lair among the weeds, and nobody spoke, all we did was make faces through the dirty perspex and grunt and wave our arms at one another, boys and girls, in a rum sort of Eden? And then Val and Enid took their knickers off and showed us their little fannies? Time I was gone, said Joe, though it was only four o'clock. And I've been thinking a lot about the Berlin Wall, said Bert, the Death Strip on the East side but the grass, the weeds, the rabbits, the birds and butterflies on the West side where nobody could build, the land they had to let be, trees sprung from seeds high up on the bombed-out tenements, sprouting out sideways, lifting up to the sky, tall ruins and the trees reaching up from that dizzy hold and that scant nourishment in rotting mortar, up and up. Thirty years, let be. And Chernobyl, Joe, I wonder do you think of Chernobyl the way I do? I don't mean the accident, I mean the aftermath, the recovery, how all other forms of life rejoiced to see the back of us, how exuberantly their lives resumed and prospered, how well they get on without us, they breed so fast they get rid of our filthiest filth within the lifetime of a man. Happy zone of recovery and flourishing, once homo-so-called-sapiens has fucked off out of it. Now don't get het up, Bert, said Joe fearfully, seeing the flecks of white on his old friend's lips. No sense giving yourself a heart attack, it won't mend the situation, and besides not everything is hurrying to hell in a handcart, only yesterday I watched a programme about water voles, doing well, it seems, on the Somerset levels, scores of sibling groups and breeding pairs released into the wild, doing very well, so the nice woman said, along the riverbank.

They turned to go in. Fancy walking to the station with me? said Joe. Bert shuddered. Half-way then? said Joe. Bit of exercise, bit of a change of scenery? I find a trot round the block works wonders when you're up to your neck in the Slough of Despond. Bert stared at him. Circles in the cul-de-sac, he muttered. Joe shrugged and was close to saying, Never mind, old feller, forget it, next time, eh? But then Bert nodded, Why not? he said, Why on earth not? Suddenly the idea animated him, he grinned, he tugged at the lobe of his left ear. Give me a quarter of an hour. Go and sit among my curiosities where it's sunny. There's a trilobite on the window ledge, far right, I found it in a stream under Wenlock Edge. And a bowl of cinders, many different colours, from Vesuvius. How abundant Earth is and how little I know about her! I bought a brief introduction to botany and on every page there were half a dozen words I didn't understand. So I bought a dictionary of botanical terms and now I'm making headway, as into a foreign language I will need for a country I want to travel in. Sit in the front room, old son. I still don't like being in the house, but just for you, to look decent on a walk with you towards the railway station, I'll have a shave and find a clean tee shirt and a pair of trousers. Give me fifteen minutes.

They paused at the open door of the sunny front room. Bert ushered Joe in and, standing on the threshold, he said, I know the noise will return. One morning I'll be in this room, the black cat will be on the desk, under the lamp, I'll be in the state of quiet, doing my calligraphy, raising my eyes now and then to the window of our bedroom, where Kay's things still are, where I never go, and suddenly my visiting cat will prick up her ears, she'll hear it first, she'll look alarmed, and at my back then I'll hear the trucks have come, work will begin again, they'll cart away the rubble and the weeds, all that unending beauty of weeds, they'll evict the lovers and the down-and-outs and begin building affordable homes for the very rich – I know that, Joe. Meanwhile, in the time allowed, I'll sieve soil, I'll make barrowloads of fine tilth and the bits that jig on the riddle at the end, the ugly wounding shards that will never rot, I'll put them in the appropriate council bin for landfill. I'll encourage a riot of life among billions of worms and insects in my airy compost heaps. And in my thriving garden I'll grow a few vegetables in among the weeds, in among the poppies and the groundsel and the scarlet pimpernel and the shepherd's purse, my veg will grow with the weeds' permission, as you might say. In a nutshell, Joe, my endgame will consist in siding with the weeds. You can tell Alice that, I'd be glad if a lady-friend of yours knew that about me. And I hope when you tell her what the quack said it's nothing bad.

The Diver

When Lucy was eleven she accompanied her father, an amateur diver, on one of his expeditions, the last as it turned out. Her mother did not want her to go. She was far too young 'for that sort of thing', and the boat would make her sick. But her father brushed these objections aside. Time she learned, he said. And Lucy herself, at that age always taking her father's part in any disagreement with her mother, made such a fuss that in the end her mother said, Do as you please then. And on your own head be it.

Mr Jarvis kept his diving gear and his boat, the *Hesperus*, at a cheerful little fishing port a couple of hours' drive away. In the heavy traffic he had to stop two or three times for Lucy to be sick, and when at last they got there she looked more dead than alive. His mate – an older man called Ike – was waiting on the quay. This is Lucy, said Jarvis. Usually she looks much better. Pleased to meet you, Lucy, said Ike.

They went aboard. The *Hesperus* had a heroic past as a landing craft at Dunkirk and Sword Beach. After the war, refitted, painted black, she became a small salvage vessel, and for quite some years Ike himself sailed her and made a dubious living in that trade. Buying the *Hesperus*, Jarvis acquired Ike too and soon, though licensed himself, mostly left things to him. They headed off, it was still early, the sea was quiet. Lucy perked up and sat in the bows eating a bacon bap prepared for her, with lashings of ketchup, by her father in the ship's very pokey galley. This is the life, eh? he said. Lucy nodded; Ike, at the wheel, kept his own counsel, as he generally did.

It seemed to Lucy that they were not making for anywhere in particular, just out to sea. She glanced back: either side of the wheelhouse the coast was diminishing. And ahead there was nothing, only the quiet sea and on it, very distant, one large ship passing across and becoming small. Her father could not keep still. He went continually between Lucy in the bows and Ike in the wheelhouse, paused at each like a man wishing to speak, but only smiled, gestured towards the horizon, chuckled, turned up his hands and resumed his inconclusive little passages to and fro. Perhaps he had so much to say he couldn't say any of it. At last he disappeared below and when he came back on deck, advancing laboriously, he was wearing his diving-suit and boots and carrying his helmet. Ike showed no interest, and continued at the same speed towards, as it seemed, nowhere in particular. But Lucy did not know what to make of her father in his outfit. He carried the helmet under his right arm, like a spare head much larger than his normal one. He looked rather warily at his daughter, as though fearful that the seriousness inside him, which he could not conceal, might be too much for her to bear. You look funny, Dad, she said. In truth, she was disconcerted by his new shape and manner. Yes, well, he said. This is the gear. Not all of it, of course. Ike will help me with the rest when we get there.

The *Hesperus* slowed, the engine shifted its note and rhythm into idling, and the sea's own voices, subdued till now, quietly took possession of the emptied space. Ike left the wheelhouse, went below, and in two or three trips assembled the rest of the necessary paraphernalia and began to dress Jarvis for the dive. Squire and knight, said Jarvis. Ike said nothing. Lucy thought of Sir Lancelot and was suddenly frightened by the real spectacle of her father being accoutred.

Has Mum ever seen you like this? she asked. No, said her father. As a matter of fact she hasn't.

They were out of sight of any land by now. Another big ship was visible ahead but, like the first, proceeding on its own course far away and lessening. This is the place, Jarvis said. Ike had almost done. The weights were belted on, the boots and gauntlets clasped watertight, the harness donned, the airline and the hauling rope coupled up. Remained only the helmet, a splendid Soviet model in copper and brass. With great solemnity, as though it were a crown, Mr Jarvis raised it high above his head, then lowered it very slowly into position. Ike bolted it to the corselet. Much distress awaited Lucy, and this was the first thrill and intimation of it. Her father, small and slight in his normal reality, now bulked enormously before her. At the same time, viewed through the glass, his head seemed an entity in itself, detached and imprisoned, beyond help. She looked to Ike – he shrugged – then back at her father, at what was still visible of his natural exterior self, encased and on view in the helmet. He must have seen her unease. His mouth made a smile and his right hand, gigantic in the gauntlet, lifted in a clumsy thumbs-up. Then he waddled to the gunwale and the iron ladder there and in a few bubbles went below. Ike stood by the ladder paying out the line and observing the gauge.

Ike said nothing. Perhaps he was shy of young girls. Lucy might have been abashed too but the disappearance of her father in a few bubbles had dismayed her and she turned to the remaining grown-up for some reassurance. Why are we here? she asked. I mean, what's special about here? Ike shrugged. Search me, he said. It's always round about here, never anywhere else. – But doesn't he tell you why it's special? Doesn't he tell you what he sees down there? I don't ask, said Ike. He don't tell. But he looks happy enough when he comes up. Then, after a pause: Well, not exactly happy. More relieved, you might say. As though he's done what he came to do and now we can all go home. – But is there anything down there? – Usual stuff, I suppose. Weed, a few fish if you're lucky. Nothing worth bringing up. To the best of my knowledge nothing ever sank hereabouts. It's deep though, very deep. Not much light. And, on the line we've got, he's nowhere near the bottom. Lucy gasped at this revelation. – So what does he do all the time? – Just sort of dangles there, I suppose, till it's time to come up.

Lucy fell silent, looking inwards. There was a gap. She entered a trance, as in a fairytale or a nightmare, she was spellbound and with her mind's eye had to watch her father who, in a helplessness of his own, oscillated very slowly in the murk over an abyss. This passage out of time continued. Then she became aware that Ike was staring at her. Sorry, she said, with a shudder. Did you say something? – I said if you hold the line I'll go and make you another bacon bap. No thank you, Ike, she said. I'll just sit here till Dad comes up again. To be honest, I'm feeling a bit sick. – Just as well sit quiet then. I don't suppose he'll be long now. And I can always give him a tweak if you're worried.

Lucy was thinking, I shan't be able to tell anyone about this. Not even Mum. Especially not her. It's too weird. And she felt she wouldn't want such things bottled up inside her. Ike kept his eyes on the gauge. Lucy watched the surface, below which her father had vanished. After a while she couldn't bear it any more. She felt she shouldn't have to. Ike, she said, please will you give him a tweak. – Of course I will, darling, if you're worried. I'm sure he won't mind. He tweaked at the line. Lucy watched his face, saw it closely attending. He gave the signal again. Must have nodded off, he murmured. Wouldn't surprise me. Not very exciting just dangling there, I shouldn't think. Haul him up, shall we? Lucy bit her fist and nodded. Ike hitched the line to the winch and very slowly began turning the handle, to bring Mr Jarvis back into the light of day. Can't hurry, he said. Don't want him sick.

Lucy watched the line slowly and with pauses winding out of the water. But again and again she glanced at Ike's face to see if she could read anything in it that would dispel her fear. He was a professional, he must know. Her father left things to him, put himself in his hands. So long a time coming up, so deep her father had been down. She felt quite unfit to witness what was happening.

His emergence was very sudden. The helmet came through, archaic, resplendent, then the shoulders, the sea streaming back into itself off the human in his costume. Ike paused the winch, so that Jarvis, in the harness, seemed to stand there half way out. His arms, visible only as far as the gauntlets, hung slackly at his sides and his shoulders were hunched up by his bodyweight hanging. That was bad enough: the slack deadweight of a father dangling from a hoist half in, half out of, the water. But far worse was his face through the Cyclops window: the eyes were shut, the flesh was a leaden blue-grey colour. He's dead, said Lucy. And she began to scream. Ike hushed her softly and resumed the winching, until Jarvis's boots were just grazing the surface. Halting again, he reached out and very gently manoeuvred the diver through the gap in the gunwale where the ladder went down. Now the last of the seawater dripped off him on to the deck. Catch hold of his legs, Ike said to Lucy. When I lower him, stretch them out so he can sit down. She did as he directed, though clasping her father's legs felt wrong somehow. Still in the harness, to prevent him from slumping forward, Jarvis sat on the deck leaning back against the gunwale. Ike knelt by him and rapped smartly on the glass. That did the trick. Jarvis's eyes flung open, showing more horror than you'd think one human could contain, so that Lucy's relief was suffused with a vague and potent apprehension of what being a grown-up might entail. Then her father blinked, shook his head in its massive casing, and smiled. He'll be all right, said Ike. It takes some people that way sometimes. Like I said, he probably nodded off hanging there in the dark all on his tod. He unbolted the helmet and lifted it off. Lucy hugged her father's head. The smell of his hair was dank, not salty. Ike winched him up on to his own two feet and took off the belt of weights. Thanks, squire, said Jarvis, rather absently. Ike brewed some tea and dug out a packet of ginger nuts. Lucy and her father sat together in the bows, not saying much. It was sunny, the sea was quiet, quite soon the coast re-appeared, and before long they were back in harbour.

Usually Jarvis would take Ike for a drink but on this occasion he excused himself and gave him an extra fiver instead. They had better be getting on home, Mother would be worried about her daughter. The traffic was easy, they went along at a leisurely pace. Are you really all right, Dad? Lucy asked. Right as rain, he said. But a bit later he asked, Does my head look any different? The question troubled Lucy, but she answered that he was quite back to normal, his head, his colour, everything. Still feels as though I've got my helmet on, he said. And my voice has gone down in my chest. Lucy conceded that his voice was not coming out quite the way it should. Sounds a bit flat, she said. But she assured him in a grown-up girlish manner that he looked fine, he would be fine, they'd soon be home. He fell silent for most of the rest of the journey, occasionally yawning and mouthing things to himself, as though putting his speech organs to the test. And he rolled his head, as though it were too heavy and not quite balanced as it should be. Ten minutes from home, he said in a voice which did indeed sound to be struggling under the weight of many dark atmospheres, Don't tell Mum I was funny. It would only worry her. I'll be right as rain when I've had a sleep. Promise? Lucy promised, though she really did not want any such secret harbouring in her for evermore.

Rivers of Blood

Stories in Two Voices

ALICE MAPENDA: I remember the silence. Thinking about it, that's what first came back to me. If I remembered nothing else, that would be something, wouldn't it, the feeling of silence? But tell me – since I am very interested in the truth – did we really walk in silence?

HARRY CLAYTON: We did. And the people on the pavements, they stood in silence. Actually, to be precise, two voices were raised against us, separate voices, an elderly man, and ten minutes later another elderly man, they shouted out against us.

AM: You remember that?

HC: No, I read it. To be honest, I'm not sure I even remember the silence, not myself. But I've been reading up about it. The papers said we walked in silence, 'the coloured people' along the way stood in silence, and there were two hecklers, two elderly white men. And apart from that: it was May Day, early evening, and it was raining.

AM: And we gathered at Rose Lane. You were already there.

HC: Yes, I was watching for you. To be honest, I was hoping you would come on your own, but you arrived hand in hand with Jack. I looked at you, the pair of you, for half a minute before you saw me. Funny how these things never die. It goes through me again and still, even now.

AM: It wasn't silent while we were gathering.

HC: No, there was the noise of an increasing crowd, that murmur, like starlings before they swarm, louder and louder, only the nearest voices speaking in words you could understand, the rest, the mass, all a murmur, the murmur of a gathering solidarity, like nothing else on earth.

AM: Unfolding the banners, handing out placards, the stewards going round. And before we set off everybody hushed.

HC: You remember that? So it must have been before we moved off that Jack said the lines. Jealousy is a horrible thing. He was still holding your hand. I can see his face, quite the most beautiful I ever saw on a man, and even then I knew in my heart that he wasn't showing off, he spoke very softly, not to you nor to me, more to himself, in a musing sort of way. Of course, I didn't understand what it meant, but even that wouldn't have mattered, only for the jealousy.

AM:

> 'O tandem magnis pelagi defuncte periclis!
> sed terrae graviora manent. In regna Lavini
> Dardanidae venient; mitte hanc de pectore curam;
> sed non et venisse volent. Bella, horrida bella,
> et Thybrim multo spumantem sanguine cerno.
> non Simois tibi, nec Xanthus, nec Dorica castra
> defuerint; alius Latio iam partus Achilles,
> natus et ipse dea; nec Teucris addita Iuno
> usquam aberit; cum tu supplex in rebus egenis
> quas gentis Italum aut quas non oraveris urbes!
> Causa mali tanti coniunx iterum hospita Teucris
> externique iterum thalami.'

HC: So you know it too?

AM: I learned it later, many years later.

HC: And he wasn't even reading Classics! Did he not do Engineering?

AM: Yes, he did. He thought it would be more useful. And I suppose he was right. Engineering would have been more useful.

HC: Rose Lane. Then over Magdalen Bridge and round the Plain. And on very slowly down the Cowley Road. Do you know I'd never been down the Cowley Road before that evening? If I ever crossed the bridge it was to go left to the Moulin Rouge or right to the river. Never once till that 1 May did I walk down the Cowley Road.

AM: Who did?

HC: I'll bet you and Jack did. I'll bet you leafleted at the Cowley Works.

AM: So what if we did? The past isn't everything. You can't live off the past.

HC: You're not like me. I have to keep persuading myself there was once a time of hope and I lived then and acted hopefully and thousands around me were doing the same.

AM: You mean to say you can't live hopefully now without believing there was a hopeful time back then, half a century ago?

HC: No, I can't. Can anyone live without believing in such a past?

AM: Millions have no such past. And most of those who do, live without ever giving it a thought.

HC: Still I do live like that. Seeing you again makes me know it. It's a way of the imagination. Convince yourself there was once a time of hope, really, here on earth. Believe it. Better still: remember it. Remember you were there.

AM: By 'remember' you mean read up about it?

HC: I remember the feeling of the occasion, I read up the real details if they're anywhere still to be found.

AM: Tell me some. Perhaps we're not so very different, you and I. Tell me a few of the details you have unearthed.

HC: Heath sacked him from the Shadow Cabinet. London dockers and meat-porters went on strike and marched to the Houses of Parliament. They wanted him re-instated, they wanted him for the next prime minister. Our little march – not that little, the biggest since Cuba, two thousand or so – our little march was eleven days after his speech, on May Day, International Labour Day, Red Flag Day. Ruskin called for it. Listen to this: 'There must be many people in Oxford who would like to express their dismay at the recent upsurge of racialist innuendo. A whole complex of insecurities has emerged, which put in question this country's entire moral and social state. The fate of the immigrants has been discussed as though they were so much scrap, to be shunted hither and thither as the vagaries of opinion – and the movements of the economy – heartlessly dictate.' *Cherwell* carried a photo of an Oxford student, an Anarchist by the name of Piers Greenwood – did you know him?

AM: Maybe. But I wasn't with the Anarchists then.

HC: In the photo he was shown on the ground being kicked by pro-Powell dockers. It was in London at a printmakers demonstration. Apart from that, the Race Relations Bill was being debated in Parliament. The Nigerian government were slaughtering Igbos with British arms and employing famine as a weapon of war. *Rebel without a Cause* was on again at the Scala.

AM: Yes, I went to see it with Jack. He didn't much like it. He said there were any number of causes. Open your eyes. Look around.

HC: To be honest, I'm not sure I'd have gone on that march but for you. And when you turned up with Jack I felt there was no point me being there and if I'd had the nerve I'd have left you to it.

AM: Then you'd have missed something good. It was an occasion, like Grosvenor Square or the big Iraq War demonstration. Surely you were glad to have been there?

HC: Yes, I was glad. Trouble with me is, I'm often gladder afterwards. Sometimes *long* afterwards. That may be because it takes me a long time to take things in. So perhaps when a thing is happening and when I'm there I'm not quite sure whether to be glad or not. That march from Rose Lane, down the Cowley Road, right at James Street, back down the Iffley Road, down the High and Cornmarket to St Giles, I thought about it on and off for several years, along with much else in that particular year, and, yes, I was glad I had been there. But only these last few weeks, knowing I'd see you again after half a century, did I set myself to remembering all I could and to reading up on what I couldn't, and then, like two or three other events in that same year, the silent march through the immigrant area became very clear and luminous to me, and I am deeply glad of it. I looked for us, the three of us, in all the photos I could uncover but was never sure of a sighting, though the *type* – you and me, at least – was everywhere visible. I didn't see Jack. He was a rarer kind and it's a pity I saw no photograph of him. There were several photos of the people along the route. They were watching with great attention. My impression now – I don't know how I felt then – is that they didn't quite know what to make of us, or of it, the occasion, but at least they knew our incursion into their territory was friendly.

AM: There was a banner – Somerville International Socialists, if I remember rightly – it said: WOULD YOU LET YOUR DAUGHTER MARRY ENOCH POWELL? Do you remember it?

HC: Can't honestly say I do – not the thing itself, so to speak. But I came across it in my reading up. If it wasn't Somerville, it was St Anne's. What did your mother and father say to you marrying Jack?

AM: We didn't tell them. I only took him home after we'd done it. I wasn't very considerate in those days. They didn't exactly shut the door in our faces but nor did they ask us to stay. So after a couple of hours and nobody saying very much we walked back to the railway station.

HC: Why did you marry him?

AM: Because I loved him.

HC: Quite a few of your sort – of our sort – had given up on marriage by then.

AM: He got citizenship, but that's not why we did it. But just as well we did, as things turned out. I was pregnant when he left, though he didn't know that. He was dead when Elsa was born, though I didn't know that. I went home and they took me in. They took me back into their hearts when the baby was born, and when I learned her father was dead they kept me safe in the land of the living when all I wanted was to go down among the dead.

HC: I wrote you a letter when I heard about Jack. Perhaps you never got it? I wrote to College, I thought they would forward it.

AM: They did.

HC: You never wrote back.

AM: But I read your letter and I was grateful to you.

HC: I supposed you thought it would encourage me if you wrote back.

AM: What have you done with your life, Harry? Forgive me for asking, I always wonder and if they're still alive and I meet them I always ask people who knew Jack what they have done since he got killed.

HC: I don't mind you asking. I do the same. I often ask myself what I've been doing since Jack died, and not only Jack, three or four others besides him, I ask myself what I've been doing, what am I doing now, in the time that has been allowed me beyond theirs. Well, I've done various things, none of them heroic, nothing you'd put up in the firmament and that people would look out for at nights and be thankful for and be steadied and orientated by, nothing like that, nothing fit to be up there among the deeds of my own pantheon of saints and heroes.

AM: What, then?

HC: This and that, different forms of the same idea, I'd say. For nearly twenty years I had a partner called Masouda. She was much younger than me but we couldn't have children. She died not long ago. Anyway, we opened a library together, we called it the People's Library. It's still going, still called that, up five rickety flights of stairs in a part of town they keep saying they'll develop one day but they never have and now there's no money so with any luck they never will. Quite a big room when you get there and all the books properly in order around the walls. People donate books, and pamphlets, newspapers, posters, all sorts of ephemera. Only last week an old lady left us a suitcase of stuff from the Munich Soviet, priceless. Once a month there's a talk and a discussion. We've had speakers from all over the world, we're on the network, it's almost the old International, the idea of it at least, the survival, the new beginnings, who knows? When nobody else offered, Masouda or I would do something. Her last talk was about women in the Commune. Everybody's heard of Louise Michel, but there were others, many others, needless to say, making a start at least in that brief interlude of a possibility of justice. I'm giving a talk on Kropotkin next Thursday. It's hard without Masouda, quite a struggle, to be honest, but it's like with Jack, I'm alive and he isn't, I'm alive and Masouda isn't, they need me, if you take my meaning, in a way none of the living do. Did you ever blame Jack for going to Mozambique?

AM: Yes, I did. Not when he left. When I was twenty-three I didn't believe in death. A year later I did, and I felt I would never forgive him for going away and dying when I needed him so much. When Elsa was old enough, I told her the whole story. She was furious. Typical man, she said. Typical stupid man.

HC: Does she still feel that?

AM: Yes, I think she does. She forgives him, but she still thinks he owed allegiance to me first, not to an idea. When FRELIMO notified me of his death – on a cyclostyled form with a gap for the name – they sent me also, wrapped up in silver paper from a cigarette packet, the silver ring I had bought him in a junk shop on Folly Bridge. It was in the form of two entwining snakes, good magic, we said, against all evil. I wrote to the office in Dar Es Salaam, asking could they tell me where and in what circumstances he had been killed, but I got no answer. I wrote three more times and never got any answer. Then when the War of Liberation was won, I made a plan to go to Maputo, leaving Elsa with my parents, to discover what I could about Jack myself. But almost at once the Civil War began, and lasted another fifteen years, and I felt very bitterly that he had laid down his life for just the usual human mess. Why do you like Kropotkin? I know I used to, half a century ago.

HC: Because he was born into privilege and moved from that into revolt. Once a *page de chambre* of Czar Nicholas I, in 1882 he came to the Durham coalfields, he went into the pit villages, he talked to the miners and their families in the hovels they rented from the Company. He wore a working man's cap, which he took off on entering. That bald head, that big grizzled beard, that look of wondering innocence, he must have appeared to them like a visitation from another world, one in which the brotherhood of man was already achieved and he had come to spread the word of it to those who needed it first and most, the poor, the labouring classes, to foster solidarity for their struggle. He addressed their Big Meeting! I often think of that. His life had a purpose and a shape, it is fit to be looked at. And here's a thing – one of those emblematic moments: Escaping from prison in 1876, he crossed Russia and Sweden as fast as possible and spent a few days at Christiania, hoping for a passage to England. Seeing a likely steamer – let me read you this bit. 'I asked myself with anxiety, "Under which flag does she sail, – Norwegian, German, English?" Then I saw floating above the stern the Union Jack, – the flag under which so many refugees, Russian, Italian, French, Hungarian, and of all nations, have found an asylum. I greeted that flag from the depths of my heart.'

AM: I learned the other day that Powell wrote poetry. Every year he gave his wife a poem on her birthday.

HC: Yes, that's right. I read up about him in the *DNB*. He married Margaret but really, in his early years at least, like A.E. Housman, he preferred young men. And he wrote like Housman: 'The years that took my youth away,/ They brought to me instead/ The hunger that from day to day/ On other youth is fed…' And, also like A.E.H., he applied himself to the editing and explication of obscure ancient texts. Few know anything about the Rendel Harris Papyri, for example, but he knew all there was to know. That seems to have been part of the discipline: a sort of chosen pointlessness, meaningful as an act against the pointlessness of human existence because you yourself chose it. A scholar, a poet, master of many languages (including Urdu), 'a fine mind', fiercely independent, nobody's lobby-fodder, in that year after the Sexual Offences Act, had he gone back to young men and classical scholarship, he might well have caused no trouble to anyone. But instead it was Smethwick again: 'If you want a nigger for a neighbour, vote Labour!' And ancestral voices, his at least, prophesying rivers of blood.

AM:

    'At length having passed through the sea's great perils
    Worse awaits you on land: oh rest assured, Trojans
    You will come to Lavinium, and coming there
    Will wish you had not. Wars, horrific wars
    I see and the Tiber foaming with much blood.
    Simois again and Xanthus and the encamped Greeks
    Again, in other shapes, and in Latium another Achilles
    Born, like him, of a goddess and nowhere will Juno
    Let you rest but you in your dire need to every tribe and
      city

Of Italy will go begging, and the cause of so many ills
Again will be a bride who is a stranger among the Trojans
Again will be marriage to a foreigner.'

HC: If it was only the Tiber. After the Siege of Magdeburg in 1631 the Elbe couldn't move for corpses – she was quite choked, couldn't take any more, halted, clogged up. And that was back then, by our standards quite a trivial slaughter. I often think of the *effort* of the old massacres, Constantinople, say, or Chios, the terrible labour of it. Born when we were, Alice, our generation, I've often said we're the living emblem of the beginnings of the makings of a fair society – the Education Act, the Labour Government, the NHS, the welfare state, the chance for all our citizens to realise themselves – then, after 1979, the counter-revolution, the systematic rolling of it back, to the state we are in now. That's one way of looking at our social selves. Another is blood – rivers, lakes, seas, oceans of blood – the inescapable, all-pervasive knowledge of the shedding of so much blood: the opening of the camps, Belsen and Auschwitz, Hiroshima and Nagasaki, the Nakba, Korea, Vietnam, Biafra, Cambodia, Rwanda, the Balkans, on and on and on, the mass graves, the trials, the films, the memoirs, the exhibitions of photographs, the forever increasing archives, the *consciousness*, the unexpungeable knowledge of what we have done, of what we have let happen. Look at us that way, we are steeped, steeped, steeped in blood and our waking and dreaming lives are brimful with the knowledge of it. A man helps in our People's Library, he shelves the books when our borrowers have returned them. He speaks rarely and with great difficulty. He has come out of Syria with his wife and three children. He tells me that when his children first went to school here he stood at the gates all morning, fearful of what might happen to them inside. Advised he must spend a night in hospital here, in England now, to mend at least one of his physical injuries, he did not dare to, he refused, he fled. Hospitals and schools, for him, are places that get bombed.

AM: Where was Masouda from?

HC: Her family were driven off their land in Palestine and finished up in the camps. She was born in Shatila. When we fell in love and admitted it to one another she asked could she come and live with me in my house but have a room of her own and not sleep together for twelve months. I agreed, though I didn't want to wait even twelve minutes. I gave her my big bed upstairs and slept on a couch in my study-cum-lumber-room downstairs. That was the arrangement and I didn't ask her why it had to be. I viewed it as an ordeal such as a lover might have agreed to in a legend. I supposed that in her tradition there might still be a *pudeur* long gone in mine. So the year passed and in that chastity I loved her more and more. On the first evening of our new life we ate together as always, then she moved my things upstairs and we went to bed. In the dark, after we had made love, she told me the waiting year had nothing to do with modesty but she had wanted to try in that time, sleeping apart from me in my house, whether she could get rid of or at least reduce the violence of her nightmares. In the massacre of 1982, when she was four, all her family – mother, father, two brothers, two sisters – were butchered. Her mother hid her under a pile of bedding. Hours later, when she crawled out, she saw what had been done.

AM: And the nightmares?

HC: No, wherever these things live in a person, there they still lived. But they tortured her less often and when they did I was with her, she was in my arms, I helped. She was ashamed and it made her miserable. She said she had not wanted to infect me with all that, she loved me, it was horrible to bring me that, as she put it, for her dowry. But over the years her sleep got quieter and deeper, for weeks at a time not once did she wake screaming. Then would come another bad phase, but it passed, it always passed. I woke more often than she did, I woke and lay listening to her quiet breath, and I was gladder of that than of anything else ever in my life.

AM: I live just round the corner from Elsa and her family. She and her husband are both teachers. They have three children. Coming here today, I was early for our meeting, so I walked the first part of the march to see what I might remember. I walked from Rose Lane to James Street and down as far as the Iffley Road. Then it was nearly time to meet you, Harry, and I turned back to the Cowley Road. The traffic had halted at the zebra crossing outside Sainsbury's and two classes from the primary school were being shepherded across by their teachers and the teaching assistants. They were Foundation Year, I should say, they were hand in hand, boys and girls mixed, and many looks and colours and kinds of dress, all mixed. They passed between a red double-decker bus and a cement transporter and the bus-driver and the truck-driver had clasped their hands and were leaning on the steering wheel and looking down at the children and smiling. The two T.A.'s, an elderly woman from, perhaps, Kerula, and a young woman from, I should say, Somalia, both beautifully costumed, were in among the children who were local and exotic, each of them distinctive and all, hand in hand, moving as a body, with a noise like a brook. They crossed over with a babbling, their language ran like a small clear river. I closed my eyes for a few seconds, just to listen, and as I listened I saw the living waters, I saw the streams of my childhood in the country of my heart. And when I looked again, there in the sunlight the children were crossing, hand in hand, safely, and people had halted on the pavements either side and were watching, all manner of people, all the mix of those streets, had halted to watch. The teachers and the teaching assistants, looking anxious, ushered their charges across and people stood to watch and were smiling. Then it was done. The teachers waved to the drivers, the traffic started up, and the children passed two by two, with the merriment of a stream, towards their school.

Seeking Refuge

THE CAFÉ IS ON THE second floor. We used the lift. Since his injury he has walked with a stick and stairs are hard for him. In the lift we said nothing. I've noticed that even if we are talking when we step into a lift – and it makes no difference whether anyone else is there or not – the closing doors always silence us. And if, as is often the case, there's a pause before we ascend, I feel in myself, and sense in him, a need to speak and a failure of all the words.

When the lift halted and the doors opened I rejoiced. There in the window, in the very best place, a young foreign couple were just leaving. I left Fahrid standing and hurried across. I was deferential, apologetic, but I wanted that seat very badly. I claimed it with my bag and went back for Fahrid. He looked lost. We're in luck, I said. And asked, The usual? He nodded.

While I was queuing I glanced again and again his way. I hoped he would be gazing through the window, I wanted him to be, as they say, 'taken out of himself'; but he was bowed over his smart phone, stroking at it with one finger.

I brought the coffees and his glass of water. In acknowledgement, and thanks perhaps, he showed me his broad face. There were tears in his eyes and he looked, as he often did (this once prosperous and respected man), to be pleading or asking pardon. Mister Phil, he said, and raised his open palms and shrugged. Drink some water, I said. It's a fine day. I like this seat. You can see the world from here. He shrugged, tilted sugar out of a thin sachet and stirred it into his double espresso.

Yes, I like that seat. At your back, either side of the lift, you have shelves and shelves of the world's fiction and poetry. On a good day, sitting at that table, I can hear the books whispering among themselves. And lying awake some nights, good nights, I recall those voices not as a babel but as a benevolent susurration, like leaves in a soft breeze, a patter of rain on those leaves, a muted babbling of streams. That's the background noise in that very civilised room, and on it you hear the tongues, many different tongues, of the present living people in conversation over their teas and coffees or whatever else their fancy is.

Under the window four streets meet and behind their meeting-place, behind railings, stands St Michael's Church with its chestnut tree, among its graves. Right there, in a sort of alcove that used to be an entrance into the consecrated ground, the City Council or the Diocese has allowed a space for busking. It is a very well-regulated permission. Each act gets fifteen minutes and on the dot each steps aside for the next. I had worked this out only the week before from a vantage point in a shop doorway and now in the window seat I wanted to watch it running.

End of May, the big tree was glorious. Oh the surge, the soft butting of the horns of flowers! Later, I admit, this tree like many, like most, of its kind in Britain, in Europe, throughout the world, for all I know, will show the ugly brown sores on all the fingers of all its hands. But now, now, the life it displayed was abundant and beautiful.

Under the tree the act was an elderly – no, an old – man in jeans, cowboy boots, a red tee shirt and a flat cap from under which his draggled white locks fell upon his shoulders. He was slapping a guitar and singing a love song or a protest song or a threnody, hard to tell which in the tumult of people and bicycles at that meeting of four ways under the café window before St Michael's Church. Florets of chestnut snowed on him when the breeze moved. His face was uplifted and his eyes were shut. I touched Fahrid's arm. Look at him, Fahrid, I said. He's doing pretty well, wouldn't you say? Fahrid smiled, but only as though he were remembering his manners, so that again I felt I could not engage him. Myself, I was brimming with words for the spectacle under our window, for the feelings it excited in me and for my hopes that it might touch Fahrid also, and help him. But in his command of English, as in everything else, there was a before and after, and I should have laboured in vain, even on a good day, and this was a bad day, to quicken in him with words an interest in present life. But I said nevertheless: Look, he is old. He is singing his heart out. Some people have stopped and are looking and listening and some of them have thrown coins into his open guitar case. And the tree is beautiful, is it not? Flowers are falling around him and even on his upturned face. Fahrid nodded, smiled, lifted his hands, and let them fall again, as though they weighed too much. Mister Phil, he said, UK is very good place.

The singer's fifteen minutes were up. His audience dissolved into the general mix. He stooped for his takings, packed his gear and moved away with a wry upwards nodding of his head to the next act already in the space.

Tight faded-pink leggings and top, bare feet, her hair fastened tight in a pink ribbon. I suppose she must have been of age, to perform, but she looked barely twelve or thirteen. Swiftly she placed a board across two blocks of wood, an old CD-player to her right and a floppy straw hat on the flagstones before her. Then she waited, in silence, smiling. An audience formed, mostly girls of around her age, mostly Chinese or Japanese, they seemed drawn as if by a force out of the hurrying crowd, irresistibly, to watch. I love that making of a space and a silence in the rush of life, a pause in it for something, a particular gift, to be offered to strangers. She reached down to start the music, waited until in its own mode it was underway, and then in a twinkling sprang on to her hands on the level board. And there she posed, upside down, and began a *pas seul*, arching, opening, spiralling, on two palms or on one, always moving, always rooted, such grace, I have tears in my eyes remembering it, that child slowly dancing on one flat hand on a board in her own arena while life passed in haste across the shopfronts or halted spellbound in an arc around her. She danced on her hands like a new creature, like a cross, a go-between, a fluid mixing, she danced to a voice which rose through the ordinary hubbub to our open window, the voice of a dead man singing, Hallelujah! Oh I wanted it to last for ever, that singing, the skinny girl upside down dancing, that ability, grace, balance of energies, shapes and poise in movement and the audience from elsewhere halted, wholly attending. That song lasts seven or eight minutes. When it ended, when she, its passing incarnation, sprang lightly as a kitten from her hands to her bare feet and smiled and bowed, Fahrid touched my arm. Mister Phil, he said. His face was as I had not seen it before, possessed by malevolence, helplessly, blamelessly visited, *afflicted*, by malevolence. Mister Phil, he said. See this. And he pushed his smart phone towards me between our coffee cups.

It was a video. I watched a few seconds of it. I felt Fahrid watching me. I saw a boy lying face down on the tailboard of a small truck. His head was towards the camera, towards me. By the truck, close to the boy, stood a bearded man. Very briefly I supposed it must be the aftermath of a bombing and the man was getting the wounded boy to hospital in the truck. But then by the hair with his left hand he lifted the boy's head and with a knife in his right hand cut the boy's throat. I saw the instant vast spillage of blood across the floor of the truck and the bearded man laughing into the camera. I pushed the smart phone back through the coffee cups across the table to Fahrid. You shouldn't watch such things, I said, they feed your illness, they make you useless. How will you help your family, who are safe in this country with you now, if you make your illness worse by watching things like that?

There was no more malice in him. He had tears in his eyes, he was shaking. His English, once with half a dozen other languages at his command, was, like his faraway house and home, in ruins now when he needed it. So I heard everything in bits, two or three terrible efforts at every bit. And I was party to it, I helped him find the words and put them in the right order. I helped him, my teacher in atrocity, I helped him as his teacher in the language for it. All in bits, with gestures, with tears and sweating, the stocky man shaking so much that when he gripped the table our coffee cups trembled. Mister Phil, he said. The boy twelve years old. He has diabetes. He is in hospital. They drag him out. They drive him to the marketplace. They – he made the gesture – before all the people. They film it. They send it round the world to all the people. Fahrid, I said. Fahrid, Fahrid, stop it. But the fit was on him. Mister Phil, he said. They kill a young man. They phone his mother and father. You can have his body if you pay. They send the money. But all they get is the head. Fahrid, stop it, please, I said. But he made chopping gestures on the table, chop, chop, chop, between the coffee cups. In slices, Mister Phil. Slice by slice they get their son back. Payment by payment. And a young girl, Mister Phil, not a woman yet, good people bring her to my surgery… He can't find the words to say what has been done to her. Ten men, Mister Phil. She shake. What can I do for child who shake like that? His face streams with tears, his head will not keep still, his hands, his arms and all his visible upper body, shake as though he were a man being racked and riddled till he falls apart.

He fell silent, bowed his head and began rolling a thin cigarette. Out on the street he paused to light it. The upside-down dancer had gone and in her place a girl was playing a fiddle while a man old enough to be her grandfather jigged around her clockwise to a certain point, then anti-clockwise back to that point, and so on and on and on. When we were clear, with some harshness I began my usual homily: Your wife has started to make friends, your children are doing very well at school, their English is perfect, your little boys want to play football for England, your daughter wants to be a doctor… But there was no real need. The fit had left him. He looked about him in the sun at the everyday thronging. We passed a group of Gospel singers, all in red, singing their hearts out. And an imam handing out cards saying Love to All, Hatred to None. And a young man in a top hat riding a wheel along a tightrope, and blowing bubbles the while. Mister Phil, Fahrid said. UK very good place. Passing the council offices he halted and with great joy greeted a motherly black woman who had come out for a cigarette. She didn't recognise him – he was one of many – but to him she was benefaction in person. Mister Phil, he said, this lady give us electricity. How that amused her! She threw back her head and laughed.

I went as far as the bridge with him. His fit had passed, my head was full of it. A party of quite small children were kayaking down the river, like ducklings they looked in their yellow life-jackets, one adult leading, two bringing up the rear. The children's concentration was fierce. They were a mixed brood, about a dozen of them, a good half-dozen origins. I waved. One little boy, Afghan, I should say, beginning to feel confident, beginning to be pleased with himself, took his eyes off the water just long enough to smile up at me. Then the river gathered for the central arch and with sudden speed he vanished from my sight.

bREcCiA

IT IS A VERY LARGE and heavy book, a double-elephant folio, to be exact. If in a library you ordered up a book of this size and weight it would be brought to you on a trolley and two assistants would lift it between them on to a table normally reserved for sheet maps. But this book has never been anywhere near a library. It might more easily be read (if 'read' is the word) propped up on a high desk such as clerks in Dickens use for their vast ledgers. But the book no more belongs in an office than it does in a library. Still, a very sturdy lectern would be ideal for it and you might stand there occasionally turning a page and looking out through a large window at whatever scene would best be able to steady your mind.

The book has three hundred and sixty-six pages numbered top right in ink. Those numbers, which, of course, may or may not have been put there by the compiler or compilers of the whole volume, are the only manuscript marks in it. Everything else is photographs and printed matter, all brought from elsewhere and assembled (pasted in) here. But, as we shall see, the book is as much the work of one or more particular authors, a work of the imagination, as is any of our poetry, fiction or drama of known or unknown authorship.

The pages are numbered, but even without numbering, in our culture at least, we should turn them from right to left, from the first to the last; and within that order we should probably expect another. In a book of palaeontology, for example, it would be a chronological order, by geological period, and within those periods then a sub-order by genus and species. And in any book made up chiefly of words, sentences, paragraphs, we should expect the ineluctable progression in time (this word, this sentence, this paragraph follows that) to be bearing forward an argument, a plot, or to be tracing, at least, a developing line of feeling. And with very few words, or none at all, chronological progression could easily be, and has very often been, achieved, by setting one *picture* after another in an intelligible sequence of events, thoughts, feelings, in time. But the vast book which is our subject here works, so it seems, very deliberately against chronological order; indeed, within the order of one numbered page succeeding another, it seems to be aiming rather at simultaneity.

Making a commonplace-book, you might scatter a few general headings through its pages – love, nature, religion, ethics, society, etc. – and gather your excerpts under them, during a lifetime, each section being then stratified, *like* a lifetime. Our book is more like a scrap-book, and yet not at all like one. Most often with a scrap-book you paste in things of interest page after page just as you come across them, until all the pages are full, the chronology is that of your own life, month by month, year upon year. Finish one book, begin another, perhaps. But in the book we are discussing here, though every page is filled, crowded even, none of the pictures or scraps of caption or commentary bear any date. In fact, one has the impression that any dates coming with a text or photograph have been scrupulously removed. Of course, many items are more or less exactly dateable by their subjects. Many are very familiar. But there is no calendar-chronology in their sequence and juxtapositioning in the book. For example: Marilyn Monroe holding down her skirt in the draught blowing up from the subway (1954) appears on page 23 among some texts or images dateable by content to 1916, 1942, 1985, and with others belonging, as it were, nowhere particular in time or place. Which seems to indicate that when the compilation of this colossal work was begun all the cuttings were there ready and waiting to be deployed. Whoever put the book together certainly did not add the individual items just as they came along, just as he or she lit upon them. Beyond a doubt, the book was not begun until sufficient material to fill it, and not only fill it but to make a whole kaleidoscope of sense, even a sort of (non-chronological) narrative, had been assembled.

When was the book made? We can't be certain. The latest dateable item is – occupying the central space on page 247 – a gallery of the fifty-five people (including the perpetrators) killed in the London bombings 7 July 2005. But among the images that can't be, or haven't yet been, dated there may well be some, perhaps several, perhaps many, which post-date that atrocity. And we can't know, of course, how long after the completed collection of materials the composing of the book itself began.

All the items are original photographs in colour or black and white; or cuttings from magazines, newspapers, pamphlets and other ephemeral publications. None is a print of a text or an image found on the web. Which does not necessarily mean that the book was composed *before* you could in an instant access countless millions of pictures and documents of human cruelty and kindness, folly and wisdom, implacable hatred and enduring love; only that its author or authors, if they were working at the book after the coming of Google in 1998, chose not to take things for their project from that infinite source.

Between its two stout covers, on its three hundred and sixty-six sewn pages, the book contains around fifteen thousand items. Once the collecting ceased, and we can't know how long it went on, the making of the book must surely have taken at the very least five years. The title of it, in a very large font, made out of black lower and upper case letters cut from newspapers and pasted dead centre on the front cover, is: bREcCiA. And those letters, upper and lower case, in a small font, are strewn in great profusion and as it were at random like a handful of black seed, all over the inside covers of the book, facing page 1 and page 366. The *Oxford English Dictionary* defines breccia as 'A composite rock consisting of angular fragments of stone, etc., cemented together by some matrix, such as lime.' A similar rock, but in which the fragments are rounded and waterworn, is called 'conglomerate'. Their particular allure, to anyone haunted by measures of time, is that, themselves dizzyingly ancient, they are composed of very visible materials far more ancient. 'Breccia' is an apt title for a book made at a certain date out of pre-existent bits and pieces. Pebbles in conglomerate are very likely older than the sharp fragments in breccia but the compiler or compilers of our book will have gone for 'breccia' because in the packed coexistence, on one time-level, of unrounded shatterings there is something quite peculiarly recalcitrant. The primeval violence is still apparent, no softening of it has even begun. 'Breccia' is a good title; and yet, as whoever thought of it certainly knew, only up to a point adequate. The old fragments in the newly forming rock are thrown together haphazardly: in the book, the material is collected and assembled with very great deliberateness, in part to create an *appearance* of randomness but even more to construct a quite particular sort of sense. On the pages the collected texts and photographs are indeed fixed, as fixed, in a sense, as is the pre-Devonian debris in the Devonian rock. The reader views the page; and the composite shape, the juxtapositions, the relations between parts and the whole, are static. The medium insists on fixity. But the spirit of the whole endeavour is quite the opposite: it is the principle of eternal instability, of 'everything moves and flows'. The fixity of texts and photos on the page allows us to see a particular shape, but the imagination and the heart and the pulses feel its undoing, its return to the matrix, its rising again into another and different fleeting incarnation. Turning a page, concentrating hard on what is offered there, steady, on the new page, we are always on the brink of dissolution, of tumbling and whirling, on and on.

This must suffice as a general description of our extraordinary book. Now, in the time remaining, let us look at one of its pages, enlarged, on the screen. Any spoken or written account of a page, one sentence following another, would unavoidably be very inadequate. The details, presented like that, come at you consecutively; but in fact, on the page, they co-exist. Listening or reading, the mind takes in details consecutively and attempts to reconstitute them into their actual relations, into simultaneity. That is a laborious process, always bound to fail. But here on the screen, as in the book itself, the image holds steady, and you see at once how the page was composed and, more importantly, *how it works*. Of course, in the time allowed now, however attentively you look, you will not get very far into the workings themselves, you will only begin to see and feel what the effects of the relations, of the co-existences, are or might be. Every page is *multiplyingly* rich. Indeed, bearing in mind the sense of the imminence of dissolution just referred to, we could say with some truth that every page is inexhaustible, it is an infinity. But judge for yourselves. Here is page 237 – abundant! abundant! – but not more so than any before or after it…

The visiting speaker – born 1944 in a small town in the north of England and still living there, lately as a widower – made his excuses – it was a long drive home in the dark – and left. Being silent and alone was for perhaps fifteen minutes such a profound relief that no other feelings had any presence in him; but then came a familiar vague regret and a deepening sadness. Why feel like that? The audience had been small, but attentive. He was a regular in their calendar, every year they invited him, every year he gladly accepted. The occasion itself, in an old institute, a philanthropic foundation that had just celebrated its centenary, was, as he never failed to tell his hosts, right up his street. He said it and meant it. True, during the years of his going there the audience had aged and diminished. The old WEA connections had long since vanished. Chiefly the U3A gathered in the Institute now and in recent years it was they who had invited him. But the speaker's despondency had little to do with that. Always after such an engagement his spirits lapsed. He heard his own voice, his fluency, his facility, and always it distressed him. But on this particular winter evening, finding his way out of one small town towards another, his dejection was worse than usual.

It's the book, he said to himself. I shouldn't have talked about it. There was no need. Indeed, many months ago, he had announced to them at the Institute that he would talk about something quite different. And two days before the event, very suddenly, he decides he will talk about the book, doesn't even have the courtesy to inform his hosts, arrives, apologises, and tells them about the book of books. Why? One element in his present regret was a sense of trespass, as though the book were not to be spoken about, or not by him, at least. Certainly, I shouldn't have displayed a page of it on the screen. And yet, why not? Out of the book's infinite store he had given away half a dozen grains. No measurable depletion. And, who knows, that very little might have *taken* in one or other listener and be already working productively in his or her third age?

The speaker was by now driving with great caution across a black moorland under a moonless but brilliantly starlit sky, a town, not his, visible as a dull luminous cloud far below on the left, headlights, rarely but too often, coming towards him on the narrow road at great speed and slipping past. His uneasiness changed, or perhaps it clarified and focussed at last on a truer concern than whether or not his speaking about the book had been an offence. He smiled in the dark. Face it, old son, he said. The house will be cold and empty, the book will be wide awake, a thousand times more alive than anything else in your home, waiting. You won't sleep. Your head will seethe like an anthill, writhe like a worm factory, all night and into the daylight. And so it will be for days or for ever now. I always said there was a crack in me. He switched on the radio, came in at the start of Schubert's C major quintet and, grateful for its wordlessness, got safely home on it.

Gone eleven. He stood in the kitchen with his coat on and a glass of wine in his cold hand, waiting for two slices of toast to leap up. He forgot them. The book was working in the earth of him. The heating had turned itself off. You don't look after yourself, she said. Frugality, he answered. Not penny-pinching. The toast leapt. The clatter hit him like a thump in the heart. The wine slopped from his glass. He began to sob. There, there, she said. Hush now. Butter them, put some cheese on them. Quieten down, go to bed, think of us quietly and go to sleep. With the toast he did as he was told. Unbidden, he filled up his glass. Frugality, he said, and strictness of regime, these are virtues, not vices. Then he carried toast and wine through into the room she had always called his study, a pleasant room at the back of the house, off the lounge, a few steps lower, facing north into a long garden, cosy at midsummer or in winter with a fire, but now empty, the open hearth empty, no shelving, no pictures, no chairs or carpet, only the solid-as-a-rock lectern facing the uncurtained French windows, the lectern, and on it, open under a bright low-hanging bulb, the book. Ten minutes, he said, till I've finished my supper, then bed, promise.

Facing pages, 182, 183. Eyes shut, he had opened the book, turned away without looking and driven off in plenty of time to address the good people in the Institute. Now he looked! There were always connections between two facing pages and overleaf too – texts or some decorative motif ran on, an image might be split – but each page and the clusters on each page could always be studied separately. That observation is at once trivial and the key to the whole thing. If you undid the book, detached all its pages and laid all the pairs of them out on a spacious empty floor, the interplay among them would be a sort of delirium. And if, further, whilst studying the visible, you allowed your mind to imagine those texts and pictures, half of the book's total, that were invisible because lying face down; and you imagined the entire stock, the visible and the invisible together, all simultaneously on view, and never forgot that no arrangement on any page was final, all, so to speak, aspired to their own dissolution, to starting again, *that* to your eyes and mind would be the vortex of the world sucking in, or the trumpet of the world blasting out, the smithereens (oh a very few of them!) of a century or so of homo sapiens on earth. Coming again to the book, the visiting speaker, now the reader, had at his back a noise like the surf of deep space. He was glad of the stout covers, the definite title, the well-sewn pages in a numbered order, the possibility of a thread, a trail of clues, a plot, a tale that might be followed in the forest of tangle. Eyes and mind, he bowed over pages 182-3.

There, dead centre, across the centre pages, sits the newsreader, a recurrent figure, sits like God the Almighty in certain medieval cosmographies with the orders of being in circles around Him, closest the angels, farthest out the tribes of mankind, and beyond them, as it were nowhere, the wild beasts and the devils. There he sits, not God but a familiar and well-loved reader of the evening news, at his desk, resting his hands on some papers and looking straight at us, familiar, but on these pages in one detail very unfamiliar: his well-known patient, serious, sometimes understandingly smiling face has been cut out and replaced with that of a woman whose once beautiful looks have been utterly changed into those of a person viewing the hitherto unimaginable worst, aghast, helpless, given up to it, only staring, quite unable to take it in, surpassed by it and knowing in her body and soul that neither she nor any other human was made to withstand the sight of what – by chance? by calling? – she is now bound to see. That face, dead centre, riven by the gully between the pages, stares out at us. And in the circles behind her, which she cannot see but doubtless senses, there is the usual fighting of the stuff of the world, of what we have done or let happen, desired or could not prevent. The seven separate rings do not *contain* this mêlée, ubiquitously it spills over, the orders themselves transgress in all directions, so that we cannot but feel that disorder was there first and always and the circles were only a shot, and a futile one, at control.

The visiting speaker, returned to his empty house, stands at the lectern in his overcoat, wine in one hand, toast and cheese in the other, and nods as though he expected what he is seeing. Drink some wine, she says. Have a bite of your food. He does as he's told. Now tell me the good, she says. He swallows. A colour photograph of a little girl, he says, and a bird, a bluetit, has perched on the index finger of her left hand, she can't believe her good luck, her eyes are wide, her mouth is a tiny bit open. And? she says. Our pair are there again. Only this time she's much younger than him. It's them alright, but she's young enough to be his daughter. – What are they doing? – Oh, strolling along. The place isn't very nice but they look happy enough. – And? – There's a black kid busking. I think it might be in St Anne's Square, in Manchester, just outside the church. He's playing the trumpet. I'd say it might be sixty years ago.

There's about twenty office workers, men and women, all white, they're in a semi-circle facing him, they're dressed like my mam and dad not long after the war, his cap's on the flagstones, he's playing with his face upturned to heaven, they can't take their eyes off him, you can hear what his music sounds like in the way they look. I'd say it must have been cut out of the *Manchester Evening News*. That's good, she says. And that's enough now. Finish your bit of supper and go to bed. You promised. Yes, I promised, he says.

But he has discovered, only an inch away from the little girl with a bird on her finger, a soldier with a cigarette in his mouth and a gun across his knees and his legs hanging over a pit that is nearly full. So it is, he says to himself. Bed, she says. You promised. Tell me one more good thing and then go to bed. There's a bit of text, he says, above the outermost circle, top left. It's been cut out letter by letter from somewhere, a fancy script, and assembled so that it runs around the curve, a good six inches, outside, where the wild beasts and the devils belong, it's some lines you know very well, you were always saying them. I can guess, she says. But tell me anyway. He recites, 'O the opal and the sapphire of that wandering western sea, And the woman riding high above with bright hair flapping free…' Now go to bed, she says. He does as he's told.

His night was not, as he had predicted it would be, sleepless. Better for him, perhaps, if it were. He fell at once into the shallows of sleep, perpetually nearing the surface but not able to rise and breathe the daytime air, sinking again but never able to get down to oblivion. The dreams came in a rush, as though, crowding elsewhere, they had been waiting for him to become defenceless. They broke in like a rapids, he was taken up and along. The haste and multitude of them was as though the entire book, all its pages visible together, forced themselves through narrow conduits in his head. Such pressure and plethora. And out then very suddenly, into a seething *in one place*, everything, every possibility, flung up and falling back, tested and failing, back into the maelstrom. Then quieter, it was the tangle wood, and through it, like Hansel and Gretel, went the pair he had spotted again and again, making their way, clue by clue. They changed. Their faces, their postures, changed, they were aging, but inconsistently, one might suddenly carry an old head on young shoulders, the makers had cut and pasted as they pleased, the woman stooped, a boy young enough to be her grandson supported her tenderly with his hand under her elbow. They were in the world of time, tracing a line from an entrance towards an exit, but they were not obeying a normal course, nor even fixed in the him and her, they swapped gender, they went half and half, all fluid, but quite slowly, as though they wanted time to wonder at it. And so, errantly, repetitively, in circles sometimes, at times straight ahead, they continued on a recognizable path, picking a way through, in much dread, but determined. And all the while, somewhere in the background, against a livid sky – in his dreaming he could see it and hear it – all the good and evil of the world struggled in their mythic unending contest, torturers and lovers, tongues and bayonets, troth and treachery, birth and murder, on and on, round and round, without the least hope, as the pair in the forest of tangle knew, that there would ever be a cessation in an outcome the angels would rejoice to witness.

He sits in his overcoat at the kitchen table, warming his hands around a mug of black coffee and staring at a blank sheet of A4. The heating will come on when the time instructs it to. Meanwhile, until it does, having crawled out of the dreaming sleep like a man flung up from shipwreck, in this coldest phase of the day before the light makes its bleak appearance, he will list from memory as many as he can of the book's hundreds of trees.

So, in no particular order, just as they occur to him: Samuel Palmer's *Shepherdess under a Chestnut Tree*; trees sprouting high out of the roofs of ruins in the wasteland along the West's side of the Berlin Wall; the apple tree in blossom, the apple tree dead and dry, in the Paradise Garden; a row of thorns bent almost horizontal, 'asking alms of the sun', on a bank to windward of a ruined farm; a giant sequoia and a dozen children holding hands around its trunk; girdled eucalyptus, stone dead or still dying, a photograph taken from a train crossing the outback between Canberra and Melbourne; the Magic Faraway Tree; willows along a riverbank in Wales, ancient leaning and split-wide-open trunks, pollarded years ago, flowering golden up the renewing spikes; a branch, just a branch, blossoming on a blue sky, just that one branch of an almond tree, as though freed of all dependency, living on air, flourishing, so carelessly beautiful, painted by Van Gogh; the strange-fruit tree, the blacks dangling in it, the whites, men and women, gathered under it, pointing, smiling; a rowan, late summer, seeded in a crack in a rock-face, jutting out and at once rising up, densely berried, orange-red; trees at Chernobyl, doing well now without us; trees in Mametz Wood. At that image he halts. It has brought to mind another. He hurries to check his memory of it in the book itself.

There he is now at the lectern, under the bare bulb, turning the book's great pages, remembering only roughly where he needs to get to, coming there slowly, with many errors, with helpless intakes of hundreds of images along the way, his heart beating too fast, panicking that he will not find it. And there suddenly it is, there *he* is, staring at it: another battlefield, the level ruined earth, the low sky, so black, and so heavy it looks about to fall, and the humans, crawling one way or another among their dead fellow-creatures, through the strewn wreckage of their equipment, and a horse, sunk half into a crater, kicking upwards with its forefeet, its head lifted high and tilting back, bellowing a vast imprecation. But no trees. Except this: assembled and transported thither, a tree as luminous as Palmer's, as innocently lovely as Eve's before God in His jealousy spoiled it, a glorious and abundant tree, branching and leafing to its heart's content, and where there might be flowers – dark red sparks of larch, dusty-yellow hangings of sycamore, creamy candles of chestnut – at every place where a nobly thriving tree might put forth flowers, there instead you see unfurling scrolls, on every one of which, composed with infinite meticulous labour, letter by letter, from scores of publications, are scraps of poems in German, French and English, a line or two that lead you forwards or backwards into the rest, lines you could continue into the entire poem, into the whole oeuvre, into its antecedents and successors, a vast tree whose flowers and fruits-to-be are opening scrolls of poems. The book has that tree full in the middle of an infernal plain under an infernal sky, sprung up and rooted among tormented creatures, flourishing. He begins to read, 'Down the close, darkening lanes they sang their way…', 'If only this fear would leave me I could dream of Crickley Hill…', 'Ich trug Geheimnisse in die Schlacht bei Arras…', 'But she would weep to see today…', 'Lou si je meurs là-bas souvenir qu'on oublie…', 'One was a pale eighteen-year-old…' On and on, hundreds of them.

He halts, looks up, muttering, And what is that supposed to do? Console? Recompense? Speaking, he sees himself mirrored in the black French window, haggard, ghastly, staring in horror at a vision of himself on a cliff on a mountain of the mind. This won't do, he mutters. Really, it will not do. A tree of poems photo-shopped into that cesspit. That really will not do.

Get dressed, she says. Have a shave and make a proper breakfast. Then go and do some shopping. Buy something nice to cook and a decent bottle of wine, for this evening. Stay away from the book for a few hours. Please. He nods. OK, he says to his grisly reflection in the black glass.

The day looks not so bad after all: frost-sparkle, a new moon, very sharp stars, and, as all that fades, blue appears, sunlight, pink vapour trails, first traffic far off, neighbours are waking, they wonder about their dreams, turn then to their daytime duties and desires, every creature after its fashion, the human, the cat, the early hungry small birds, all the intelligences, they wake and go about their business, every one different, every one my kith and kind.

He makes himself presentable. The face in the mirror looks no worse than most first thing with a day to go out and meet. You'll do, he says. It is a passable, a fair-to-middling imitation of a man in his rightful mind. He knows of eyes that would see through his into all the turmoil, but he knows also that he will not be suddenly accosted on the street and see them looking into him. No book for a few hours. – No book. – Promise? – Promise.

Closing his front door, he says good morning to Mrs Opposite just leaving for school with her two small children. He sees that she does not think him very untoward. He wears an overcoat and a cap and scarf. He is normal. Are you there, love? he says over his shoulder. Yes, love, I'm there, Sorrow replies.

It is Thursday, the library is open for two hours, elderly ladies manage it on a rota. He goes in with his shopping. They welcome him gratefully. He reads the newspapers. Then he does a bit of research. This elderly man who has done some reading in his time and whose head of late has been especially crowded with an upsurge of things he had forgotten he had in him or was fearful of entertaining, this quite well-read citizen acknowledges almost joyfully that he knows not a millionth part of what there is to know in the books on the dozen shelves which he sits facing now with his poor bits of shopping beside him.

You're back early, she says. – I got tired. – Eat something. He does as he is bid. I think I'll have a nap, he says. Must you? she asks in the worried tone he cannot bear to hear.

Again the dreams fall upon him as though, lost in an outer darkness, like ghosts wanting blood, suddenly they have a place to go: his head, his heart, all the tracks in him to every part of his compliant body.

It feels like the release of his sperm towards her womb, milt down the river, pollen down the wind. And as if the rush contained a mix of seed, a plethora of species, and would cross-fertilise with zest and plants would be born to sing, cats to walk upright and set off on adventures and humans would recover the use of their gills and cruise the deep oceans echo-finding one another. Riot of miscegenation. And fearful imbroglio of good luck and bad, good deeds and evil.

He wakes feeling cold and not knowing who or where he is. Lies there a while outside the covers on his side of the bed. Witness, he mutters. This time that is what it was all about.

He sits in his overcoat at the kitchen table sipping a cup of black coffee. Come spring, he says aloud, I shall spend two hours every afternoon in the garden. Promise. Meanwhile, I will have another glance at the book.

There are witnesses on every page. Once you start to look for them, they are legion. Some kind, some not. Some pleased by what they see, some appalled. On page 1, for example, towards the bottom right hand corner, there's a black and white – in fact, rather murky – print of the old men spying on Susanna at her bath. Not far away, in what looks like a family photograph, a seal has come up head and shoulders in a small deep bay, close to the shore, and is looking very quizzily at two little boys in swimsuits who are staring back entranced. In this book, birds and animals, cut out from who knows where and strategically placed, are often seen watching, often from page to page. They take it all in. And on every page a searchlight, a

CCTV camera, a watchtower, a guard with binoculars, a peep-hole in a prison door, or the conning tower of a submarine will be discovered if you look long enough. A good part of page 83 is taken up with an engraving of Bentham's Panopticon and, in large letters, his own description of it as 'a new mode of obtaining power of mind over mind, in a quantity hitherto without example'. Around that image, occupying all of the page's remaining space, is a luxuriant revelry of foliage and flowers with many cheerful creatures, humans old and young among them, endlessly disporting themselves. Another very characteristic montage is to be found on page 33. The well-loved picture of the virgin and the unicorn has been cut out and pasted exactly into the central circle there. She is seated, holding a mirror, in which the unicorn's head and horn have appeared. But behind the fabled creature and not yet come into the girl's mirror, on page 32, outside the circle but stepping very definitely towards it, is a child-soldier with an AK-47. The book abounds in such juxtapositions. Is that the truth of it, in endless variations? No, no. Only one of the truths, only one slant of the truth. Caspar David Friedrich's 'Wanderer above the Sea of Fog' is there (p. 87) and Goethe at his window in Rome, looking down on the Via della Fontanella (p. 361). The one is contemplating a new coming into being of Earth herself, the other the glorious motley of life on the street, and their backs are not covered and they are not threatened. And go to page 29 for a photograph of a man handing perhaps his grandson a lump of Wenlock shale in which, embossed on the surface, spread like a butterfly, is a trilobite. The boy stares in amazement at the fossil, the man with loving wonder contemplates the child's amazement. Much like that. The world abounds in things like that, and so, seeking the truth, does the book.

On pages 178-9, a third of the way down across the whole double-spread, runs an extract from a cartoon, provenance unknown, entitled *Walt Whitman and Mephistopheles*. In each frame Walt is represented by a different photograph, always whiskery and long-haired but with or without his wide-brimmed hat and flowing necktie. Mephisto is throughout Gustav Gründgens, as he appeared in that role, greatly impressing Hermann Goering, in the 1932-3 season at the Staatstheater am Gendarmenmarkt, Berlin. Here are a few bits of dialogue (issuing from either mouth in speech bubbles). Walt: 'I am the man, I suffered, I was there.' Mephisto: 'My arse.' Walt: 'I do not ask the wounded person how he feels, I myself become the wounded person.' Mephisto: 'Oh what bollocks!' Walt: 'That is very unfair. I was in the field hospitals during the Civil War, I tended the sick, I comforted the dying.' Mephisto: 'You like young men. Nothing wrong with that. So do I. But I don't go creeping over battlefields after them.'

The Newsreader appears on the left-hand page, diagonally above the cartoon and as though circling it, in what might be a bathysphere or a space capsule. He is the most constant witness, to be found somewhere on every page, always recognizable by his decent suit and tie, his upright posture and his hands that rest on papers on his desk. But, as already noted, the author or authors of the book have made pretty free with the poor man's head. He appears (not in any chronological order) as a screaming baby, a toothless crone, Medusa, Pol Pot, Richard Nixon, the Eumenides (three heads on that occasion), Idi Amin, Marie Curie, and in many metamorphoses besides, the most terrifying being the woman at the heart of the book who is seeing what she cannot bear to see. These borrowed personae are fewer, and it may be less powerful, than the night after night ageing and saddening of his own familiar and well-loved face. Night after night he reads the news and his face is marked by it like a small and once beautiful and fruitful planet that is assaulted year upon year by drought, famine, flood and fire and plague and cataclysmic wars. Some pages, mercilessly, have him saying, 'And I must warn you that our report contains images which some viewers may find upsetting…' And at his back cluster the pictures which have accompanied our growing up: the fork-lift trucks at Belsen, the little girl on fire, the child with a belly bigger than her mother's was and her eyes blacked out with flies, on and on, night after night, and his kindly face takes the stigmata of it all.

And on page 125 we see a child, a family photograph, who saunters through a forest glade around which a vigorous 'Massacre of the Innocents' is taking place. She is talking to her doll and seems to be pointing things out to her – clearly, from her expression, not what is being done among the leafing trees. Turn a hundred pages and you come to that photo of a Viet Cong soldier being tortured while American G.I.'s look on. In a column by it is Graham Green's comment: 'The strange new feature about the photographs of torture now appearing is that they have been taken with the approval of the torturers and published over captions that contain no hint of condemnation. They might have come out of a book on insect life. "The white ant takes certain measures against the red ant after a successful foray."'

Enough, she says. I think we understand by now what this book of yours is all about. Another ten minutes, he answers. He hears her sobbing. And then, I promise you, I'll sleep. He keeps his word, more or less. Sleeps in his clothes under his overcoat on his side of the bed, sleeps, wakes, sleeps, small difference which, both states are feverous, they run together, he dreams in both, his mind runs in the current, swirls in eddies against the current, in both. And at the back of his mind is the conviction that he is continuing the endless creation of the book. He contributes from his own life as though from a stranger's or as though from other books. And turning the pages, seeing them turned before the figure of himself who stands under the bare bulb at the lectern, he reads the texts there, views the images there, as though all of them had sprung from his own most secret and uniquely living soul. Strange that fusing and separating, running alongside, or as two-run-into-one. He is the reader and, as author, inexhaustibly out of the pages he hauls the makings of many books.

In passages of authorship he becomes again the visiting speaker. Thank you, he says. I am very glad to be here. Speaking to your Society has grown over the years to be the most important engagement in my calendar. I am a familiar and I trust you to forgive me that I arrive and speak to you on a subject quite other than the one agreed months ago and announced in your programme for the year. My subject is a book called *bREcCiA*, it is my book of books. It is a large and heavy and abundant book. Yet weighed against reality it is a speck of dust, the blink of an eye, a pipsqueak. And what can I give you of it in the time allowed? An atom, an atom's atom. Or say a grain of sand, a grain of sand in a nutshell.

Being among friends, let me speak personally. I am bounded in a nutshell, I count myself a king of infinite space, and I have bad dreams. Singular, I am plural. Here and now, I am back there and then and in both locations forever imagining a future. Who would be without the future perfect or the heartrending conditional perfect? No one. And yet, strictly speaking, there is only the present tense. I should have had her when I was in health… Rent his heart then, rends my heart now, in the present. And yet, and yet… The body ages, step by step I am approaching my extinction. Driving here I calculated that this is my twenty-first visit. Twenty-one years I have arrived like Father Christmas or Father Time and addressed your dwindling company. I have mottled hands, my dear wife has passed away, driving in the dark flusters me. And yet and yet… The soul in me, my thinking, feeling, remembering, imagining, quick little anima, born with the body, dying with the body, becoming the one she is by virtue of the subtle senses of the body, continues sprightly in the interval of corporeal life allowed. Quick as flame, various as water, and as unfixable as the wind, she dances in the present and comprehends my past and future things. My course is linear, from the A of birth to the Z of death – but hers? Repeat: conceived together, we die together. But in the meantime she will not, cannot, toe the line, she is errant, she is vagrant, she goes off at tangents, she doubles back, she loves spirals, labyrinths, the ways that loop and coil. We are lovers of footways, she and I, but while I see the col and the track that climbs to it and carry in my head an estimated time of arrival there, she, my anima, animula, animula vagula, wisp of a creature, lightly carries with her every path I have ever trodden and forefeels those – may they be many! – I tomorrow, this year, next year, sometime will yet tread. We are one flesh, she and I.

A good idea of the spirit and practice of the book is given by the majuscules, at least one on every page, which the author has cut out, I should say, from the fancy calendars that carry you through the months via images to be found in illuminated manuscripts. There you see letters whose strict function is to begin the word that starts the sentence on its more or less lengthy journey to a full stop. And that letter, far from hurrying you on your way, is a world in itself and there you linger. Friends, how I have grown to love tendrils, curlicues, the big 'T's' that are rooting and branching, the 'E's' making a lattice for roses to climb up and fauns to spy through! Glory be to the makers of distractions, all designs that will not allow you to rush ahead, intricate threadings it takes the eye a good ten minutes to follow, the dead letter sprouting, the spirit of anarchy giving it life. And the doodles, the marginalia, a devil showing his bum to a nun playing on a dulcimer, and the yearning, the yearning, dear God release us from boredom, my fingers hurt, my cock wants a say in my obedient life of chastity, O westron wynde…! And yet willy-nilly I am a text proceeding, I am a sentence hurrying, or dawdling through many subordinate clauses, to the period. I am a page, I get turned, turned, turned, till the last. And yet, and yet… This book of books, you reach page 366, you turn, turn, turn the pages back again, it makes sense backwards or sideways or up or down, sucked into the centre or flinging out beyond the borders and the edges. You will die, he will die, she will die, I will die, but this is the meanwhile, this is the book of the meanwhile, of life to be lived in the time and space allowed. Waves drive only apparently across the surface of the ocean to extinction, in truth they are the made-visible passage of an energy, they lift in its dance, that is everlastingly here and now. Floating in the midst of it for an interval, time hurrying us on, we see what looks like, feel what feels like, the life everlasting. No wonder the soul leaps up! Consider the wind: certainly it passes and carries with it leaves, papers, balloons, birds and horizontal sheets of corrugated iron out of sight. But passing it manifests itself in waves and pliant trees and clouds so that, briefly, we see what it means in practice, the law that everything flows. Friends, I am beginning to believe the domain and condition of the dead to be like that: energies crossing a space and their myriad and changing appearances jostling wildly before our very eyes. Or let us say in the living it feels like that and in daydreams and nightdreams and visions looks like that, when the party wall between us and them is breached and we are flooded. Lose a loved one, and your common years, many or few, assault you without order or sequence and at every new surfacing of every image or scrap of story or conversation, you murmur, So it was, or ask, Was it really so? And if so might it not have been otherwise? Why were we lucky or unlucky?

He sinks and dreams, and Yes, says Walt, I sing the elements in their totality and in every facet of every one of their countless manifestations. That's my boy, says Mephisto. Sing it like it is, sing the fire, Walt, old friend, fire in the hearth and the crematoria, the campfire in the dark wood, two close friends by it, talking, fire through the letterbox because the daughter loved the wrong man, on our way to the bread shop we smelled the blackened house, oh fire, indeed there's a lot to sing about, there's napalm on the children, heretics burning for Philip's nuptials, and a thousand suns in the streets and homes and schools and marketplaces of Hiroshima, the citizens cast on the walls as shadows, oh the candle flame in a coil of barbed wire. Sing water, poet, water in her cupped hands, lifting it to my mouth, sing the clear seawater, the long thongs standing vertical nine feet high, sinuously swaying as we, quiet as we could, rowed over them, sing the long icicles I fetched from a hillside cave, to show her in our warm house on the valley floor, how we lay listening to the river and the rain and after the rain the increased and joyous nearness of the streams, sing waterboarding, sing the craters of Passchendaele, a sludge of corpses, sing the ocean gyre and the Pacific trash vortex, sing the Chernobyl rain, the Niger delta, and the surf breaking on Cornwall black and heavy, harbinger of more to come, in the spring of 1967, sing the glass of water thrust into the hand of the refugee who, safe and sound, relives the worst that man has ever done to man, drink this, friend, you are safe, your wife and children are with you, safe, drink this, the fit will pass. Walt Windbag, sing the air they could not breathe for chlorine gas, the air taking into it the puffs of smoke that say we have a new pope and the crematoria are working overtime, the Holy Ghost, the coming of the gift of tongues in a rushing mighty wind at Pentecost and her soft breathing when I wake in the night and listen and bless my life, sing the bright air in the frost-light, the zephyrs over honeysuckle, the wind finding his voice in the swaying tree-harp, the air at the summit, so sharp in the lungs, and bubbles uprising as we dipped in the cooling tarn far far below, exchange of breath, oh love's inspiriting, so that a lover can murmur to the as yet unborn what love is like and next day witness and be given the words for his mother on her deathbed cheyne-stoking. Sing Earth, Walt, Gaia altogether and the handfuls on the coffin lid, and the soil my father in his army blouson sieved for the garden of a Sunshine House so that fruit and flowers and vegetables would grow for the first time in his life as the work of his own hands, sing that sweet tilth, Walt, and the pits of Katyn Wood and Srebrenica, Pol Pot's, the stolen lands, the Nakba, sing the ploughlands before Guillemont and what the plough turns up there year after year, sing Demeter, goddess of the corn-bearing earth, and Erysichthon whom for his sin she punished with a greed the whole earth could not satisfy and he devoured himself. All this I swallow, says Walt, it tastes good, I like it well, it becomes mine.

And Jesus answering said, 'A certain man went down from Jerusalem to Jericho, and fell among thieves, which stripped him of his raiment, and wounded him, and departed, leaving him half dead.' And the Priest and the Levite passed by on the other side. Well, be thankful then for the Good Samaritan to balance things out a bit in that Golden Age of crucifixions. For, dearly beloved, along with the principle of everything flows I give you also the law and promise of Ontological Pointlessness, of random throws and accidents, of casual lots, the haps – the neutral-tinted, the good and the bad – scattered impartially over the deserving and the undeserving but the good landing mostly on the undeserving who see to it that they will, and, if challenged, point to Scripture, 'For whosoever hath, to him shall be given, and he shall have more abundance…' Meanwhile the son of a carpenter was out and about among the tombs where the poor mad people ran to and fro, cutting themselves with stones, and he ripped the evil spirits out of their mouths and flung the hedge-fund managers arse-over-tit from the temple of the Mother Goddess and forbade his sweet friend

Lazarus to lie any longer in the arms of stinking death, he wept, and hauled him forth and healed the sick and gave back skipping and dancing to the lame, and sat him down, human to human, with whores and drunks, and fed the hungry, blessed the peacemakers and comforted a grieving mother and father, saying, She is not dead, but sleepeth, and proved it with the magic words, Talitha cumi. But he was up against Herod and Ivan the Terrible, the Spanish Inquisition, Bloody Mary and most of the popes and Uncle Joe and a pair of Adolfs and Dr Mengele and millions in pursuit of their Manifest Destiny who carried his teaching into terrae incognitae, empty lands, and coloured them red with the blood of the ignorant and thoroughly stained the lovely places with syphilis and his worship. It is still touch and go, says Mephisto, after two thousand years of mass, which will come out on top, love without frontiers or cluster bombs. Sing, Walt! He sings.

The visiting speaker wakes, he is flung up like a ship-wormed log on a beach nobody combs, he lies on their bed, his side of it, the overcoat slipped off him, he is cold. Get up, love, she says. Have a shave and make yourself some breakfast. A coffee first, he says. And a glance at the book, I had a few thoughts about it during the night. Please, she says. Just go and close it. Perhaps you will be quieter when it's closed. How much longer? he answers. I tell you, love, I don't like it here in our empty house, my head is full to bursting, full as a poppy head but with every sort of seed, some nice, some horrible. – I heard you saying to yourself, Come spring, I'll work two hours in the garden every afternoon. – It's not spring yet. – But you have to promise you'll get through to spring because then you'll be all right working in the garden and with other things like that. So do you promise me? – I do.

Autumn Lady's Tresses

IN THE SHORTENING DAYS when the visitors had left, and around the solstice and in the lengthening days before they returned, Mrs Phipps might appear at dusk or at dawn and walk for a while on the turf before the School House or on the empty beach behind it; but for most of the spring and all of the summer and a part of the autumn she was strictly nocturnal. So it is no wonder that the girls, spying out from their hiding-place over half an arena, an arc of bay and the little headland where her old house stood, never once in all the years of their coming to the island – until their last – saw her. And the encounter with that lady towards the end of that final holiday was altogether a thing impossible to imagine beforehand and very hard to understand or even believe when they thought about it afterwards.

The island was small – barely a mile long – and from the start Gwen and Polly, promising not to go to certain places or do certain things, had been given the run of it. They were out for hours, and returned to their separate families, hoarding secrets.

Summers in childhood last for ever. And childhood itself is more a *state* of life than a phase. Outside that state, away from the island, time ran on, of course, and grown-ups measured its passing as they were bound to: dead-straight, tick-tock-tick-tock, on and on. But the girls returning to the island, itself and themselves a year older no doubt, re-entered the blessed state of summer whose particular years, re-lived in memory years later, could hardly be distinguished but made an entire zone in which they, as children, sun-burned, salt-licked and scratched by brambles, had run free.

Their spying-place – a large rock cleft in two – was on the west coast. West and east, though not half a mile apart, were very different. All four winds and all their quarters blew at the island but those from the west brought the ocean in with them. Very warily Gwen and Polly would approach. They came over the hill and sat there on the crest, as it were innocently, for a while, and climbed down only when they were sure no one saw them. But on their first arrival *that* year, the year of the apparition of Mrs Phipps and their last together on the island, they sat far longer then usual and gazed in disbelief at the transformation of the familiar scene below.

Where there had been turf and a path, now, on pale sand, there were tidemarks of dead seaweed, an enormous blanched tree trunk, the tangled wire and staves of a fence, plastic bottles, milk crates, fish boxes, and stones, stones, stones, many of them larger than a grown human being's head. True, the sea was back where it belonged, moving very quietly in the small bay, but the low dunes between it and terra firma had been levelled, so that you might assume the salt water would extend its reach again whenever it pleased.

The boatman said it was like nothing on earth, said Polly after a long silence. He said they went to rescue the School House lady but she wouldn't come out. She told them to go away and leave her in peace. Peace! said the boatman. All hell let loose, more like.

Nobody in sight, Polly helped Gwen down off the hill into hiding in the split rock. So every year they returned to this place, a cave at the back of the mind, that in daydreams and nightdreams often they had visited during their time away. And there they sat, shivering a little, huddling close, perched on a hillside, behind a curtain of ferns, tall stalks of dead fox-gloves and the clustered red berries of honeysuckle, and this late-summer return was stranger than any before because of the winter's extraordinary storm, its litter still clinging in the gorse and brambles below and its after-smell in the den itself.

There in hiding they were children of paradise spying with a thrill of secrecy on the everyday. And how strange it looked! How comical, fascinating and mystifying were the grown-up characters to the children observing them unseen. Clockwise or anti-clockwise some appeared and lingered or, without halting, passed and were never seen again; others an hour or a week or a year later reappeared and paused or as steadily as a second-finger, clockwise or anti-clockwise, went their ways. A stout man circumambulating the island hove up and vanished at terrific speed, elbowing furiously as though through a hindering crowd. A young woman came very slowly into view, a book in her hand, her thumb in its pages. She leaned on the white log amid all the wreck and gazed out to sea, occasionally shaking her head. And there were trysts, likely and very unlikely pairs, who met, embraced, and wildly, in a sort of panic, surveyed the terrain for a place to hide.

Each girl held a reporter's notebook, Polly's lined, Gwen's unlined. Polly recorded what they saw in words, Gwen in pictures; and the plan was always to marry them up one day in a book of books, a unique tome, in which the late-summer life of a small island facing west across two thousand miles of ocean would be preserved till kingdom come. Year by year, their skills and styles changing, the record grew and was housed separately, words and pictures, in their mainland dwellings. But the girls moved house, they left home, they settled elsewhere, moved again, settled for a while in another elsewhere, and amid such displacements one half then the other of the account was lost. But of Mrs Phipps there was no account to lose. Neither girl felt able, not on the occasion itself nor ever later, to sketch or make any notes about that lady.

It was a sunny day, late afternoon, very hot, the sea in close but quiet, the horizon hazy. Stillness, a hush, the space below the hill felt vacated and as though into it now, on to the stage, nothing familiar would be allowed. The semi-circle into which the sea had trespassed, the smothering white sand strewn with pebbles, stones, weed and all manner of wreck, that eerie theatre was waiting for the apparition of Mrs Phipps.

She did not enter from the School House, through the garden gate, but from the beach, through the midpoint of the levelled dunes, and slowly and very deliberately bore towards the hillside cave in which Gwen and Polly, huddled close, were hiding. She took nine paces, and halted, her eyes fixed on the cleft rock. She was tall and upright, her long hair, grey-white in colour, fell from under a flimsy pale scarf to below the bosom of her long and faded floral dress. The hem was wet, her feet were bare. She knows we're here, Gwen whispered. But the lady turned and, facing the sea, raised her arms to shoulder-level, opened them like a pair of dividers, and very slowly, head down, retraced her nine paces. Then her arms, as though weary, in hopelessness, fell to her sides, she turned again, strode forward and quite suddenly, as though collapsing, sat on the littered ground and hid her face in her hands. Gwen and Polly watched. It was one of those moments – the luckier you are, the later they first come – when children see with certainty that grown-ups suffer.

Mrs Phipps looked up. You two, she cried, I know you're there. Her voice had an antique tone and accent, but breaking, so that the adult it belonged to sounded like a child near to tears. I've watched you spying on me. Everybody spies on me. Keeping an eye on me, they call it. I call it spying. Well, come down here with your spying eyes and help me find what I have lost. Stand with your back to the rock that is rent in twain, he told me. Hold your arms out so and within that angle, looking carefully, you will find them, in the turf below the bracken below the rock. *Spiranthes spiralis*, little spirals, faint lights come up out of the dark, pale tresses, a small host of them, year after year, summer ending. I know where to look, I have always found them. And now see what a desert! Nothing but sand and stones and seaweed and bits of hateful plastic, no grass at all, let alone any sight of the darling flowers. Come down here, you sharp-eyed little girls, and help me!

There was no way down from the den except quite steeply through the tangle of honeysuckle, gorse, bracken and brambles. It was hard for Gwen, Polly helped her.

Mrs Phipps beckoned them closer. I had an owl for a friend once, she said softly. He blew in from the Lord knows where. He stayed two years. We walked out together night after night. Then he flew away, Lord knows where to. Now the bats and the moths are all my company. The flowers are like little torches, they come up out of the darkness that is under the earth and after a while in the sun they go back down again. But now they haven't come up, I've looked and looked, I've scrabbled around with my bare fingers – see what a ruin I've made of my pretty nails! – and the flowers he showed me are smothered and that is that.

Her eyes were a soft grey-green. Rapidly, in a low voice, she said: We were married as the War ended. And at once they sent him away to Palestine. But very soon I went to join him. It was a troopship, full of young wives. We were three weeks at sea. How bright Port Said looked after five years of London in the black-out! The quay was crowded with young husbands. I saw mine before he saw me. I waved and waved. We travelled overnight to Lydda, such a mixed and lively little town, and were fetched next day in a swanky car to Jerusalem. Three nights we spent there, in the King David Hotel, what fun! And then, would you believe it, we toured through Jordan and Syria on a little train. Such an adventure, so very young we were, we stopped where we liked. We had lunch with Bedouins in their tent, we saw the ruins of Jerash, and in Aleppo he bought me this scarf and all manner of bangles and beads and a beaten tin pot inscribed with a blessing in Arabic. Oh Aleppo! Oh the souk in the ancient heart of Aleppo, thronging with the costumes and colours of old humanity and joyous with many tongues!

She halted. Her raddled face was shining. Her lank hair, long as a mermaid's, hung over her bosom in silver-grey twists and spirals. Gwen noticed particularly the salt around the hem of her dress and that her feet were stained brown from the oils in the banks of weed she must have trodden through. Then she said, very flatly: We came here when our first child was born. Year after year my husband had come here with his mother and father. And in our first year, late summer, he showed me where to look for the Autumn Lady's Tresses.

Without a further word, she turned and walked like a somnambulist towards the sea. Gwen and Polly watched her out of sight. The sun shone. They felt cold.

Years later, far inland, Polly, the survivor, wakes out of a deep dream and lies alone then, eyes wide open in the darkness. She feels she has surfaced from the seabed, with the island and her best friend Gwen in her arms. There with her are the spying-place in the cleft rock, the old lady, her travels through the Holy Land to Aleppo, its souk and citadel, its mosques and arches, gardens, baths and cooling fountains. And there also, buried under the winter's sand and wreck, are the pale little orchids, the torch flowers, grey-green little rods spiralling upwards with faint lights. Polly lies in the dark, shaking her head in wonderment at the depth of her grief. She sinks again, dreaming, musing that the island, so small a bit of terra firma, for so many tears must surely be weighted with the sorrow of the whole wide world.

When I Was a Child

VIEWED FROM ABOVE, as it might be by a vulture, the lay-out of the House of the Brothers and Sisters of Mercy was clearly cruciform. In the east were a capacious chapel and the Brothers' quarters. In the south the Sisters lived, the girls and the very youngest children had their dormitories, and there was besides a large classroom, a sickbay and a mortuary. North were the boys, another classroom and a couple of workshops. The kitchen, refectory, storerooms, offices and two reception rooms were arranged down the long western axis that ended in a double door through which all but the very important visitors to the House were obliged to come and go.

The horizontal and the vertical axes did not intersect but opened into a large arena, the heart of the place, open to the heavens, and here around the circumference were a piggery, stables, hen-house, tool-sheds, a barn, and much else less easily named. In this space, on the first Sunday of every month, the Special Punishment Days were held. A high brick wall, spiked along the coping, enclosed the whole property, making a shape which, with the cross of buildings, might look from on high like a crusader's shield. The land outside the cross and within the walls was given up chiefly to the cultivation of edible produce; and out from the angles of the cross, splitting the cardinal points, dead straight paths led through the worked terrain and scraps of playground to four locked gates into the outside world.

And in that world? South, very far away, known to be there, never visited, was the Ocean. North, distant but not *so* distant, was the city whose lights the eye of faith, if permitted, saw flickering when cloud obscured the pitiless stars. West, distant but bulking nearer at sunset, were the Red Mountains. Children glimpsing them at that hour if the big doors opened to let a visitor out, never forgot their apparent nearness, and Father Dominic liked to allude to it in his sermons. East, behind the chapel, the outback began and was, Father Dominic said, empty and everlasting. You believed him, for the apse of the chapel was itself built into the confining wall and through transparent spaces in the lurid east windows, standing on tiptoe, pressing your forehead against the cold glass, you could see that the level emptiness did indeed stretch into eternity.

Matins was held every morning, summer and winter, at eight, and on Sundays vespers too, at four. And before vespers boys and girls were separated into their Sunday schools. The Lord's Day was also distinguished by music at matins. The House never had a choir to speak of, the very elderly Sister Cecilia worked the harmonium for the hymns, and the congregation sang along after a fashion. But at Sunday matins music of a different order was provided. It came from LP recordings of Religious Favourites, 'Ave Maria', for example, or 'The Chorus of the Hebrew Slaves', played on a bright red Dansette machine, the gift of a patron, a wealthy farmer, a visitor to the house. It stood on thin black legs in the nave and was managed by one of the prettier children, a favourite of the moment, who heard none of the music but stared throughout it fearfully at Father Dominic for a sign from him to turn the volume up or down or halt the performance altogether. All the children, not just the minder of the Dansette, watched his face. He had cavernous sad eyes, which he closed while listening, and bulldog jowls that sagged, as it seemed, under a weight of sorrow. Once he had let a whole side of the record play, a full half–hour of song, and had given no sign and in the dreadful silence afterwards had waved the whole congregation away without any sermon, hymn or valedictory prayer and blessing. Accustomed to much, everyone present, in their different ways, had been quite peculiarly terrified by that occasion. But usually after at most five minutes of ethereal harmonies, Father Dominic would signal for silence, heave himself into the pulpit and preach a sermon.

His particular subject was Purgatory. This is where we are, he said, gazing down and round, all of us, young and old, nuns, priests and laity, sisters and brothers, little daughters and sons, pure in heart or a prey to demons, amid so much lovingkindness here in this House we are all in Purgatory, and we pass from here to Heaven or Hell. Which shall it be? Who shall decide?

The answer to that second question, spoken privately to those among the children on whom his especial attention fell, was: *I* do. He told them in all humility and as though the burden of it oppressed him more than he could say, that he was charged by God Himself to consult his own conscience and experience and to take soundings also among the Brothers and Sisters of Mercy, and come to a judgement. He must sort the sheep from the goats, the wheat from the chaff, the gold from the dross since the Almighty Himself, overwhelmed, had no option but to delegate and had turned for help to His servant Dominic. Yes, said Father Dominic in private in the dark, trust me, at the footstool of the Lord what I say goes.

On one unforgettable Sunday, the first after Ascension and, as it happened, the first of the month, Father Dominic halted the Dansette midway through the 'Alleluia Chorus', clambered fast into the pulpit and without his customary commanding minute's silence began in breathless haste to speak. Ask yourselves, he said, each and every one of you, this question, Where have I come from? In the interest of truth I will answer for you. Out of sordid misery you have come, out of dirt and hunger and mortal peril. We have rescued you from loveless and violent circumstances, out of the clutches of drunkard fathers who beat you and mothers who wore fur coats and told you they were too poor to keep you. We took you orphaned out of the ruins of family life, we fetched you in off the streets of the Mother Country's festering slums. You were conducted hither by our guardian angels. You were rootless and we planted you in the good earth of a Christian life.

He paused, then in a steadier voice continued, My text today is 1 Corinthians 13:11, 'When I was a child, I spake as a child, I thought as a child: but when I became a man, I put away childish things.' Dearly beloved in Christ, you are here to grow up. You have been brought to this place of salvation so that you may put away childish things and learn to speak and think as adult men and women. In this asylum of love and good order you learn a craft or a trade so that you will have a place and be useful in society and will pass on to others what has been given to you. It is expected of you that you will do as you were done by. You are here for a purpose. In a world all adrift you will employ your talents for the good of your religion and your race and so doing you will shine forth before men and your works will be pleasing to the eyes of the watchful Lord. He leaned forward and down, the jowls on him quaked, every child present felt seen through and through by Father Dominic's small eyes that were like frightened creatures spying out from caverns of darkness at a patient predator. Leaving, male and female coming together in the aisle, Sister Grace whispered to Brother Anthony that the Father had spoken with the tongues of men and of angels in equal measure. Indeed he has, said Brother Anthony, giving her a wink.

Father Dominic, in the hour before supper, visited the sick-bay. One of the younger nuns, Sister Agatha, was on duty.

He came in silently and caught her bathing the face of a boy of seven or eight whose name was Stanley. He stood a while watching her and only when the boy opened his eyes and stared in terror over the Sister's shoulder did she realise Father Dominic's presence. He bowed, and withdrew to her desk at the door and sat there leafing through her reports. When she had done with Stanley she emptied the bowl at a sink against the wall and threw the stained lint and cotton wool into the bin beneath it. She had filled the bowl again with warm water, added disinfectant, and had taken up a clean towel and more lint and dressings, but set it all down on a trestle table when he beckoned her. I see that it is hard for you, Sister Agatha, he said when she stood before him seated at her desk. She nodded, saying nothing. Your notes, for example. They need not be quite so full. Nor so precise. The only record that matters is in the child himself. If he remembers, then we have done our job. Sister Agatha said nothing. Do you have a question, he asked? Yes, I do, she answered. Since you ask. Why must they be set to fight one another, these poor boys, and always a big boy against a much smaller one. Ah, he said, *that* question. And I suppose you were going next to Daniel in Bed 5? Yes, I was, she answered. He has been flogged and must lie face down. The flogging, said Father Dominic, is a practice we copied from Eton. The Masters there delegate the punishment. Older boys flog the younger who in their turn then will flog the youngsters coming on. As to the bare-knuckle fighting – our use of it here – boys will fight anyway – but our deliberate practice, I'm not sure where that came from, but certainly, together with the Etonian flogging, it works very well. We are the Church Militant, Sister Agatha. We are making child-soldiers for Christ. We bind them together in complicity. We make of them a force to be reckoned with. They will never break ranks. You deprave them, said Sister Agatha. Father Dominic smiled. She was indeed unsound. You? he said. Who is this 'you'? *We*, Sister – *we*, the House of the Brothers and Sisters of Mercy, all of us working together. And if you say 'deprave' I say that you are forgetting the Fall. They are born depraved. We bring their fallen state into the light of day. Only thus can we enlist them in the long march towards redemption. I must see to the child in Bed 5, said Sister Agatha. Do, said Father Dominic. With my blessing. He rose, but standing at the door he added, Not everyone is fit for the work of this House. If you feel you cannot be one of us, you are free to leave. But remember your vow of silence, Sister Agatha. God is listening. Keep your mouth shut.

In the House of the Brothers and Sisters of Mercy solitude, except as a punishment (in the cellar under the mortuary, for example), was forbidden to the orphans, and discouraged among their keepers. Always at least two or three were gathered together, and three or four times a day the whole community, excepting only the sick and the very young, assembled. This was House policy and at every meeting of his Inner Circle Father Dominic extolled its virtues. Between the Wilderness and the Sepulchre when was our Saviour ever alone? he asked. And muttered in his soul, Always, always, never a moment of human nearness.

The day's three meals were taken communally. Supper, with candles in the winter and the sun-lit stained-glass windows in summer, was truly, as Father Dominic said, a love feast. He sat with the Brothers and Sisters at High Table under a blue and gold Assumption and with portraits of previous Fathers and paintings of some notable martyrdoms close on the white-washed walls around them. The children, the two sexes and all ages permitted to mingle, sat below in silence but for their disobedient sidelong whisperings that the Monitors found hard to locate and punish. A girl with red hair, for example – with the remnants of red hair, to be exact, the lovely fullness of it having been cropped because the Devil was in it – Jezebel, the Sisters had named her, she had a birthmark over her heart where the Devil had kissed her, and for her own good, the saving of her immortal soul, they would beat her often and long with a strap, a cane, a chair leg or whatever else came to hand – this child of fourteen, insolence incarnate, kept up a sardonic commentary to left and right, never turning her head and never the least movement of her lips betraying her.

One practice at supper – a *tradition*, Father Dominic, its inventor, liked to call it – was that a child would be summoned at random to the High Table and commanded to recite the House's Latin grace. The randomness was critical, Father Dominic insisted. One would be chosen, all must be prepared. The rules were lenient enough: two hesitations were permitted, as well as two mistakes if at once corrected. Failure beyond that and the child was caned on the spot and sent to bed supperless. Then another quite at random would be called up to recite. On Jezebel the lot never fell since it was known that she could rattle off the whole thing flawlessly – Benedic, Domine, nos et dona tua, quae de largitate tua sumus sumpturi, et concede, ut illis salubriter nutriti tibi debitum obsequium praestare valeamus, per Christum Dominum nostrum – and then backwards, if let. In discussions concerning the progress of their charges, the Brothers, Sisters and Father Dominic himself often cited her as the best exemplar of *corruption* they had ever witnessed. Once or twice over the years a newcomer to the Fellowship had wondered what end these recitations served, what good did they do? Soon answered, said Father Dominic. Preparedness to be chosen is beyond doubt a virtue; some trepidation does no harm; and – here he would smile, to show that the House did not always take itself too seriously – reciting without error a script you don't understand a word of is excellent training for any position, however low or high, in the Church.

Billy, aged fourteen, still wet the bed. This vice had first manifested itself in Nazareth House, a sort of prep-school for the House of the Brothers and Sisters of Mercy, into which he had been committed by his desperate mother when he was three. The nuns there, some of them quite muscular, had done their damnedest by the usual means – prayer and thrashings – to exorcise his evil, but had failed. Deported then across the ocean into the care of Father Dominic he had undergone further treatment quite beyond what his already fearful, but still childishly limited, spirit could comprehend. Kneeling all night at his clean bed in prayer, a Brother standing by to clout him round the ear if he nodded off, for example. Or having an electrode fitted to him that sprang alive and shocked him *there*, if in his innocent sleep he watered it. Things like that. All in vain.

Billy was small for his age; in truth, a weakling. But not unattractive, said Brother Theodore to Brother Philip as they stood side by side at bedtime spying through the dormitory louvres before they did their rounds. I do like his big ears. Billy's age should have qualified him to be senior partner in the fist-fights but his physique held him back, he would never advance from being thumped to thumping. The Brothers and Sisters discussed him and agreed that he should be guided towards other options.

The Brothers were very big men, six foot and over, broad-shouldered, immensely strong. So small and weak himself, Billy could not understand why these male adults in authority over him needed to be so big. So little of their strength it took to deal him the maximum he could bear. They rose from their heavy black shoes, through the black soutane to the white cravat, so very tall, even to see him they had to bend, and to hear his little pleas they would have had to kneel.

Whenever Brother Theodore met Billy (and for a while he went out of his way to meet him) he would ask, Who's been fiddling you? Or, Who've you been fiddling with? And since he wouldn't take no one for an answer and since he had ways of making Billy talk, this child like all the other children soon offered up a name to be the holy and living sacrifice the gods that day or night demanded. So, needing loyalty, the children were joined together by betrayal. Taking Sam or Derek or Charlie up into his lap, Brother Theodore would say, Billy tells me there's been some fiddling between you? That there, he said, is my truncheon. Better do as he bids. But first my pesky blackheads need some attention. The favoured boy with his thumb and finger would erupt the several pimples on both wings of the Brother's nose into the snow-white handkerchief he provided. Strange preliminary, peculiar to the House! With Brother Philip it was nits, with Brother Hubert things in his ears. There are examples of similar service elsewhere in the animal kingdom. The Egyptian plover cleans the crocodile's teeth, the tick-bird rids the rhino of his ticks. But in those instances there is give and take, the arrangement is one of mutual aid: both birds are paid for the good they do their host. Did the Brothers give nothing in exchange for the relief they had from Billy and the bartered friends? A lollipop now and then, once or twice some chocolate. Better still, for an uneasy interlude, almost affection, almost a tenderness. But the highest reward the boys and girls hoped for was to be chosen to serve at one of the private dinners Father Dominic gave. Two or three of the Inner Circle would be there, together with three or four important sponsors, patrons, visitors and protectors. The children were allowed not just the crumbs that fell from the table but also, and generously, the leavings on the silver plates and in the cut-glass bowls. They ate in haste with their fingers on the landing. Now and then one of them brought along a paper bag to fill for some lost soul in even greater need.

There was a solitary black boy in the House. They called him Wagga. Singular in his blackness he was remarkable also for having artificial legs, his own having been lost as he tried to run away across a busy road. A renowned surgeon operated on him gratis, the cost of new legs was borne by a local charity, and, accepted into the House of the Brothers and Sisters of Mercy, Wagga got around much like a luckier child and kept up a cheerful patter in English and in a native tongue. Brothers and Sisters, directed by Father Dominic, were always on the look-out for peculiarly fitting punishments for their charges; and it was Brother Emmanuel, God bless him, who in conclave, at Pentecost, suggested that in Wagga's case the routine punishment for serious offences – speaking in barbaric tongues, for example – should be the temporary confiscation of his artificial legs. Strapped in then, Wagga sat upright on his chair, to watch glumly the usual day go by. But a big girl known as Dippy May, whose innocence shielded her from some things, in full view of everyone crossed the common room, unstrapped the boy and carried him with her in her arms all day. And not a Brother or Sister said a word. Thereafter whenever Wagga lost his legs Dippy May sought him and unconfined him and carried him in her arms the long day long. Father Dominic smiled. See how we bring out the good in the most unlikely people, he observed. And noted the example for possible future use.

Abruptly Brother Theodore was tired of big-eared Billy. One last time he nibbled at his lobes then flung him to the floor and rose and kicked him, and kicked him again, hard. Sister Agatha, who would soon leave the House, tended him and went and pleaded with Brother James, who ran one of the boys' workshops, to give him a chance in there when he was well enough and let him learn how to repair and maintain bicycles. For waking one night in tears when she had gone to him he had told her that in a dream his mother had come to him and promised him a brand-new bicycle for his next birthday. Brother James had a soft spot for Sister Agatha, he would miss her, he confessed, and he agreed with her that Billy had supped more than his share of horrors and of course he must come and learn the lore of bicycles. Why do you stay? she asked. He blushed, shook his head, covered his mouth.

The child now managing the Dansette for Music at Matins was a girl of ten or eleven called Ellie. She was very pretty, and her face showed the constant fear by which that gift was always haunted in the House. She dreaded being chosen for anything; and when Father Dominic came into the classroom one morning and appraised her for what seemed like an eternity and nodded then to Sister Frances and exited without a word, Ellie bowed her head and sat there blankly suffering agonies. The class continued around her, ended, her classmates were dismissed and she sat covering her eyes as though that might make her be *not there*. Sister Frances, bulking large, came and sat at the small desk beside her and told her Father Dominic's wish. Now don't be silly, child, she said. It is a great honour, you should rejoice. And that afternoon Sister Laetitia took her into the Chapel and showed her how the Dansette worked. It's very simple, she said. You will be told well in advance the name of the piece and what track it is. Let's say it's 'Jesu, Joy of Man's Desiring'. Side B, track 5. Now we'll have a practice. I'll be Father Dominic, I'll sit by the pulpit, and when I raise my little finger you raise the needle with the little lever, the disc spins, you lower the needle at track 5, the music begins, and you watch Father Dominic like a hawk for his further instructions.

Ellie got the hang of it and came through one Sunday and then the next 'with flying colours', as Sister Laetitia said. And on the following occasion, the first Sunday of a new month, the catastrophe was not her fault.

The choice was straightforward, just one piece, side A, track 1 of a new LP, More Religious Favourites, Allegri's *Miserere*, as much or as little of it as Father Dominic should decide, easy for Ellie to begin, easy to halt, when he signalled. That Sunday, he looked no worse than usual. Week by week the heaviness of his countenance was increasing, but imperceptibly to all except his nearest observers. He took his seat − his throne, the Brothers and Sisters called it − close by the pulpit, gave Ellie the signal and slumped then, in his usual fashion, into an attendance within himself upon the words that must come to him for his sermon. But after only three or four minutes of Allegri, his eyes, in their vast dark sockets, opened wide, he stared like a man in a nightmare at the Dansette and at the pretty child Ellie standing by it. He seemed to be seeing what no one else in the Chapel could see. He looked row by row first at the children, then beyond, left and right, at the Sisters and Brothers, all of whom felt discovered in their particular sins in a general guilt. He shuddered, he heaved himself to his feet, immense, but as though a bodily frame twice as big would be inadequate to bear what he had to bear. He threw back his head, with each hand covered an eye, and roared, thrice, he howled, out of the depths of him. Then looked at his world again, took cognisance of it, and strode, lurching, towards the music.

Ellie fled, fast as she could she ran away down the aisle, and near the door of the chapel flung herself into the lap of a nun and covered her ears. This Sister, to whom in fifty-five years on earth no such appeal had ever been made, forgot entirely where she was, and in an ancient tone and accent murmured, There, there, child. There, there, love. And fondled her blonde curls and pressed her close.

Father Dominic meanwhile had reached the Dansette and lifted it, still uttering *Miserere mei, Deus*, above his head. And now from that height, with all his strength, he hurled it down at the chancel tiles. In the crash and splintering Allegri ceased. Father Dominic vented the rest of his passion on the wreckage of the upturned machine. He ripped off its spindly black legs and flung them left and right in among his flock. Then kicked and stamped the red box and the disc inside it to a cheap mess of metal, plastic, plywood, vinyl and a few wires. That accomplished, he leaned with his right hand against the pulpit and in an off-key sort of voice, a little breathless, but level and perfectly audible, he said, There will be no sermon today. And henceforth there will be no Music at Matins. We have had the Devil in our midst, in our sanctum, our heart of hearts. I have trampled him down to where he belongs. But, dearly beloved in Christ, he is as cunning as he is strong. He walks about among us, seeking whom he may devour. Therefore be vigilant. Watch and pray. We shall assemble, undeterred, at eleven for the Punishments.

Leaving, the two sexes coming together in the aisle, Sister Grace whispered to Brother Anthony, He takes it very hard. Indeed he does, said Brother Anthony. Tollit peccata mundi. Usual time tonight?

Sister Agatha missed Father Dominic's anguish. She was waiting at the junction with the State Highway, for the bus that would take her at least some of the way to the city and her old convent, the only home she had.

Like many agents of Church and State before him, Father Dominic believed that serious crimes and sins should be punished in public. A hanging, a beheading or a burning in the public square was a proven deterrent and a powerful aid in the unending struggle against corruption. In that spirit, but in a milder form, he had some years previously instituted the Special Punishment Days; and, drawing all the Brothers and Sisters into the organization and the staging of them, he felt fortified by their solidarity and could better support, he said, the Cross of every month's first Sunday. Most often it was straightforward and did not take long. A boy was flogged (with all humane precautions) for stealing and eating corn from the hen-house; a little girl stood in her wet shift on a bale of hay and read out the confession of her disobedience and dirtiness, and since she had been made to write it herself and to read it out in a loud clear voice, the exercise could rightly be called 'teaching her a lesson'. And all the other children, arranged in a circle around the flogging stool or the hay-bale, all looking in, all witnessing, they learned too.

But one night, having accompanied an important patron to one of the dormitories and returning late to his white-washed cell and lying sleepless under the flickering lamp of the crucifix, Father Dominic, drop after bitter drop, had swallowed the conviction that all his charges were corrupt, all, toddlers and teenagers alike, they were equally vicious, and to call out one or two for sins as trivial as stealing food or answering back or wetting the bed was a waste of everyone's time and displeasing to the Lord. Over several nights then, twisting at his nightshirt, he rifled the dungeons of his mind for ways and means of making real and visible the idea of the collective punishment of general sin. He fasted, he watched and prayed, he lay face down on his damp pillow, summoned up and discarded a thousand possibilities, came near to despair – but woke at last one sunny morning out of cloacal dreams into clarity and certainty. That's it! he cried. And felt the truth and boldness of his vision in the tremendous galloping of his heart.

At breakfast, by the nod and the wink, he convened an extraordinary meeting of the Inner Circle, swore them to secrecy, and announced, This is how it will be. He relished their horrified amazement. You'll see, he said. It will work wonders. Your Brothers and Sisters will learn with the children, *as it happens*. Henceforth we shall be as one, sinners young and old working together for redemption. None of his privy council dared object. He knew their hearts and their works and deeds as they knew his. Team spirit, he called it, *esprit de corps*, collegiality, fellowship, the family, the very Church.

The children loved a horse, called White Star after a blaze on her forehead. She had worked many years on a farm where some of the older boys had once been sent to labour and learn about the land, animals and machinery. When the farmer died his widow sold up and went to live with her children and their children in the city. And leaving she gave White Star to the orphans as a pet. It became their responsibility to look after her, brush her and comb her, keep her well fed and watered, lead her for exercise within and sometimes, as a treat, outside the walls. And in turn, favouring the youngest, with infinite care and attention, they rode her. She was gentle.

Father Dominic saw the wisdom of allowing this deep affection and had shared his thinking with the Brothers and Sisters at a particularly memorable conclave for Advent. A child who loves, he said, is more open to punishment than one who does not. Obvious really, he added. When you weigh up. And he felt no need to repeat the maxim when he informed the Inner Circle of what, after nights of torment and prayer, he had decided for the next Special Punishment Day. He described exactly how the event would be choreographed and instructed them to make the necessary arrangements. Agreed? There was silence. One by one he looked all seven in the eye, saw into their blackmailed souls, four men and three women, at each he stared and each in turn nodded. So be it, he said. And bowed his head in the customary prayer and blessing.

That month's first Sunday happened to be Epiphany, and the sun, in that country, was already fierce. The children were issued with straw hats, the Brothers and Sisters with white parasols. Father Dominic himself wore his red sombrero. My one affectation, he would say with a smile. And indeed it went well with his black soutane. The children sat cross-legged on the dirt ground, youngest at the front, in a semi-circle facing the piggery. The Brothers and Sisters, the sexes mingling, stood arced behind them. The stage, so to speak, was the earth the pigs had churned. They, sows and the tusked boars, were cooped in their separate sties along the back and could be heard squealing, grunting, snuffling.

The chapel bell struck eleven. White Star was led out by a boy called Ezra. He was old enough to have left the House but had been kept on with two or three others of his kind, as a trusty. He unfastened the strong gate, led White Star through, closed the gate and brought her slowly to the centre of the empty hemisphere. There they halted and faced the audience, Ezra looking to Father Dominic for what must follow. Father Dominic strode to the gate and beckoned Ezra. The mare stood patiently where she had been led to. The flies were bothering her. She shook her fringe and mane, swished over her back and flanks with her tail. She was patience itself, amiable, trusting and to be trusted. Standing there she received love from the children as though they were an arc of it and reflected back on to her in her grace and innocence and gentleness all their fervent love in a cool collected beam. Over the gate Father Dominic handed Ezra a thing in sacking. With this Ezra returned to White Star, unwrapped a shotgun, and fired both barrels into her belly. She was smitten with astonishment. She raised her head to the skies and gave a cry that was louder and lasted longer than could ever have been imagined in her. And fell then sideways, showing the entrance wounds out of which blood leapt with the force of spring-waters out of the hillside after a deluge. She lay there kicking and writhing as though trying to stand again, as though wanting to prove by a miracle that it had not been done to her. Slobbered at the mouth, baring her teeth, showing her tongue. Ezra glanced towards Father Dominic, who nodded. Ezra ran to the sties, very nimbly unbolted them one after the other, got then at top speed to the gate, and over it into safety, as the boars and sows, not fed for a week, burst forth and fell upon White Star. Father Dominic surveyed the crescent of children. They were wide-eyed and open-mouthed. That is good, he said to himself. They are taking it in.

That night, face down on his narrow bed under the crucifix, Father Dominic acknowledged in his soul that he had led the House across a frontier into a zone he had no name for but from which there could be no return. I know this, he said to himself, and it is my duty now to induct the Brothers and Sisters into the truth of where we are with our troop of children. The mark – the picked-clean carcase of White Star – was evident and he refused any suggestion that it might be cleared away. What the pigs hadn't eaten the vultures had. One sow took to dozing in the capacious rib-cage. When she yawned and went elsewhere her piglets made a game of running to and fro through it. Half a dozen vultures perched almost permanently on the chapel roof. Their patience suggested they were sure there was more to come. Despite the fierce and disinfecting sun, the arena stank.

These details and others Father Dominic incorporated into his next sermon. Striving together, he said, the two sexes, all ages, we have made incarnate the spirit of Purgatory. Dearly beloved, keep always at the forefront of your minds that our arena of punishment – the deed and its relics and the lingering stink of it – is like the Paradise Garden in comparison with the Hell that awaits us if we do not push onwards now through further pain towards redemption. His face lately had assumed the look of congealed cold porridge, jowled and dew-lapped it sagged with weights of tribulation. Through his grey lips as he spoke his congregation saw a tongue that had the appearance of some fat worm-creature struggling desperately for freedom out of the pit of him through teeth forced open wide. But his little eyes gleamed from their hidey-holes as bright as jet. Leaving, the two sexes coming together in the aisle, Sister Grace observed to Brother Anthony that Father Dominic was looking champion, all things considered. Indeed he is, said Brother Anthony. And added, OK for tonight?

Father Dominic himself brought Billy to Brother James's workshop. He escorted him in, with a fatherly arm around his shoulder. The child is convalescent, he said. Some quiet work with his hands will do him good. Brother James bowed. He was slightly built and he stammered. Father Dominic thought him a poor specimen of a Christian Soldier, but whenever in the Inner Circle it was suggested he might be got rid of, somebody would say, and Father Dominic would agree, He does no harm. The half dozen other boys in the workshop, variously occupied, glanced only surreptitiously at the visitors. They knew better than to stare. Besides, it was nothing new. Father Dominic nodded, patted Billy on the head, and left. Billy made no move. He stood with his hand over his mouth, looking out. It was a characteristic gesture in the House of the Brothers and Sisters of Mercy. Children sat up in their rumpled beds at night, in the dark, rocking to and fro and very softly moaning – that too was a mark of being there. And especially in bad periods (as after the killing of White Star), throughout the day they might cover the mouth, as though they were afraid and ashamed of it, for what it might take in or say. Even in Brother James's workshop some newcomers made that sign for a while, and might even, in extreme cases, try to use only one hand for work requiring both.

There was very little talking in the workshop. The boys loved Brother James for his stammer. Some days he did not dare try speech at all. He carried a pad of white paper and when speech deserted him, or he feared that it might, he wrote his instructions, advice, encouragement and praise in simple words in beautiful copper-plate for each boy in turn, moving from bench to bench. And he was besides adept (and graceful) at demonstrating exactly what a particular passage in a work required. The children learned from watching his hands. There was a noise of busyness in that room, peaceful. And almost silently Brother James did his rounds. Never once had he asked a boy to uncover his mouth. When they wanted and felt able to stand before him open-faced, they would. It had happened, and the joy of it dwelled in him, that the first thing he saw on an uncovered face was a smile.

Brother James motioned Billy to follow him. On a bench in the far corner, under a window, he had already set a bike upright, each wheel in a clamp. The window, having bars on the outside, was the only one in the room that an adult or child could see through. Light came copiously through all the other windows, but they were set in a row high up under the ceiling. Brother James took out his pen and paper and wrote large and clear: Welcome Billy! Today we will learn what all the parts of a bicycle do. And perhaps we will even begin taking it to bits. Then he was anxious. By no means all the children even of Billy's age were good readers. If they were poor, he would have to mime or try speaking.

That night after supper – at which, as always, he had suffered the torments of the damned – Brother James wrote a letter to Sister Agatha. He began by saying that he had not asked permission to write the letter, he didn't want Father D. reading it, and he hoped she would feel flattered by this, his first act of serious disobedience in seven years in the House. I shall ask permission to take a little trip out, he wrote, on my moped, an hour at most, to lift my spirits, and to intercept our postman at the junction. Wish me luck! Then he turned to the subject of Billy. The child moves me greatly, he wrote. He is so full of goodwill. All he asks is to love and be loved. But his terror stifles him. His legs and chest are still badly bruised. I see him shocked by pain if he forgets and makes a sudden movement. But his eagerness will prevail, if let. Within an hour he uncovered his mouth. I had the bike up on the bench, to show him all the parts, how the seat and the handlebars could be adjusted to suit him, how the brakes worked, how they would need to be checked from time to time and the worn pads replaced. And so on. There is a deal to learn about a bicycle! And heart and soul that child began to learn. My dear friend, he forgot his misery and only remembered it again, and covered his mouth, when a Monitor came to fetch him to Bible study.

There Brother James paused. He had called Sister Agatha 'my dear friend'. He thought seriously of burning the page and starting the whole letter again. But then on an unusual surge of confidence, and viewing with pleasure his own flowing script, he muttered to himself, Let be. And he continued his account of Billy's initiation into the workings, maintenance and repair of a bicycle, and concluded, He next comes to me the day after tomorrow. I shall ask permission to let him try riding up and down the path through the vegetable garden, or even, if we both feel brave enough, through the north gate and a few yards up the little road. For why learn all about a bike if you can't ride it? He signed his letter: Hoping you are happier and altogether better off where you are now. Affectionately, James. Then he sat a while wondering at himself. She would be in her old convent, he supposed. He would address the letter there. Would she be allowed to receive it? Grown man, grown woman, ruled like helpless minors. He added a PS: You asked me why I stay. Because I stammer, because I thought in a religious house it would not matter, because I have nowhere else to go, because I am a coward, because I am quite good at making and mending things, because I think some of the boys can be helped by me.

Brother James, granted an hour's leave of absence, chugged on his moped to the junction with the State Highway and sat there under a smooth blotched tree for the postman, Mick, to appear. The House was very visible on the flat land. At a distance and in the excitement of his escapade Brother James saw the building, its community, its mores, its isolation, with spasms of sheer horror. From this trance – a gap in which his consciousness was wholly filled with the House of the Brothers and Sisters of Mercy – he was startled by the red van halting and Mick saying through the open window, You got something for me? Brother James opened his mouth but no words came out. He pointed to the name and address. Mick nodded. I'll do my best, he said. Old Mother Maggie is very watchful but there are ways and means. You go back now. I'll sit here and have a smoke.

Slowly returning, Brother James reflected that within a month of his first entering the House he had begun a life of secrecy and deceit. Not for any advantage, only in self-defence, so as not to perish. And in that struggle his worsening stammer was an asset. Often he couldn't speak at all and nobody wanted to witness his agonies. In the confessional box, doing his honest best to compose himself and to speak as though in silence, he did well enough. But then Brother Anthony, in friendly fashion, took him aside and said that on the whole it was wise not to be too candid 'in there'. Make a few things up, if you like, we all do, but keep your own secrets. Father Dominic delegated the confession of the children and the House's few secular servants to his Inner Circle. But he saved all the Brothers and Sisters, and the Inner Circle, for himself. It was generally assumed that he used what was whispered into his ear for the closer management of his flock; which made them reticent and evasive in their confessions and liable to shift a few of the more serious sins on to one another.

Father Dominic knew this perfectly well. He encouraged both their being economical with the truth and their betrayals (in a soft voice he asked for names). By leaving them with sins unsaid, and tempting them to add a few more (bearing false witness, for example), he thought to keep them in fear, in a web of it. Knowing their sins and their terrors, he felt himself to be the centre which held the House together.

Father Dominic appeared again in the workshop, so silently that Brother James and Billy, at the bench in the far corner under the window, were only made aware of his presence by the gradual ceasing of all the peaceful noise of work. They turned. Father Dominic smiled. You look surprised in a mortal sin, he said. And addressing himself to Brother James, he continued, This will be Billy's last lesson. I see that he is quite restored to health and doubtless your teachings have helped. I am sure he will be grateful to you. But now Brother Theodore has some further use for him. Billy went white and began to shake. Brother James tried to speak but halted, blurting, at the first syllable. He reached for pen and paper. No need for that, said Father Dominic, waving a dismissive and nicely manicured hand. I think I can guess what you would say if your organs of speech would let you. And I disapprove of your seeking to circumvent that God-sent prohibition with foolish little notes. Brother Theodore has done more for the *ultimate* good of this child's immortal soul than you ever will in a thousand years of footling with bicycles. Now see to your other charges. You do wrong to make a favourite of this one. He turned to leave, but halted and said, It is a while since I heard your confession. Will you come to me at four? Reverend Mother Margaret tells me you may have something on your conscience. He nodded to Brother James, and then to Billy, and strode away.

Brother James went from bench to bench, praising, gently correcting and advising, with pen and paper. Every child saw his trouble. The power of speech had deserted him. Perhaps for ever, he thought. Would I mind so very much? The class ended, the boys trooped out, all except Billy who stayed at his workplace, gripping the set of gears he had been assembling. When Brother James stood by him, he said, staring at the gears, in a low voice but very clearly, I stole one of them knives you use for leatherwork, sharp as a razor. I'll cut my wrists tonight if you won't help me, sir. I won't have that filthy devil at me again. Brother James wrote, What do you want me to do? Billy turned, and looking up full into his face, said in a rush, Please leave the north gate unlocked, I'll get away on my bike, I've thought it all out, sir, I'll go up the little road where you took me to practise, to the junction you told me about and the highway you said leads all the way to the city, I'll only ride at nights, I'll hide up in the day when it's so hot and they might be looking for me, I've stolen some food, I'll carry it in my paniers, I've got my water bottle, I'll fill it up at places along the way, I'll ride fast, I'll be travelling light. When I get to the city I'll live on the streets, I'll beg, people will have pity on me, they'll give me pennies for food, I feel sure of that. Only for six months, I'll be fifteen then, I can come out of hiding, they can't bring me back here against my will when I'm fifteen, the other kids told me that, it's the law, I'll be free, I can do as I like then, I'll get a job, I'll make my own way, I've thought it all out, I had another dream, Mam came to me and said, That's the thing to do, Billy, and ask Brother James to help you, he's a good man, he'll stand by you, and you will, won't you, sir, I'll cut my wrists if you won't, but I know you will, because why else would you teach me about bikes and help me make one good and strong, 3-speed, with a bell and paniers and a basket, a pump and dynamo lights, nobody's had a bike that good before, it'll be a life-saver, I'll ride away on it, I'll live a proper life thanks to you, Mister Brother James, sir. Brother James very slowly shook his head, in wonder, not in refusal. Yes, I'll do that for you, he wrote in flowing copper-plate on a clean white sheet. This is how we will manage it. He wrote, and handed Billy his instructions. As Billy read them, rapidly to himself Brother James in the silence behind his stammer said, If you die on the road, I'll be responsible and I can't save you in this place from the devil Theodore or from the very sharp knife in your own hands, so I'll do what you ask of me, I obey you, you'll be on my conscience for ever if you die and I'll be gladder than I've ever been in my life before about anything if you live, Billy, child.

Billy wasn't missed until late morning of the following day. There was a convention in the House that no child should be declared missing till it had been established beyond reasonable doubt that no Sister or Brother was privy to his or her whereabouts in some room or other. Those enquiries, having to be discreet, took a while. In Billy's case, Father Dominic made an announcement at supper. A child has absconded, he said. We will soon find out if any of you knows anything about this sin. If you do, you will be punished. But not so severely as you will be if you don't admit it now. But that punishment will be as the gentle rain from heaven in comparison with the punishment that awaits the sinner Billy when we fetch him back, as we surely will. I shall myself flog him to within an inch of his life and leave him out under God's wrathful stars all night. So be warned. That is what will happen.

Next day, hooded entirely in a black cape, the adult flogging frame was set up in the punishment arena. There it will stay, said Father Dominic. Many times a day you will see it waiting there, until the child who belongs on it is captured and returned.

A week the frame stood in the arena, close to the picked skeleton of White Star (still a curious shelter for a sow to doze in or her piglets to run through as a merry game). Half a dozen vultures perched on the chapel roof. Now and then one took off and lazed in wide circles over the House. The others sidled along. And a second week, and a third the draped frame stood there waiting for the child. In his absence, during that waiting, day by day its significance began to change. Perhaps it would wait in vain? Perhaps he had escaped? Then overnight the frame disappeared and on the following Sunday, a Special Punishment Day, Father Dominic prefaced his sermon (on the soul's longing for cleanliness) with another announcement. I am very sorry to have to tell you, he said, that our dear little brother in Christ, Billy Big-Ears, will not be coming back. His remains have been discovered in woodland close to the State Highway. He has been torn to pieces by dingoes, coyotes and hyenas. Carrion birds have fed on him. Of the whereabouts of his immortal soul we cannot speak.

The punishments that day were nothing out of the ordinary. Two boys were flogged, with all humane precautions, for lewdness, by a third about to leave the care of the Brothers and Sisters of Mercy and go out into the world. The normal stool, more suited to the sinners' size, was used. A girl of eleven was caned by Sister Ruth for stealing milk. Another two, both slightly older, stood on hay-bales hooded in wet bed sheets. Like little Madonnas, Brother Anthony observed. Wagga, who had his legs at the time, lay with his head in Dippy May's lap while she fondled his black curls.

Supper, however, was very much out of the ordinary. Neither Father Dominic nor any of his Inner Circle were able to be there. All were dining privately in the Large Reception Room with an alderman, a judge, a bishop, a cabinet minister, a financier and a colonel. In hindsight Father Dominic conceded that he ought not to have abandoned his flock. The dinner, arranged to discuss what they called simply Protection, was of great importance. Still, he should have put the good order of the House first, or should at least have appointed somebody fitter, more *compos mentis*, than Sister Cecilia to preside at supper in his absence.

Sister Cecilia forgot to summon a child at random to say grace. And when politely reminded of the tradition by Brother Serenus, she pointed vaguely – she was almost blind – in the direction of Jezebel, who before anyone could intervene sprang on to the dais and at terrific speed, with relish, loud and clear and with no error or hesitation recited the whole thing backwards, thus: Murtson Munimod Mutsirhc rep sumaelav eratsearp muiuqesbo mutibed ibit itirtun retirbulas silli tu edecnoc te irutpmus sumus aut etatigral ed eauq aut anod te son Enimod Cideneb. That done, breathless with triumph, turning her back on the High Table, Jezebel addressed the children, first in a preacherly tone but soon, faster and faster, in the voice all who sat at mealtimes in her vicinity knew as that of the side-ways sardonic whisperer of scurrilous truths. Dear brothers and sisters mine, she said, you have heard from the Blessed Father Dominic the awful tale of our little brother Billy being eaten alive by hyenas, coyotes, dingoes and I know not what else and that his poor shivery soul flits now this way and that and can't find the way home. But I have heard from a little bird who knows the true story. Listen, listen. Our Billy is not in the least dead and torn to pieces. He was cunning, he was strong. He rode by night and he hid by day and the men in black looking this way and that could not find him. He camped in the woods, every morning he measured out his rations with the utmost care, at nightfall, sly as a fox, he set off pedalling and sped along the road by the light of the stars and his whirring dynamo lamp. Imagine him! On and on he went, riding and hiding. He saw owls, he saw sleeping sheep, he saw a small bear, he saw the eyes of wild cats and rabbits in his beam but never a cruel human out to catch him and bring him back here to be flogged to within an inch of his life. Five nights he rode, five days he hid, and came at last all in one piece and in good spirits into the city where no one knew him from Adam and he was safe.

Here Jezebel was seized by the arm and told to hush her blasphemous mouth. But she wrenched herself free, ran along the dais and bending towards the wide-eyed children, she continued: Probably you don't believe in the kindness of strangers, especially not strange men, but here is a Gospel truth of a bedtime story, listen, listen, with luck, if let, you will sleep better tonight, here is a fable of kindness and the little bird told it me so it must be true. Billy stood with his famous bicycle on a busy street, he was hungry but more than hungry he was lonely, having been a hero he had become a child again and unmanly tears were running down his cheeks. The Monitors stepped nearer, Jezebel made the sign of Halt, Stay Where You Are at them with her left hand, they saw her fierce red hair, her white determined face, they halted and stayed where they were, and listened. So Billy stood in tears on the alien street outside a café looking in and his sorrow was seen through the window pane by a large man drinking coffee and reading the Sporting Times. That child, he said aloud, lowering his newspaper and shaking his hatted head. Maisie, love, see there that poor little nipper. And rose to his feet and opened the door and went to Billy and said, Come in here, son, and have a cup of cocoa and a sticky bun, lean your bike there, Maisie won't mind, we can keep an eye on it, come on in here and keep me company for half an hour. And Billy did, he sat at the gentleman's wobbly formica-top table and partook of a mug of sweet cocoa and a large sticky bun and Maisie, the proprietress, shook her head and said, Poor kid, where's his mam, I'd like to know. Billy didn't say much, only, Thank you, mister, and he did look very mistrustful and disbelieving but that was due to his poor upbringing and he's not to be blamed for that. And the big man rose, he wore a loud checked suit and a red bow-tie and was altogether a sight for sore eyes. I'll be off, he said, tipping his trilby to Maisie and then, bowing, also to Billy, and uttered these parting words, Give this lad what he likes, love, if he rolls in here again and put it on my tab. And to Billy he said, Chin up, Sunny Jim.

Jezebel was fetched out of her class next morning to see Father Dominic. He'll have your arse, said the Monitor conducting her. I'll have his balls, said Jezebel.

Seated, his big desk between himself and the girl, who stood, Father Dominic said, I'm told you abused Our Saviour in the grace last night. And that you then spewed all manner of lies out of your filthy mouth at the children. My mouth is filthy, Jezebel replied, only on account of what has been stuffed into it from time to time in this place without my consent. But what came out of it at supper was nonetheless Gospel, trust me, Father. You will eat nothing at lunch and supper today and instead, in the public view, you will rinse out your mouth with soapy water and Sister Ruth will cane you. Jezebel nodded. That will be all. You may go back to your class. But Jezebel stood, and smiled. I said you may go, he said. His eyes peered out of their caverns at her red rags of hair, her white face, her smile, and finally, as though against their will, they looked into her eyes. She held his gaze and said, We live in fear in this place, Father Dominic, as you know. All our waking hours we go in fear and our dreams are fearful. So I have seen a lot of fear, in the eyes of the children and the Brothers and Sisters of Mercy, oh such a lot of fear. But in none have I seen the fear I see in you. We hear that over the eats last night you discussed Protection. You need it! You will need it! Everyone knows, everyone in this Merciful House knows everything and nobody will forget the things they know.

Father Dominic looked down at his hands that were clean and white, the long fingers ending in well-tended nails. Then he sighed, shuddered, raised his head that month by month was heavier to bear, his chins, his jowls, the sags beneath his eyes, all pendulous, all dragging him down. That is the whole point, child, he said. That you, that none of you, should forget it. We desire a love of the Risen Christ that will last till your dying day. We desire you to be heavy with the love of God and all his Saints and all their martyrdoms. Only burdened thus have you the least hope of forgiveness and a chance of heaven. And, in you, I embrace all of us, nuns, priests and laity in this House of Correction with the children in our care. Jezebel saw his tongue and retched at the sight of it, the worm in captivity in him, feeding off him, writhing for escape from him. Like I said, she said. You are shit-scared, the lot of you. But you, by a long chalk, are the shittiest-scared of all. It crossed my mind the other night, I saw your face in a dream, or perhaps it wasn't a dream, and I thought to myself it must be Matthew 18:1-6[1] that's giving him the shits. Might it be that, Father Dominic? Funny we never studied that bit in Bible Study or Sunday School. He looked her in the eyes. You see what you see, he said. And what a creature like you sees, is of no consequence. Doubtless you think you have a tale to tell, you and your little bird. You will be with us for another three months, you will be a thorough whore by then and nobody in the world outside will believe a word you say.

Jezebel smiled.

A Retired Librarian

THERE ARE NINETY-THREE houses on The Heights, detached and semis, mostly early Edwardian, various in appearance, and if you bought one for £30,000 thirty years ago you would very likely get thirty times that for it now. People do want to live here! Or – an increasingly popular option – they wait for a death, buy from the absent inheritors, knock the dwelling down, put three in its place, and let others live in them for a great deal of rent. So ninety-three is a provisional tally. Perhaps we are ninety-nine by now. It is a very desirable area. Builders knock on your door and bid for your garage. They could slot a house in between you and your neighbour on its plot. Agents hover in helicopters measuring your garden. Sell them the bottom bit, they'd get a couple in there. Very likely we are a hundred and nine by now.

On The Heights, like everywhere else, bad things do happen. No. 3's car got stolen for use in a drive-by shooting on the lowlands a mile away. One sweet Easter Sunday an old lady cycling to Early Communion got knocked off and had both her legs broken when two young men (not a quarter of her age) crashed by the post-box, the police pursuing them, just as she turned. Things of that sort, over the years many such things. Quite often in the small hours the searchlights of police helicopters come feeling through your gardens for fugitive asylum-seekers from the Mountjoy camp or for the errant sick from the Frideswide psychiatric hospital whose wall borders the north side of The Heights.

Arriving thirty years ago, you would certainly have been told that Mrs Delamare's golden retriever Turpin had, until his recent death of natural causes, slept most days all day on that same post-box corner in the middle of the road where The Heights, continuing peaceably to a quiet dead end in the golf links, has an exit right, between 14 and 16, steeply down Meadow Road to the water table. A million times the shade of Turpin has been flattened since he lay sleeping on that corner in the flesh. He is less present now, less possible, even less imaginable than a trilobite in a wafer of Cambrian shale. Yes, parking is a problem: both sides, wherever you can. Now and then the Fire Service sends a couple of engines down the remaining narrow passage, just to be sure it would be possible, in an emergency, to reach the golf course. Often it isn't possible. They email the Residents' Association to say that something must be done about it.

The Heights are only relatively high up. You will not flood up here (as you most certainly will in several zones below) and if you dig half a grave-depth you reach sand not clay (your fence posts will not hold). Is the air better? Possibly. The lead-free and the diesel have less fog to hang around in. Houses on the south side – the evens – look out over their down-sloping back gardens to the illusion of open country beyond the town's limits. You see woodland, low hills, quite big skies. But really in these parts the towns do not have limits. Our town is hooped by a double ring of clogged or slowly moving iron, but outside that, in the pretty stone or brick villages, live people whose business is in town and who must get in and out and spend hours of every day in the endeavour. So the town extends its iron feelers, innumerable, far-reaching. And the quite large skies are a thoroughfare for heavy aircraft, making for choked airports that smell of old perfume, or for the military bases that service the distant theatres of our wars.

The Heights have always had more than their share of writers, musicians and artists. The best in that last category lived at No. 26; and for most of what we know of the *interiors* of The Heights we must thank her, Fay Cocker, who one sleepless night, listening to the coughing foxes, decided that her next big project should be to make an artistic record of the road, house by house and all their inhabitants, with photographs, drawings, paintings, and snippets of commentary and conversation. She woke her husband, a once and, as he insisted, future traveller by the name of Sid. Good luck to you, he said. Collectors' items in time, I shouldn't wonder. His own business, on which he was often away, was roadkill. He knew where to find it, and how to add to it, and he had a receiver always glad of it, for cash, at the back door of a hotel. Such stories! said Fay. I might find out why that trio at 73 look so smug. I saw her yesterday with another bull-worker under her arm. She murmured further on the subject. Sid left her to it, slept, dreamed unlikely fictions of his own.

Fay had her big idea a year or so before anyone supposed that the ninety-three dwellings on The Heights might multiply. Of those ninety-three, she viewed the interiors of only sixty or so, the residents in the rest being never at home or never answering the door, or telling her candidly they did not want her snooping. Still the sixty-odd who co-operated made up a handsome volume and a record of sorts, it must be said. Their fridge magnets and the jokes and reminders they pinned on their kitchen notice boards were especially telling. It was going very well and Fay was full of it. Then quite suddenly the era of extensions, demolitions and rampant building began. Gross mansions arose, and under their lawns gymnasia, saunas, wine-cellars and guest suites shoved the wormy earth aside. Fay lost heart, there was no keeping up; and even in the service of the truth she would not force herself to contemplate the habitats and habits of the incomers.

It was enough to glance through their vast uncurtained windows, into the cavernous living-rooms where they stood around, entertaining. They had, she declared, money in inverse proportion to taste and neighbourliness; and she did not want them in her book.

Before giving up, Fay had some notable successes. For example, she was the only person on the road ever to get inside No. 28, the semi conjoined to hers. More than that, the liver-alone in there, a Miss Felicity Calder, a retired librarian, rarely seen, allowed herself to be photographed and sketched in her dwelling-place, on the stairs, to be exact, and even contributed a comment: 'I quite like living here.' Fay was discreet, never boasted, said little about her subjects – The book speaks for itself, for *them*, she would say – but much later she did let slip that Miss Calder had wanted to know would the Record be generally available, would one be able to buy it in a shop, even in another town? In fact, with immense care and at considerable expense, Fay paid for it to be published by a friend of hers in Aston Clinton, an ancient-letter-press enthusiast, who made a meagre living out of her First Folio postcards, for sale at Stratford and the Globe. Fay recouped some of her outlay from the subjects themselves, and advertised spare copies on her website at £45 a piece. The Librarian, said Fay, had seemed disappointed that it would not be in the shops. Will anybody buy it your way? she asked. They might, said Fay. Quite a lot of people visit my website.

The photograph showed Miss Calder, a white-haired woman in her late sixties, wearing a soft beret the colour of her lipstick, a black tight-fitting polo-neck pullover, a wide red skirt, white ankle socks and stout black shoes. She sat halfway up her stairs, along both sides of which, stair by stair, were stacks of periodicals and on every stack stood a two-litre mineral-water bottle. In her face shone a willed girlishness, a determination to match the clothes. In the Record itself, that photo was set side by side with a crayon sketch whose only colours were black and red. The hair, face, hands, lower legs, were scarcely there, the costume prevailed, as did also the pose, the sitter-on-the-stairs, arms folded, leaning slightly forward, listening, watching out, like a child who can't sleep and comes down as far as she dares, wanting the comfort of her mother and father, but daren't go down to find them, fearing they will be cross, that she will get no comfort, more fearful still that the living room will be empty, they will have gone away, they will have ceased to exist. The Librarian's features were only very lightly touched in. The face was all but empty, but the small marks for the eyes, the nose and the mouth, sufficed to make an expression of absence. That sketch is my best, said Fay matter-of-factly, quite without personal pride.

Fay saw all but one of No. 28's downstairs rooms but was not invited to climb the narrow way to those above. Still, the character of the retired Librarian's life was obvious, there on the stairs. They were throwing them away, she said. And I couldn't bear it. All that work. So they let me bring them home. There are rather a lot, but I did want *complete* sets, whenever possible. And the water bottles? Well, I do worry about fire. I suppose everybody does. And I'm a repository, you see. All that work is in my safekeeping. I suppose it's all on-line, said Fay. I suppose it is, said the Librarian vaguely, with no interest. But that's not the same as being here really, is it?

Some of Fay's subjects showed her busily around their houses from cellar to attic as though she were an estate agent or a reporter-cum-photographer from *House and Garden*; but at 28, even downstairs, her two visits, both in summer, were uneasy. She felt that in Miss Calder a savage *pudeur* was being combated by a determination to expose herself, or a portion of the evidence of her life, for a purpose which she, Fay, could not fathom. This is the study, said Miss Calder, opening the first door on the left. The room was in darkness, Miss Calder switched on the light. In the thickly curtained bay window Fay saw a massive mahogany desk, a green-shaded lamp on it, a carved wooden inkstand, a fountain pen, two or three sharpened pencils and a stubby pipe. Before the desk stood a severe black chair, almost a throne. Two walls, floor to ceiling, were dark with books. What else was in that room? A thin faded-red carpet, a tiled fireplace, an art-nouveau mirror-glass screen before it in the hearth, and a large complex engraving over the mantelpiece. Piranesi, said Fay. Yes, said Miss Calder, my favourite of the *Carceri*. She had a thin posh voice whose roots felt wistfully at times for its deep-down native stratum in the North. She switched off the light and closed the door. I don't go in there much, she said. I work in here – she pointed to the closed door of the adjacent room. That's where my catalogues are. And upstairs, of course. Mostly I work upstairs. But come through into the kitchen. Let me make you a cup of tea.

The small kitchen-dining-room was light and neat, all things where they belonged, all clean and to hand, ready to be used. I'm mostly at this end, said Miss Calder. There, with a view of the garden, she had a small pine table and a chair. She had laid out two quite dainty cups and saucers, a pretty milk jug and a silver sugar bowl, for the visit. Was your father a scholar? Fay asked. Good Lord, no! said Miss Calder. He was a navvy. He got killed on my seventh birthday. I suppose you thought those books might have been his.

Fay sat at the little table, Miss Calder stood by her, both drinking tea and looking down the garden which had long since gone back to nature. I love my garden, said Miss Calder in a detached sort of voice. Then: Will you have to see me again? For your book, I mean. Will you visit me again?

Two weeks later, at a quarter to four, Fay rang her neighbour's bell. Come in! she heard. The door is unlocked.

Miss Calder sat posed on the stairs. Shall you take my picture straight away? Then we can have tea. Fay photographed Miss Calder and made a quick sketch of her to work up later from memory and from the photo. Then she sat again at the small kitchen table, her subject, in costume, standing beside her. They drank tea and admired the sunny garden. I'll let you into a secret, Miss Calder said. Since I'm to be in your book, I feel I ought to tell you a little more about myself.

There's a summerhouse half way down. Of course, you can't see it from here, not even in winter when the leaves have fallen. But it's there, believe me. And that's where I go to be quite alone. At nights I go there, summer and winter, once or twice a week, especially in winter, for an hour or so, two or three some nights, if the spirit says I should. I've got a chair in my summerhouse, and a small table and a little silver oil-lamp which I light when I go in and then turn off when it's time to sit in the dark. There's no glass in the windows and the roof wants mending. Even in summer I have to wrap up well and in winter I take a hot-water bottle with me. There's nothing much to see, the trees are in the way. I look at the sky when I arrive and again when I leave. I have learned the habits of a few of the constellations, I know where to look for them at different times of the year and of the night. And the moon in all her shapes. But mostly I sit still in the dark and listen. I nearly always hear owls and I nearly always hear foxes. Quite often, there's a badger, he brushes along the wooden wall, I can smell him, he comes and goes with quite a crashing. And the best thing is, nobody in the whole wide world knows I'm there. Nobody even knows about the summerhouse and so nobody could even imagine there's anybody in it. That's how unknown alone I am. And now I've told you. Will you promise you'll tell nobody what I've just told you until I'm dead? Fay promised. I shan't mind after I'm dead. In fact, to speak the truth, I'd be quite glad if you did tell people after

I'm dead. Fay stood up to leave. One night, said Miss Calder, three years ago in that very cold winter, I sat in my summerhouse till my hot-water bottle froze. It froze solid, hard and cold as a stone. I must have been in a state of suspended animation. I've read about creatures who can do that and come back to life when the right time comes. And when I woke up – it was just getting light – I could hear the whisper of frost on every single dead twig and on every single blade of dead grass. And I pressed the stone-cold frozen hot-water bottle against my female parts, to bring it back to life again, so to speak. And even that poor miracle was beyond me, though I had kept vigil through the coldest night for perhaps a hundred years, like one of Mother Mary's exceptional saints.

On the way out, pausing by the stairs with their burdens of learned journals and plastic bottles, Fay asked Miss Calder did she have a speciality, what sort of scholarly knowledge did she treasure most, what subjects did the thousands of learned articles treat? My own subject was English Literature, Miss Calder replied, but two occurrences in my private life – one, bad enough, being the death of my mother – prompted me to shift to the sciences and among them to those having no, or no necessary and inevitable, application to human life. So I grew to appreciate quantum physics, sub-atomic particles, astronomy, the lives and deaths of galaxies, entomology, palaeontology, and especially microbial life in the Pre-Cambrian Age. Of course, I gave a home to runs of periodicals in other branches of science too, because, as I told you, I could not bear to let them be incinerated. And I catalogued – am still cataloguing – everything I got into safety under my roof. But out of the nineteenth century almost to the end of the twentieth in English, French and German, I read for preference the writings of researchers in the inhuman zones aforementioned.

For the next two years Fay had only very occasional glimpses of Miss Calder. Once or twice she opened her door to take delivery of a parcel just as Fay was coming home. And now and then Fay lingered on her own doorstep to see if canvassers for religion or politics might get an answer at 28. That door did open – and closed immediately. Fay saw Miss Calder's white hair, and remembered with a pang the scarlet beret. Often at nights, especially when Sid was away on business, she thought of Felicity Calder in her hidden summerhouse.

The developments began, the traffic of destruction and construction clogged The Heights. No. 88, a fine detached house in a generous garden, was trucked away as rubble to a tip. Fay closed the Record, worked quietly at it over the winter in her own front room, and in spring took it to her friend in Aston Clinton. Sid fetched the copies home in his pick-up. Prettier than roadkill, he observed. But less of an earner, in the short-term at least. Fay began deliveries next day, and went first to No. 28.

Miss Calder seemed glad to receive the Record. She turned at once to her page, studied the photograph and the sketch, and nodded in a coolly satisfied fashion. And you didn't put words into my mouth, she said. Of course, I knew you wouldn't. I knew I could trust you not to misrepresent me. Fay did not like to mention payment and was very relieved when Miss Calder herself asked what she owed. Twenty pounds? Fay suggested. Of course, said Miss Calder. And in a couple of minutes she returned with the note. Have any purchases been made through your website, she wondered. Not yet, said Fay. But it's early days. The book is just out. I came to you first with a copy. For a lingering moment Fay saw again in Miss Calder's face that mortal combat between the desire to be revealed and the will to suppress all revelation which she had witnessed during her two previous visits. Would her neighbour not let her in? Would she not suddenly, there on the doorstep, ask a favour, beg for solace? Just perceptibly Miss Calder shook her head. Thank you, she said. I do thank you. Shall I tell you if anyone buys a copy? Fay asked. And would you like to know who, if anyone does? That won't be necessary, thank you, said Miss Calder, already closing the door. Nothing like that. If it happens, it happens. I'm sure you will be glad of any sale.

The months passed, The Heights got worse. Then one morning in November, soon after breakfast, a clear bright day, the sun enhancing, not yet diminishing, the sparkle of the frost, Fay looked up from some close work in her bay window and saw a large elderly man swaying at her gate. He was bearded, rather florid, and wore rimless glasses, a broad-brimmed leather hat and a long overcoat. He carried a stick, he had raised it and was flailing with it. By the look on his face he was all at a loss. Fay stood up. He seemed not to see her, seemed in truth to take cognizance of nothing outside himself. Everything still going on was inside. He struggled exclusively in an inner state, in his legs, his belly, his chest, in his head, in his flailing and waving arms. The stick he agitated kept no time, made no sense. Then, in manifest bewilderment and pain, he heaved himself clear of Fay's gate and lumbered down the line of his direction as far as Miss Calder's. There he halted, leaning over it until, whether by his design or not, it opened, he tottered forward and, out of her sight, Fay heard the crash of him falling.

This visitor to The Heights lay flat on his face, his stick and his hat flung from him, arms outstretched, halfway down Miss Calder's path. Fay stood at the open gate and from there, the prone man between them, stared at Miss Calder who, in the costume she had worn for the photograph, sat on the second step of her staircase, the periodicals and the water bottles climbing behind her into the upper zone. She has overdone the lipstick, Fay thought. And one ankle sock is pulled up higher than the other. Miss Calder's look, passing over the fallen man, was quite the coldest thing Fay had ever confronted. She backed away from it, feeling for the gatepost behind her. It's not him, said Miss Calder. I'll phone for an ambulance, said Fay. Miss Calder stood up. Yes, do, she said, quietly closing her door.

As Fay returned to her neighbour's path, the man made a snuffling noise, shuddered, and thereafter was entirely silent and still. She felt for a pulse on his left wrist and could find none. His feet were turned awkwardly; the inside rim of his leather hat was black with grease; his bald crown showed; blood was seeping out from under his face. Fay realised the helpless great weight of him, how powerless he had been to resist the force of his own body. He had not been permitted to sag and be let down slowly but had gone over stricken, felled, a deadweight, flat out, hurling at the concrete. How useless the flung open arms! Their embrace and surrender, how flatly they had been refused!

Two ambulance men knelt by him. Heaving together, they turned him over. Jesus! said one. His own mother wouldn't know him. His face was suffused a dirty purple, his glasses had smashed into it. The nose looked broken, it bled into and over the slightly parted mouth. The men unbuttoned his overcoat and laid the great folds of it aside. He wore no jacket, sweater, waistcoat, only a rather grubby white shirt. No pulse at the neck. They slit open the shirt, he wore nothing under it, the breast plumped up like a turkey's, almost hairless, smooth, very white, like something that shouldn't be looked at under the sun. An indecency. Perhaps the ambulance men had thought of attempting resuscitation, and now there seemed no point? They laid the stretcher close by him. Oh he was a weight even to lift only a little and shift sideways. Fay knelt and supported his head. She had the heaviness of it in her hands, and the closeness of his empurpled and battered face in her vision, and the smell of his mouth in her nostrils, for weeks. They laid the stick between his legs and the leather hat on his now covered breast. Then the doors closed on him and he was gone.

That night Fay woke hearing sirens getting closer. Then came a thump whose nature and sense she could not grasp. She lay wondering, smelled smoke. Next thing her front door was smashed open and men shouted she must get out. She pulled on Sid's big overcoat over her night clothes, thrust her bare feet into wellingtons and stumbled down her path to the street. Three engines, blue lights, doors and bedroom windows opening in the houses opposite and a concentrated force of water driving into the holes where the door and the windows of 28 had been. The fire inside roared like a furnace at full strength. Flames leaped and cavorted as though the water, the contrary element, were exciting them into everchanging new forms of life. There came explosions and the endlessly varied sounds of breakage and collapse. Smoke was issuing from under the eaves of Fay's own house. Among the fire crew no unnecessary words were spoken and among the spectators for long periods none at all. Two firemen went into 28 with apparatus but could not live in there and backed out. Nothing in that dwelling could be saved, all the effort went on containment. Fay's roof burst, fire leaped free into the frosty air. But from a ladder, already above that level and to one side, a fireman directed such a power and quantity of water he soon converted flames into filthy smoke and steam. So they preserved Fay's semi, whilst everything in her neighbour's – the gentleman's study, the room of the catalogues, the neat kitchen, the thousands of learned articles, the single bed and whatever else was hoarded in the upper storeys – all of it, with Miss Calder's slight and costumed person, burned.

Fay phoned Sid. Come home, will you. Yes, I'm OK. But come home. He arrived an hour later, by which time they were damping down, most spectators had gone back to their safe beds, and the main lingering evidence was the smell. He parked by No. 1, which was as close as he could get, found her and stood by her, stroking the sleeve of the overcoat, speechless. She had a fireman on her left and was saying to him, She always worried about fire, she kept bottles of water on the stairs, two on every step. White spirit, lady, said the fireman. Sixty litres of it. Must have gone up like a bomb. And another strange thing: we're pretty certain she phoned us before it started.

Sid walked Fay to the pick-up. Admiringly he pointed out the cars the fire engines had wrecked as they forced through. Alf and Rosie will put us up, he said. Rosie will lend you some things. We'll drop this off – a hump under a blanket in the back of the truck – for Jake on the way. Reversing out of The Heights, he added: I'm thinking we'll go on the road for a while, till it's all sorted out. And even then, who knows, that might be our best move.

Late next morning they were back at the site, which was taped off, police and firemen busy. I'll leave you to it, said Sid. Ring me when you're ready. Fay stood there in her wellingtons, a red woollen dress of Rosie's, Sid's overcoat and his old black beret. The damp stench made her weep. She couldn't be let into her house. Tomorrow maybe. A police inspector asked would she mind telling him about the death, before the fire, at Miss Calder's door. It wasn't quite at her door, said Fay. In Fay's account to the inspector Miss Calder did not speak nor even appear. Her door remained shut. Who was he? she asked. No idea, said the inspector. No ID on him whatsoever. And his face won't be much help either. No fixed abode, from his general wear and tear. His hands were soft, said Fay. Then, almost to herself: What happens next? He stays where he is, said the inspector, contemplating the blackened ruin of 28. In cold storage. And if nobody claims him, he gets a decent cremation. And how's my friend Sid?

Fay was allowed round the side of her house into the garden. The back did not look very much damaged. Perhaps her work would be all right. Nobody looking, she went quickly down to a place near the bottom where Miss Calder's fence had rotted and fallen. From there, pushing in through what had once been quite a formal terraced garden, and making more noise than a pair of badgers, she soon found the summerhouse. The door was hanging open on one hinge. She sat on the simple chair at the simple table. Through the empty window, even in daylight, she could see only trees and undergrowth grey with old man's beard; and through the holes in the roof, small fragments of very blue sky. Absolute stillness, not the least breath of a breeze, no stirring, and only as a rumour could she hear even The Heights, and the world below her fainted towards utter silence. Out of a trance or sleep she woke and found that her hands had enclosed the small silver lamp on the plain table. She pocketed it.

Fay phoned Sid. He'd be there in ten minutes. Waiting, she was sidled up to by a man of whose appearance, later, she remembered only the muzzle, which sniffed and twitched. Too sad, he said. Not at all what you'd expect round here. And I understand there's no family, or only a niece in the States, who'll be glad to dispose of the place, too much of a worry at that distance, I daresay. And yourself, Mrs Cocker? Very distressing it must be. Take my card, will you. Ask what you like. The two plots together, you know.

Fuck off and drown yourself, said Fay.

Sid arrived. We'll need a skip, he said. I'll give Andy a ring. He owes me. Looks not too bad from the back, said Fay, taking his arm. Where's the truck? Ah, said Sid. And he led her halfway down Meadow Road to a 50s camper van. Traded it in for this, he said. Do all right for now, maybe?

Driving back to Alf and Rosie's, Sid expounded in an ecstatic mutter his vision of the life of Riley that lay ahead.

Insurance, selling up, a million quid at least, studios for her in Connemara, on Coll, under Skiddaw, at the end of the Lleyn. A big house somewhere above Appleby, he might go back to the horses. And they'd have a small yacht somewhere warm. Fay listened, half-listened, smiled, sobbed. I sold two through the website, she said when he paused. Neither looked very likely. One was an uncle of Mrs Bradshaw at 55, he lives in Dundee. The other lived in Brisbane, but wanted it posting to Hounslow, for her grandfather. The trouble with you, said Sid, if you don't mind me saying so, is that you feel people's stories have to make some sort of sense. Whereas in reality it's all accidents, that make no sense. Stick to your paintings and sketches. They really do make sense. They'll be collectors' pieces, more than ever after this. Fay took out the silver lamp from the pocket of Sid's overcoat and clasped the bulb of it, warming it, in her two hands in her lap. In the bulb was oil, moistening the thirsty wick. The glass sheath was like the stem of a hyacinth, through which it would flower. You would have a slim column of protected flame, you would have a small sufficient light and an aura of light and warmth in the shelter of any room you chose to dwell in.

Rue de la Vieille-Lanterne

1

THAT NIGHT HIS VOICE came up out of him, chanting and singing very loud, so that before long, for the good of the other inmates, an attendant entered and conducted him downstairs to a more secluded room, and locked him in. There his dream continued. He suffered it. The room had eight walls, he stood at the centre, turning to follow the images as they appeared, clockwise, on each. He saw all the beauty he had ever seen in his life before, but it was hacked, mutilated, piecemeal, and below it, written in blood in an Eastern script he could read with ease, the interminable chronicle of the world's violence writhed. And he knew: I am being shown this because I am responsible.

Dr Blanche came in. It was daylight, the everyday light. Blanche wore his everyday good nature and carried a cup of coffee and a brioche on a silver platter. Eat, he said. Drink. Then I should like to introduce you to a person whom you may perhaps be able to help.

He led him to the garden room, which was the surgery. There in an armchair, two attendants standing by, sat a young man. His feet were bare, very white and shapely, his hands lay quietly in his lap, his eyes were closed, a length of rubber tube dangled from his right nostril. Nerval thought him as beautiful as a fallen angel. He was a soldier, said Blanche. He

153

was in Africa. Now he won't open his eyes or speak. Nor, so far as I can tell, does he hear any sound. Worse still, he will not eat or drink. So we feed him liquid chocolate through a tube.

Nerval was transfixed. The mute soldier seemed to him another self, a younger brother, who had pushed on with the quest, to the final door, and sat there now, beyond the world's interferences, at the very mouth of God, listening. He will help me, he said aloud. Blanche shrugged. One another. Who knows? Then he withdrew, signalling to the attendants that they should follow him. The garden room shone with the light from outside.

Nerval kneeled before the soldier and took hold of his feet, which were cold. In such proximity he felt himself to be bulky, almost gross, the young man seemed slimmed in body and spirit for the crossing over. He contemplated the shut eyes, the closed, tightly pursed, lips, took the hands, also cold, and pressed them to his forehead, desiring a transfusion. No good, not close enough. He stood up, fetched a chair, seated himself so close that his and the soldier's knees interfitted, and bowed his forehead so that it pressed against the bowed forehead of the man who had escaped the empire of the senses. And in that posture, conjoined (so to speak) with a twin at the brows, Nerval began to whisper the chronicle of himself, the recurrent episodes of his suffering, the exaltations, the wanderings, the need for asylum, the need for flight, and his fear of the freezing that would come to him again soon, as it did every winter, from the river in Silesia which his dying mother had crossed when she was twenty-five. He felt assured that this presentation of his life passed with no diminution of its truth out of his brain into the young man's brain, through their brows; and that although he uttered it in words it passed not as words but as the current and pulse of them, from soul to soul. He had no sense of any passage of time, and was astonished when Dr Blanche came in and said it was noon, the soldier must have his semolina, and he,

Nerval, was invited to table with himself, the physician, and two or three others among the patients whose conversation might be amusing and of interest.

That night Nerval dreamed such a dream that when he woke his face was wet with tears of joy. He had seen the soldier, or his double in the other world, they were walking together in open country under a sky blazing with stars. They halted, the young man touched the older man on the forehead, addressed him as 'brother', and opened his eyes, they shone under the stars as though in daylight and their colour was periwinkle-blue. Nerval took a stick of charcoal and on one of the very few remaining spaces on the walls of his cluttered room he wrote: Last night you came to me.

Blanche mentioning that the soldier was a countryman, Nerval broke off the chronicle of his own ordeal and, still holding the patient's hands, still brow to brow with him, in a slow murmur he began to sing. Day after day then, for hours at a time, he sang the ancient songs he had collected from the Valois, his native land: love songs, elegies and ballads, in many different voices, the whole stock, beginning again wherever he pleased, remembering more, steeping himself in the country, its three sacred rivers, its countless haunted springs, still waters, deep forests, its festivals, struggles and sufferings, so many named places, so many named persons. He stood outside the door of the garden room until Blanche opened for him and let him in. The attendants were wiping the last drops of chocolate or semolina from the dangling length of tube, they removed the bib, arranged the young man comfortably, bare-footed, eyes closed, lips tight shut, the quiet hands folded in his lap. Left alone then, Nerval fetched his own chair, sat close, bowed the soldier's head to meet his at the brow, and softly and slowly began to sing.

So this intercourse continued until the first day of October, the trees in the garden – acer, hazel, beech – flaming in the colours of their dying, and on that day came the breakthrough. Leaning back from the young man, Nerval fixed his eyes on the shut mouth and sang:

> Aux quatre coins du lit
> Des bouquets de pervenches
> Et nous y dormirons
> Jusqu'à la fin du monde…[2]

The soldier's lips moved. Nerval paused, watched them closely, sang the four lines again. Waited. Again the lips moved, but this time in obedience to the larynx, the tongue, the palate, the teeth, to make words. Quite without expression, as mere repetition and very softly, the soldier said:

> Et nous y dormirons
> Jusqu'à la fin du monde.

Nerval shuddered. It battered him like Pentecost. He exulted. After long absence he felt himself chosen once again to be the servant of the Good Angel, to raise a fellow sufferer out of torpor, to enable him to partake again of the life that had gone missing. Informed, Blanche nodded. Good, he said. You will help one another.

The following days strengthened this hope. Nerval sang a quatrain, stared hard at the young man's lips until they stirred and performed a repetition. From that, under Nerval's tuition, before and after the singing, these lips progressed to the exchanging of simple courtesies. Next, for one second, shocking his companion with ineffable joy, the soldier opened his eyes: they were periwinkle-blue, alien, like those of some lost and future race of human beings. A day or two later he opened them as any person might, looked around him, spoke unprompted a sentence now and then – all, it must be admitted, the looking and the speaking, without expression. He addressed Nerval familiarly, called him brother, without gratitude or wonder, simply as fact, they were intimates of longstanding, so it seemed. Still, of his own volition, he would not eat.

After the feeding, Blanche allowed them to walk in the garden for a while. They walked arm in arm, saying very little, or they sat side by side on a bench. Once, very beautifully, a blackbird sang, which Nerval brought to the soldier's attention and he nodded. Then he said, I am thirsty. Please will you fetch me a glass of water. Nerval obliged, handed it to him, he raised it to his lips, but could do no more than that. He seemed to own neither the idea nor the art of drinking. Yet he said again, in a vague distress, I am thirsty. Nerval took the glass from him. Why is it, he asked, that you cannot eat or drink? It is because I am dead, said the young man. I died a year ago in Mortefontaine. I am buried there. Nerval said, If that is so, where do you believe yourself to be now, at this moment, with me, here in this garden? Where do you think you are now? In Purgatory, said the soldier. I am in the process of my expiation.

Next morning, unshaven, half-dressed, white spittle at the corners of his mouth, Nerval entered Dr Blanche's consulting room unbidden and demanded to be released. It was, he said, quite intolerable that he should be incarcerated one day longer. He was a man of letters, he had commissions, obligations, which he could only fulfil at liberty in the city. By what right do you confine me here among the mad? Blanche spoke soothingly to him, bade him be seated. He was making good progress, soon, soon he would be well again. I beg you, my dear friend, let us not undo the good we have done. Be patient, let us have faith in one another. But Nerval could not be quietened. He stood up, paced to and fro, muttering to himself and clenching and unclenching his fists. Inspirations come to me, he said, and I cannot rightly hear them. I am being harmed in this bedlam. I demand my release. I wish to be among my own kind in the outside world.

For two days, uncouthly, Nerval put his demand to Blanche, in the end threatening him with a judicial process if he did not accede to it. Blanche was grieved. Father and son, Esprit and Émile, over many years, in Montmartre and Passy, they had cared for him, coaxed him out of the pit, out of the terrors in his head, enabled him to write again and to be his gracious self among his countless friends. The injustice wounded him, the son, as it had in the past the father. Very well, he said. Find two competent persons who will certify that they understand you wish to leave here against my professional advice and who support you in your wish nonetheless. I cannot be held responsible for any bad consequences. Further, I must have from someone who knows you well a promise to accommodate you for as long as may be necessary. Once I have those documents, you will be free to leave my house.

By the evening of the following day Jules Janin, a journalist, and Louis Godefroy, a lawyer, had written the letters Blanche asked for. And next morning from Mme Alexandre Labrunie, Nerval's aunt, came the offer of a room in her house at 54 rue de Rambuteau for as long as he liked. Shortly before noon that day, 19 October 1854, Nerval left his doctor's house, 17 rue de Seine, carrying only a battered valise and promising to have the contents of his room sent on after him very soon. He wore the famous black *redingote* of the many pockets, all of them stuffed full with books and work in progress. He looked aged, corpulent, altogether unsteady. Embracing Blanche, he began to shake with sobs. My dear Gérard, said Blanche. Think again. But he would not. He shrugged, as though it had to be. Turned and shambled like a bear the short distance to the *quai* and there boarded the omnibus just leaving for Paris, Place du Palais-Royal. He lived all his remaining days and most of his remaining nights on the city's streets.

2

The problem was not lodgings. He had friends all over Paris who at any hour of the day or night would have welcomed him in. Two or three women kept a room ready and waiting just for him, kept it clean and neat, with a desk to write at, and always a vase of flowers changing as they came in their seasons to the market, a room that was light and airy, with little amenities, touches they knew he would like. His friends had an image for him: he was the bird, the swallow, who flits in at the window left open for just that entrance, and rests, and flits out again, vanishing. He was not Jesus Christ: always within walking distance, Nerval had where to lay his head.

Nor was money the problem. He boarded the omnibus to Paris in stained and crumpled trousers, his coat, kerchief, battered *chapeau claque* might have been a huckster's, his shoes were down at heel and leaked at the soles. But he wore the ring of Isis on the second finger of his left hand, he could have pawned it for clothes fit to appear in at any ball. He got money easily: whatever he wrote, the best journals and reviews would publish it, and they paid well. True, when he had money he got rid of it blithely, no friend ever asked and was refused, and to strangers also, if their plight moved him, he gave with both hands. But scores of men in Paris were in his debt, all would have repaid him with interest for some past kindness.

Neither money nor a lodging was the problem.

Swallow – or swift? He was likened to both. Both are waited for and when they come in on the winds of spring their arrival surprises like a thing that, after all, it was beyond us to imagine. The city loves them around her towers, steeples and attics. The streets, deep down, are glad of them above in the free air. They are travellers, they divide their year into hemispheres. A swallow might well land on your sill, look in, bide a while. But a swift never would, never could. Once launched, once evicted from the nest, they cannot land. They live in the air, they hunt and mate in the air, they ride its invisible pathways, they sleep on spirals down, down, and wake before they crash. The swift, *apus apus*: 'footless'.

He frequented various reading rooms, one under the south arcade in the Place des Vosges. There especially, they let him be. He read the journals, or sat quite abstracted, or wrenched a wad of tightly written pages out of an inside pocket and worried at them. At some point during any visit he would ask politely for a few sheets of paper. None who attended him ever forgot. Among the testimonies is this: I gave him the sheets, he thanked me with excessive courtesy, and from my desk on the far side of the quiet room I watched, I was ashamed to, but I did. I remember it now with fear and pity. He was sweating and his hands were shaking. He laid the sheets in a neat pile on the right, took up his pen, sobbed like a man breaking into pieces, and began. I saw him quieten, in that public room, I saw what it was like in him when for a space, in another respite, he wielded his pen against collapse. He wrote steadily, never pell-mell, with an unhurried certainty. His trembling ceased, on his face when he paused, looked up, waited to see the shape of a sentence and to feel for its rhythm, in his expression during those moments there was – forgive me this language – something seraphic. He looked conscious of his blessing, of his *being able* – which is why I should not have looked, I should have looked away, attended to my registers, but I did look, I watched, I couldn't help myself and now I can't regret it. I saw a man in the possession of his gift, doing what he was born to do, near the brink with no diminution of his powers, but near the end, near the ruin. He wrote, and I have read: I must command my dream, not suffer it. Still now in the light of afterwards I see him in the public reading room for the last interlude doing precisely that.

He wrote in reading rooms, in cafés, in the rooms of friends. In the cold of that coldest winter for many years he wrote in churches, in their pews, on their steps, he wrote on benches in the public gardens and the cemeteries. And when he was not writing he was walking. Head crammed with the matter of his writing, he walked the streets, never idly, never strolling. Afterwards, many could remember seeing him and could tell you where – on the corner of the rue Malebranche and the rue Saint-Jacques, crossing the Pont du Carrousel, by the west door of St-Merri – and all agreed, if he saw you he would return your greeting, if you collared him he would bide politely as long as you held him, but in truth he was never at leisure, on the streets he had to keep moving, he looked hunted, some said, others said hunting, he looked hunted by or hunting after certain very compelling phenomena that nobody else could see. He saw the English girl on the steamer from Marseilles. She was biting into a lemon. He perceived that she was consumptive and would not live long. He saw her in the sea at Naples, she was swimming towards him, she vanished, rose again and stood with the water up to her small breasts, smiling, pleased with herself, and offering him on the platter of her outstretched hands a golden fish. The last time he saw her was at Herculaneum. He was underground, staring at the girl Proserpina with flowers on her left arm, staring and staring until he felt the cold draught of the Underworld on the nape of his neck, the hairs stood up, he turned and saw the white-faced English girl in the costume of Proserpina biting into a lemon with her small sharp teeth. And his mouth filled with the clear bitter juice as though it welled up from his beating heart. Turning into the rue Basses-des-Carmes, he saw his way blocked by the possessions he had left in his room in the house of Dr Blanche. It was Faust's study, tipped out, all the mouldering tomes, the filthy alembics, all the learning in a jumble that made no sense, the sum total clutter to date, all the reading, all the bric-à-brac, all the souvenirs of travel in Europe and the East, there piled high, so that he could not proceed further down the narrow street. It was the condition the Illuminati call the *capharnaüm*, lumber-room, mêlée in the brain, bedlam. He blundered into a café, asked for cognac and some writing paper and wrote to Dr Blanche. He addressed him as 'dear friend', begged his forgiveness, and beseeched him to burn the contents of his room. But at once erased that sentence and instead, detailing every item he could bring to mind, asked that each be sent to the person whose name he set next to it. Thus:

A Florentine console supported by a winged sphinx: Alexandre Dumas

An 18th-century bed with a baldequin of red lampas: Jenny Colon

A narghileh from Constantinople: Heinrich Heine

Panelling from the rue Doyenné: Théophile Gautier

A pilgrim's gourd: Mme Labrunie

A colossal wall map of Cairo: Francis Wey

An Arabian burnous: Henry Millot

A wedding chest, decorated with huntresses and satyrs: Sylvie

A bow and arrow from the Valois: Mlle Angélique de Longueval

A notebook of songs and music from the Valois: Mathilde Heine

And many things and many people besides. He asked that the blue cashmere shawl be sent to his mother in the Catholic cemetery in Glogau.

Leaving the café he saw that the contents of his room had vanished from the pavement. So his letter to Dr Blanche had been instantly effective. He felt an old pride in the power of the written word. His belongings having been dispersed as legacies to every loved one in his pantheon, now his way was clear – Place des Anglais, rue Galande, to the Seine. He hurried. Not a soul on the Pont des Arts. What hour must it be then in this sleepless city? The river came towards him, engrossed by the freezing rains, crazy with flotsam and queer lights. These were the days and nights of his mother's death. He knew that behind his back, dead soldiers of the Grande Armée were arriving from either bank, lying down, awaiting burial, the bridge was becoming heavy with them. He would not turn and look, he felt the cold of them on his back and the cold of the great river passing in silence beneath him. Now – he knew it – his mother began her crossing on an unsteady cart. She was feverous, she had been among the many dead, she had breathed their breath and was crossing now to her place of burial. He would not look, he stood in the river's draught and shook with cold as though his frame had no more covering than a skeleton's. He waited, bowed over the parapet, till his dying mother had gone by and the soldiers had vanished in the thin air.

Stéphanie Houssaye died 12 December of consumption. Nerval appeared at her funeral two days later in the Madeleine. It is not even certain he knew it was hers, not until he recognised friends among the mourners. He had taken to following any cortege he happened to encounter on the streets. He stood at several opened graves. Mourning with strangers for a stranger had become a part of his expiation. Strictly speaking, there *were* no strangers. But learning whose funeral he was attending in the Madeleine, he felt a profound grief, and further pains of conscience. Mme Houssaye had kept a room for him and he had disappointed her. He stood in a side chapel, looking on. Come in off the streets and now weeping helplessly, he was a spectacle. Nobody else showed such a helpless sorrow. His face was chapped, the tears made it look raw. As the service ended, he fled into another night already beginning.

He was seen in the Salon littéraire, 67 rue Sainte-Anne, on Christmas Day. Instalments of his work just finished and of things still underway were appearing in the journals. Early in January he appeared at the Odéon, at a performance of Dumas' *La Conscience*, between two strikingly beautiful women, said by some to be mother and daughter. He wore the black *redingote* and looked like a creature from elsewhere. He left abruptly during the second act, head down, mumbling excuses.

He spent entire days and sometimes the nights tramping the wastelands between the faubourgs and the gates of Paris. Alfred Delvau, author of *Histoire anecdotique des cafés et cabarets de Paris* (Dentu, 1862), records that one night in the Cabaret de la Canne, himself the only visitor, on the city's rim, by the abattoir, between the *barrière* Rochechouart and the *barrière* des Martyrs, Nerval came in, his thin black jacket caped with snow. The two men, not exchanging names, talked for hours. Delvau wrote up the encounter afterwards, by then, of course, knowing who the stranger was. He remembered his courtesy, the grace of his gestures, his chapped hands, his perfectly formed sentences ('fit to be written down'), the snow melting and at length a faint steam rising, from his clothes. They swapped stories of the vilest places in Paris they had ever drunk, eaten, slept and been entertained in. Also, they imagined the afterlife. If there must be one, said Nerval, let the soul in it still have something to strive for. But frankly, he added, some nights I pray there will be none. He had known such happiness, he said, he had such memories of the sweetness of life, it would be a torment to him as a shade. Then he bowed, shook my hand, and made his exit into the still heavily falling snow.

3

He wrote: I was author and hero of my own novel. The gods were reading me. They watched with interest to see what I would make of myself. To which, with some asperity, one of his actresses replied: You were good at situations and at plots and sub-plots, one thing leading to another. But you were quite hopeless at dénouements. When did you ever bring anything to a conclusion? You were all beginnings and little forays hither and thither. That's what you enjoyed and that's what you were good at: inventing situations full of possibilities. To be absolutely honest, I doubt if they were watching you from Olympus. Gods and goddesses love endings, in my experience. And the bloodier the better, I might add.

In his head ('everything is in my head') he continued this conversation as he hurried with apparent purpose down one street or another or, through the *terrains vagues*, orbited the city's knotted heart. In truth, it was no conversation. One woman after another rose up and told him straight he was no good at endings. Dearest friend, you have a morbid horror of dénouements! He concurred. Every woman he had ever loved – and they were legion – had been right about him whether at the time they had delivered their verdict or not. Few had, in fact. They loved him too much. Even now in the cold, beyond the faubourgs, on the new boulevards, in the ancient fetid alleys, among the ruins and the sparkling new temples of commerce, where he passed, they followed, accusing him. He was a fleeing comet, they were the Furies on his tail. What nonsense! He sat in a draughty mausoleum in Père Lachaise, he summoned them up, he whistled them out of the north, south, east and west, some out of their early graves. And he gave them their parts, he wrote their lines, he coached them in their delivery, so that it would be irrefutably clear what his life-fault was and he would see once and for all what a mountain of amends he had to make.

He walked out to the *barrière* de Pantin, which is an exit into the Valois. Should he or shouldn't he, for the old virtue of those places? He could not. He was weary, he was cold and weary to death. He turned without volition and let the lodestone of innermost Paris pull him in.

He found himself in Montmartre, rue de l'Abreuvoir. It had stopped snowing, under a slant moon and more and more stars he halted in familiar whereabouts. Close by was the city's one surviving vineyard. The vines will survive the deep cold, they bide their time; when the year turns, they put out feelers, they bud, they leaf, they fruit. Silence. Stillness. Before long the cattle and the horses will come down the cobbled lane to the trough hereby and drink. The secret gardens will overflow their walls. There will be festivals on the homely streets, games and dancing and singing, joyous solemnities. Oh this *quartier*, oh this village above the city!

Very faintly, he heard one of the small hours striking. He walked around the walls of the house and garden of the Folie-Sandrin, to the front gate, rue Norvins. He might pull at the bell for ever and no night-attendant would open to him. It was long ago, and besides the Doctor himself was dead. But oh, the gardens of that place, the abundant flowers, the gracious trees, the eternally self-replenishing fountains! He thought of them as lost to him, of himself as shut out from them, and his heart raced with gratitude to the father and his people gone from there and to the son and his people still in Passy, makers and custodians of asylum, physicians, ministers to minds diseased. What pain his antic disposition had dealt them and would deal them!

In childhood, motherless, he had been ripped from the Valois into the city. Time and again he went back there, by coach, omnibus, railway train and on foot, again and again, ever more in love, ever more ('petit Parisien') debarred. He slept in her woods, haunted her waters, forfeiting her, by neglect and failure, by growing up, until she was lost to him and thereafter, in one lodging and another, he must write about her. In which, now, trudging through the snow in leaky shoes around the *maison de santé* of the late Dr Blanche, he felt the breath, almost the shaping up, of some consolation. In a consciousness almost without name or particular identity, he rejoiced in the sleeping idyll of Montmartre and in the magical moon- and star- and sunlit domain of childhood in the Valois. His hands were too cold to search his pockets for the pen and any scrap of unscribbled paper, but he felt the sentence to be safe and sound: Reasons for joy, whether I live or die, are the asylum gardens, my doctors, father and son, and my constant returns to the country of my heart, my *knowledge* of it, cognizance through the feet and all the senses, love, love, my love.

This is the *rallentando* before the hurry to the end.

Like many an insomniac in the sleepless city he wandered till he found a café still open or just opening, sat himself down near the stove and ordered a grog. When his hands were warm enough, when they came back to life and would *work*, he retrieved from an innermost pocket a couple of sheets on which he had composed a prospectus for his *Complete Works*. Looking over it gave him great satisfaction, the scores of titles, nearly thirty years of publication. He added a few more 'subjects', some half-finished, some never begun but burning like super-novae in his head, and among these the Queen of Sheba whom he thought of as his own, he knew her, he could write her out, page after page, whenever he pleased. He laid his head on his arms and slept, warm. The patron let him be. When he woke, the place was busy with men taking a drink on their way to the day's hard labour. They saluted him, so he felt, as one of their kind, so that he blushed with pleasure, with a modest pride in himself, and returned their salutes. To complete the prospectus, he added, under the heading *Reflections. Philosophy. Religion*: 2 vols of manuscripts. Then hurried away in the trodden snow to the rue Notre-Dame des Champs, to M. Jacob, agent of the publisher Dutacq, who had promised to publish him 'entire', and to pay him well. Afterwards Jacob remembered him as, yes, quite mad, but never wittier, never in better humour.

In the remaining nights the cold worsened. During that of 23-24 January the police found him with his jacket undone (all the bulging inner pockets visible), outside the Madeleine, clinging to the railings and chanting a paean or supplication to the Great Goddess. Quite gently they forced his frozen fingers open and conveyed him in a carriage to their station at Châtelet. There he raved, and lifted up his voice again. They strapped him to a bedframe in a cell out of earshot. Next morning, apologetically, with great courtesy, he asked would they send a note to M. Henry Millot, a childhood friend, 13 rue du Départ, who would vouch for his identity and take him off their hands. They obliged. Early afternoon, very surprised (he had not seen the man in question for twenty years), Millot was brought to him, recognised him for who he was from the engraving by Eugène Gervais published in *Les Contemporains* the year before. Yes, he would take him home, he would look after him, it would be an honour.

We sat together in a café on the rue de l'Hirondelle, said Millot afterwards. He drank a cognac and a glass of St Émilion, enquired most courteously after my wife and family, and did not seem very mad, only now and then rather abstracted. We had been there an hour or so – the lights were already lit outside – when he stood up, excused himself, approached the bar and was directed through into the back yard. That was the last I saw of him, disappearing as though for two minutes.

He had seen the face of the young soldier who had served in Africa and was now in Purgatory unable to eat or drink. How certain he was, and patient! This is my ordeal. I have to pass through it. He felt again the joy of seeing the young man's eyes come open, so strangely blue, oh such joy! He knew he was ill, and he saw no reason not to call the illness madness. And he knew that the fateful truth shone through the mask of madness, his truth, his fate, killing perhaps. Cowering away from it only augmented his self-contempt, which feeling drove him not to run from, but in search of, that very truth. In equal measure he longed for and dreaded the signs of an outcome. They were beginning to multiply, the markers, the pointers, faces, letterings, birds. How long still? Such a lot of wrong self he had to slough off before he could even say for certain: now the ending has begun.

In that final day and in that final night the needle of his soul swung helplessly through every degree for the lost north.

He ran to the Morgue, a Greek temple in appearance, on the quai du Marché-Neuf. It was warmer in there than on the streets, light and airy, and populous too, people of all conditions, native and tourists, some with their children, strolled in the hall, and through walls of glass viewed the naked dead of all ages and conditions on marble slabs. He asked an attendant for a sheet of notepaper and wrote to his aunt: Once I have triumphed, you will have your place on my Olympus as I have my place in your house. He added that she should not expect him home for supper 'because the night will be black and white'. Leaving, he saw a barge mooring. He waited, though he knew what it meant. The drowned arrive by boat. Pandora was lifted out and carried past him on a stretcher. She drifted, singing, said the bearers. You'd never believe it, the weight of her now. He ran to the Pont Notre-Dame, working his ring loose, and – propitiation, harbinger? – flung it where the girl had come from. Flash of light. Nothing.

He remembered that three or four years ago he had received payment from Heinrich Heine to translate more of his poems into French. The work was unfinished, the advance never paid back. He began to run towards the rue d'Amsterdam.

He had no money to repay the debt, nor could he promise to complete the commission, all he could do was beg forgiveness. What number of such failures debars you even from Purgatory? He hurried, as though the clock would strike: too late! But at the fellow-poet's door he turned away. Had he not, on precisely the same heave of conscience, made precisely the same foot-journey during an earlier sojourn in the Underworld little more than a year ago? Repetition, eternal repetitions, a very simple machine, very few possible actions, round and round, again and again and again.

He was weary to death. He remembered a priest who had told him of another priest whose particular gift was the swaling away of madness with his waxen hands. His name was abbé Dubois and he had his parish somewhere in Gentilly. He set off in that direction, rolling his shoulders, perhaps to propel himself more forcefully through the flurries of snow.

As though in a dream (a dreamer dreams he wakes), he found himself in a curiosity shop in the rue de Valois, stock-still, merely waiting. He turned, clockwise, very slowly, searching, and soon saw what he did not know he was looking for. Only then did he notice the proprietor observing him. The very thing, sir. It belonged to the Queen of Sheba. I have a certificate saying so. Not expensive, said Nerval, making the purchase.

He crossed the river with no thought of drowning. He saw the abbé Dubois' white hands, felt them on his burning head. But in the rue de la Reine-Blanche, nowhere near Gentilly, all the virtue went out of him and he entered a café where an old woman was singing to a sick child and a ragpicker was reading the tarot. Nerval looked over his shoulder. Happy man, he said. Ordered wine for the woman, the ragman and himself. Sat apart by the stove and fell asleep. When he woke, the child and the ragman were both sleeping. The woman smiled at him. He drank off his wine, bowed to her and the *patron*, and in no hurry now began the return into the heart of Paris, to a street that while he slept had surfaced from the back of his mind.

4

From behind the ruins of Châtelet prison, leaving the slaughterhouse and carrying its blood and offal, the rue Pied-de-Boeuf after forty yards or so joined the rue de la Boucherie which itself, running parallel to the Seine, narrowing, darkening and descending, entered the rue de la Vieille-Lanterne. Lover of beauty, it was to that corner, in the zone of the dungeons, torture-chambers and places of execution, of the abattoirs and tanneries and of the gutters and sewers by which they passed their slops into the river, that in the night of 26 January 1855 Nerval walked through the dirty snow to die. People lived in that underworld, they had their being, went about their business, through slits they saw the sky or, on their level, the river bearing away the ordures and the drowned. He had been down there before, often, as though to assure himself that a place existed in which his nightmares and his horrors would always feel at home. That world, that real world of the city's streets. This street dropped lower by a flight of a dozen steps. Here there was a public baths (only think of its waters), a locksmith under the sign of a large key, and a lodging house under the sign of a lantern. Seven steps down was a landing, just to the left of which a sewer spilled out through a grille from the *marché* Saint-Jacques. The locksmith had a pet raven, it perched on the key, and uttered the words J'ai soif! again and again. Dr Blanche said afterwards: he saw his madness face to face. He went where he would see it, on a date (twice thirteen) that fitted because it was doubly ill-omened. The crow said: Your gift has left you, you will thirst for ever. There were five further steps, to the very floor. There he found a stone, placed it on the bottom step, climbed up on it and threaded a cord which he believed had laced the stays of the Queen of Sheba, around the third bar of the sewer-grille; and of the two ends he made a noose. Against the cold – which had dropped to 18 below – he was wearing everything he owned: the black *redingote*, two calico shirts, two flannel waistcoats, grey cloth trousers, patent leather shoes, reddish-brown cotton socks, a black collar, his black collapsible top hat. In his pockets were scraps of his writings, his old passport to the Orient and a white handkerchief. The day was beginning its efforts to get light, hopeless down there, on the floor, between cakey walls, under the locksmith's thirsty raven. He took off his hat, fitted the noose, firmly replaced his hat. Then kicked the stone away, swung out and tolled there, choking, his feet only a couple of inches above a resting place. When they found him, just before six, in that cold, he was still warm and his right hand was still moving. They bled him, uselessly. They carried him over the Pont au Change, displayed him on the marble in the morgue and sent for Gautier to come and identify him.

That same year the rue de la Vieille-Lanterne and all its foul connections, the leprous habitations, the cloaca, the slurried public square, the places of butchery and flaying, all were obliterated. It has been calculated that the grille he hung from in his comical hat was just below the curtain of the present Théâtre de la Ville (formerly Théâtre Sarah-Bernhardt) – in fact, exactly below where the prompter sits and helps the actors and actresses in their nightly comedies and tragedies, when they forget their lines.

Neighbourhood Watch

YOU NEVER SAW THE mother. You saw the father, the son and the grandfather, but never the mother. Well, hardly ever. Once in a while Mr S. drew up passenger-side on, and in less than thirty seconds a person in black, very probably his wife, mother of the only child, daughter-in-law of the grandfather, passed from the front door, down the garden path, through the garden gate, into Mr S.'s black Austin, and away.

41 Parsons Road is a corner house. It stood then on quite a large but rather barren plot. Mr S., in his chatty fashion, told Tomek the postman, the neighbours and anyone who, passing, showed the slightest interest, that he had plans, patience, patience, one day it would be beautiful. First, said Tomek, I suppose you'll finish off those trees. Very first, said Mr S. I promise you. And he stood by his motor car looking up at them. They were the tall lopped trunks of what had been three overwhelming leylandii. They stood side by side, only a few feet between them, for all the world like remnants of Golgotha. Each towards its top, at a point of torsion, had forked and with the fat stubs of that fork stood now gesturing through the circling kites at heaven. The previous owners of the property, failing, getting out in a panic, had settled with the tree-surgeons for only that amount of surgery on those three trees. The money had sufficed for a fourth, isolated at a little distance from the grisly trio, to be taken right down to a comfortable stump on which the

grandfather, early every morning, wearing a white fez and a black silk dressing gown, smoked the cigarettes he was not allowed to smoke indoors and took a tot of something. Yes, said Mr S., bear with us. They will be felled. And topsoil, said the postman, pointing at the lawn. Your predecessors did more harm than good, I'm sorry to say. We'll make amends, said Mr S. Believe me, sir. We'll bring the place to life again. Herbaceous borders, said Tomek, raised beds, a proper bit of lawn for the grandchildren. That sort of thing. Mr S. beamed. Exactly so, he said. You need a few tons of topsoil, said Tomek. And I've got a mate who knows where it's to be had.

The S. family had moved in towards the end of April, very discreetly, overnight. Mr S. had one cousin who ran a taxi firm and another who traded as 'Man with a Van'. They shuttled to and fro. So there was no daylight spectacle of wide-open pantechnicon and private possessions. The near neighbours woke, as from a dream, with a lingering sense of hushed, almost surreptitious, busyness. At daybreak, in a light frost, there was nothing to be seen. But behind newly hung and drawn curtains Mr S. and his family were in residence.

That corner, that very house, stood on the joint of two school routes. Down the hill, turning left at the three flayed and beheaded trees, came babies, infants, toddlers and children up to Year 6 with parents and guardians, making along Parsons Road to St Mary's. And in a contrary stream along Parsons Road, turning right at the trees and climbing the hill, came Years 7 to 13, unaccompanied, heading towards St Bartholomew's. These two throngs of young life passed through one another in the colours of a commonwealth of many races, creeds, ancestral lands and tongues. Mr S., up early, stood at his gate, smiling and unnoticed. Behind him the grandfather, an old sleeveless jerkin over his silk, sat smoking the day's first cigarette. When the children were all gone by, Mr S. looked up at the three dire trunks and said to his father, You'd expect a few leaves sprouting all the same. I've seen them doing very well on less than that. And to himself, as his – the head of the household's – decision, he added, I'll have them down, as soon as can be.

Across the road at No. 42 lived an elderly couple who doted on their grandchildren. Indoors the wife arranged and re-arranged her hoard of photographs and works of art. But the husband made his love external in a multitude of garden gnomes at various tasks and pastimes with all the necessary tackle. And on the walls, roof and chimney stack of his semi he affixed a display of Christmas lights that people came from miles around to see. Arriving in April, Mr S. could not have known the magnitude of the illuminations in store for him. Several frames and outlines were left in situ from one year to the next; but they were skeletons, ghosts of the real thing, which itself, when it materialised, exceeded belief. You wait, said Tomek. It's like a nuclear power station exploding. I wouldn't live here for a fortune. Your one hope, boss, is that he falls off the chimney and breaks his neck. He fell off last year but as luck would have it he landed on a blown-up Santa and suffered only minor injuries. Live and let live, said Mr S. mildly. All very well, said Tomek. But that gentleman is raving mad.

St John's Day, and still not a leaf on the three gibbets. Mr S. confided to the postman that his son, studying management at the local College of Further Education, had 'mental health issues'. I'm sorry to hear it, said the postman. But you'd never guess. Whereas with him over there it's as clear as daylight that he's barking.

It was obvious to any outside observer – Mrs May, for example, at her bedroom window in No. 39 – that Mr S. loved his black Austin with all his heart and with all his soul and with all his might. He made limited use of it; his trips, as any neighbour idling in a front garden could have told you, were only local. But without fail, every day except Friday, he put on a pair of white gloves and spent a good half hour washing and polishing it and hoovering its insides. He stood back, admiring, stepped forward, stroked the bonnet and the roof. His motor car! He parked it with the greatest care and always, if possible, exactly outside his house; very close to, but never quite touching, the kerb; and always, except on those rare occasions when he collected and returned Mrs S., driver's-side on to his garden gate. If he couldn't get the home space, he parked as near to it as he could. His distress then was clear to every witness. He appeared at the front bedroom window and stood there waiting for the only berth that gave him peace of mind. Seeing it vacated, he hurried, visibly close to panic, to fetch the vehicle from where he had been forced to leave it back to where it belonged. You could imagine him ceasing to drive it altogether so anxious was he to keep it always safe at his garden gate. In this harmless compulsion he was terribly on view, terribly at the mercy of anyone who might have wished him ill.

The son did indeed look rather nervous, but Tomek was quite right: you'd never have guessed he had issues with his head. Smartly dressed, he walked briskly from the house soon after eight and returned soon after five. He was dark, quite small, very slim, with very fine features, extraordinarily appealing eyes, and with his father's punctiliously manicured hands. He said good-morning and good-afternoon to the daily neighbours and looked for all the world like a young man who, if not exactly happy, did have a purpose and was pursuing it. His grandfather, however, had a manner most thought downright rude. In all weathers, sometimes wearing a second jerkin or holding up a black umbrella between his head and the kites and Heaven, he sat there on the dead stump, smoking and sipping, at the young man's going out and at his coming in. Passers-by, cheered by this disreputable character, raised a hand in salute or smiled or said hello and got nothing in reply but a look; and the look, that he expended on the adults and the laughing, larking, singing children alike, was baleful.

Ah, those children! There were girls in headscarves and gowned to their ankles, beautiful as Sulamith; others in skirts as short as they could get away with, leggy, mouthy, unbiddable. Two black kids posed for a selfie against a laburnum. Most had leads in their ears so that while they dealt with the outside world they heard a wildly elating music in their heads. One girl carried a white cello on her back, large almost as herself. You saw adolescence on a boy's upper lip, heard it in his throat, saw it in the looks and uncertainty of the girl he couldn't keep his eyes off. And through this crowd shoving towards St Bart's came the contraflow of parents and grandparents with slings and push-chairs and toddlers by the hand and older siblings on scooters, passing towards St Mary's. Oh the revelry of it, whatever the weather! Twice daily, that torrent of possibilities passed before the Three Dry Trees and under the eyes of Mr S. Senior whose only look on the world was baleful.

Midsummer. Soon they would disperse. And gather again, same-and-different children, not in Creche but in Nursery, not in Nursery but in Foundation, in Year 7 not 6, Big School not Little, their losses made up with newcomers, a constant tide of zest against the hurts and disappointments, the betrayals and the trauma, the always new children, the joyous revolt of the living against the dying and against the dead who should bury the dead. Heedless, headlong, the children, upsurge of the last-hope future, we nearer death salute you!

Boss, how you love that motor car! said Tomek. I do, sir, said Mr S. And let me tell you why. That beauty is one of the very last all-British models ever to roll off an assembly line. I count myself lucky to own her. Tomek nodded. You ready for your topsoil yet? he asked. Not quite yet, Mr S. answered. But soon, very soon. And Mrs S.? Haven't seen her for a while. Not ailing, I hope? Not ailing, I thank you. But much as she usually is. Tomek was without guile. Some people he liked, some people he didn't like. But he was quite without guile. And Mr S. sensed this. Thank you, sir, he said, his eyes more pleading than appealing, his manner more placatory, more apotropaic, than polite, the whole gesture of his body more suppliant than engaging… You are very kind, he said. Life is not always easy. We do our best, Mrs S. and I, and our dear boy who has his peculiar troubles, and my father who lately has not found it easy to be a member of the human race. But what good fortune to land up here! Here indeed – in you, sir, for one – we have met with the kindness of strangers which is a very present help along the way. In his far too open face Mr S.'s eyes were red-rimmed and watery. His smile was a plea for mercy. The news, you know, every day, many times a day, the terrible terrible news. Tomek patted him on the shoulder. The news isn't your fault, Mr S. Mustn't take it personally.

The fond grandfather at No. 42, everything ready, everything checked and checked again, at 6 pm on the second Sunday in Advent pulled the lever under his stairs. Mr S., forewarned but forgetfully absorbed in his own concerns, was out cleaning his Austin's glove-compartment with one of those miniature hoovers some use for crumbs on table-cloths. He felt a shock as though No. 42 had flung the whole voltage through his, Mr S.'s, slight corporeal frame. The lights came on not just with a dazzling brightness but also with a din and with frenzied movements. Troating of bolting reindeer, clarions of flapping angels, glug–glug–glug of obesely waddling turkeys. And over it all, high up on the chimney pot, Santa himself was shown in a searchlight, raising one red leg over the hole, to go down, and ho-ho-hoing as loud as Beelzebub. A jack-in-a-box sprang from his sack, shrieked, and vanished.

The neighbours came out into the road, drivers on the hill

halted, the First Night Gathering began. Every year – this being the seventeenth – No. 42 caused a universal astonishment; and although his grandchildren had long since lost all interest, indeed had emigrated with his children to Thailand and Saudi Arabia and after various fallings-out never saw one another and never 'came home', still he had a congregation, it was in the Town's calendar, faithfully he got a write-up in the local paper, you might google him, if let, in Timbuktu and there he would appear on YouTube, with comments. His wife showed herself at the opening night and again at Epiphany when the spectacle closed, but otherwise kept mostly indoors with her knick-knacks, photographs and fading works of childish art. The first evening was by far the jolliest. 42 crossed the road for a better view and stood outside 41 with a can in his hand, to receive the customary congratulations: Amazing! Best yet! Like nothing on earth! Lager and pork chipolatas circulated. Until his stroke three years ago the very stout man from No. 28 had stood between Mr and Mrs 42 and sung 'There'll always be an England' as loud as he could, which was very loud but against Santa and his troupe and a sort of fairground music rising in lieu of smoke out of the chimney, quite inaudible. The council, until the Crash and the onset of Austerity, had made No. 42 a small grant towards his considerable costs. He was good for trade, they said. He put the town on the map. He did no harm. He was part of our heritage. The Town would be the poorer without him. There was never any trouble.

This last observation was gospel. 42 and his wife went early to bed. The sound-effects were turned off at 8.30, the lights dimmed at 9 and, on a timer, faded out with a sigh at 10 o' clock exactly. Never any trouble. Among the spectators, drinking slowly, the first astonishment soon subsided into a sadness they would have been hard put to explain. Unlike the Reverend Thomas's firework show in the Big Field a month before, 42's Santa-Fest exhausted its repertoire very quickly – in three minutes, to be precise. Santa, one red leg in the chimney pot, flung back his bearded head and bellowed Ho! Ho! Ho! His jack-in-a-box sprang, screeched and vanished, his elves tittered, and all the rest of the cast made their movements and their noises. Paused. And, led by Santa, went through them all again. And again and again, till the depletion at 8.30, the dimming at 9 and extinction at 10. It was all mechanics: ingenious, but merely repetitive. Whereas the Vicar in the Big Field gave you twenty minutes of the abundance, variety and essential unpredictability of fireworks effulgent on the starry or cloudy heavens. *Feux de joie!* And after them came the bonfire, an *auto-da-fé* of the year's wrecked furniture and fences, always an inferno beyond compare.

Still, credit where credit's due: No. 42 did his bit for the community and would be remembered and missed when death by old age or some tragic accident obliged him to desist.

But that seventeenth year's illuminations, splendid as they were, lodged themselves in the public's memory and imagination more on account of 41 than of 42. After the initial trauma dealt him by the starting-up, Mr S. stooped out of his Austin, switched off the handy little vacuum cleaner and stood staring at the explosion of traditional ideas there realised on the walls, the roof and the chimney stack of No. 42. The maker himself, standing by Mr S., gestured with his can towards Santa, the reindeer, the angels... Not bad, eh? he shouted. Mr S. looked ghastly, his complexion shifted through many shades of sorrow in the flashing and running and pervasive unsteadiness of hundreds of garish lights. He held the hoover in his white-gloved fist like a truncheon. But in truth there was nothing of the law about him. He rested himself, as though he might collapse, against the shining black body of his motor car, and stared at the show as if hell had opened up before him and he must burn in it for ever. Forgive me, sir, he said. I am obliged to go indoors. He turned, leaving 42, indifferent, at his gate.

The Three Dry Trees were flung into a semblance of surface life by the pulsing and the emanations of the electric spectacle. Chiefly they ran red, but took on also blotches and shimmerings of white, yellow, puce and a peculiarly viscous and putrescent green. The grandfather, a cigarette in one hand and a tot of rum in the other, sat on the stump – grinning! More than that, he looked – but because of the din could not be heard – to be chortling. Happiness, albeit of a baleful kind, capered on his unshaven face, his filthy white fez and his black silk gown.

Then his son, Mr S., came down the garden path carrying a meat cleaver in his bare right hand. He had torn his face with his nails and the blood ran in tears from his eyes. Behind him, on the doorstep, stood *his* son, the college student, restraining and seeking to comfort the mother. At the gate, 42, in great self-satisfaction regarding the work of his brain and hands, knew nothing until Mr S., in the unearthly din, whispered, Pardon me, sir, into his ear, and shouldered him aside. Ali and Janice, the two Community Police Officers, standing outside No. 29 and enjoying one another's company as they always had and – so they hoped – always would, for the first time ever at this harmless celebration saw that they were called upon. Mr S. raised the cleaver in both hands high above his head; looked up at the Three Dry Trees behind whose chopped and gesturing fists hung a lopsided and peakish-yellow moon; shouted, loud enough to be heard, Allahu Akbar!; and with great force and precision brought his heavy weapon down into the highly polished black dome of his beloved Austin. Wrenched it free, and demolishcd all the windows. Crouched like a hunchback, and moving anti-clockwise slashed all four tyres. The black motor car sank lower with a gasping exhalation. Janice and Ali approached.

Excuse me, sir, said Janice. Mr S. ignored her. He beat with the cleaver at every curve and ornament of his pride and joy, at the silver headlights, the heavy silver wing-mirrors, the old RAC badge, every beloved grace and appurtenance went under the cleaver. He pulled open the doors, eviscerated the seats, brained the dashboard, hacked the rosewood car-radio to smithereens and eternal silence. And all the while, through bloody tears, he sobbed to himself, Allahu Akbar!

On his stump, luridly lit, the grandfather chortled. Santa guffawed, the jack-in-a-box, the elves, the reindeer, turkeys and angels came to a crescendo of their own noises of glee and derision. The son stood with the grieving mother on the doorstep. He had pushed back the covering of her face and head and was stroking her cheeks and her white hair. There, there, Mother, he said. There, there now. It's only a car. He's done no harm. He'll be all right. We'll all be all right. It's only another car.

The Phone Call

THE PHONE RANG. I'll go, he said. Normally he left the phone to her but they were cross so perhaps he wanted to put himself even more in the right. She remained at the table. This keeps happening lately, she thought. Oh well, what if it does? He came back: It's for you. – Who is it? – He shrugged: Some man. By the time *she* came back he had cleared the table, washed the dishes and was watering the beans – *his* beans – at the far end of the garden. She stood in the conservatory, observing him and trying to make sense of the phone call. A long summer evening, birdsong, everything in the garden doing nicely. But she could tell, or thought she could, that he was watering the beans much as she supposed he had washed the dishes: to be indisputably in the right. She could almost hear the voice in his head, the aggrieved tone. Not really pitying him, nor herself either for that matter, but because she did not want it to go on till bedtime, she walked down the garden and stood by the beans that had grown high and were crimsonly in flower. She smelled the wet earth. He turned and came back from the water butt with another full can. That's good, she said. He said nothing, but he did nod his head, and she saw that the job, which he loved, was softening him. When he had emptied the can, he said, One more.

She waited, watching him, thinking about the phone call. Over his shoulder, as he finished the row, he asked, Who was

183

it then? Some man, she answered. He said he'd met me twenty years ago, on that course I went on. The husband put down the empty can and looked at her, mildly enough. What course would that be? – The course you gave me for my birthday, the poetry course in the Lake District. You said I'd been rather down in the dumps and a course writing poetry in the Lake District might buck me up. All my friends said what a nice present it was. – Oh, that course, the husband said. And the man who just phoned was on it with you, was he? – Well he says he was, but I can't for the life of me remember him. I said I could, but that was a fib. – But he remembered you all right, enough to phone you up after twenty years. – To be absolutely honest, I'm not even sure he did remember me, not me myself, if you know what I mean. He said he did, but I'm not so sure.

The husband turned away to put the can back by the water butt where it belonged. She watched, wondering more about the man who had phoned than about her husband and his questions. Did he have a name, this man? he asked, returning. Yes, he did, she answered. He said he was called Alan Egglestone. But I honestly don't remember anyone of that name on the course. I remember who the tutors were, and two or three of the other students, but I don't remember an Alan Egglestone. Then the husband said, Well it was a long phone call with a man you can't remember. You must have discovered you had something in common, to go on so long. Yes, she answered, I'm very sorry I left you with the washing-up. I couldn't see a way of ending it any sooner. I didn't have the heart to interrupt him. Now the husband looked at her as though, for some while, he had not been seeing her for what she really was. Don't look at me like that, Jack, she said. I'm not looking at you like that, he replied. I just don't know what you could find to talk about with a complete stranger for so long. Perhaps you've been on his mind for twenty years.

Perhaps he's been writing you poems for twenty years. I very much doubt it, she answered, beginning to feel tired, and not just of the conversation about a phone call, but, as happened now and then, of everything. Jack must have seen this. It was pretty obvious. Nobody else of his acquaintance lost heart quite so suddenly, quite so visibly, as his wife. I'm not getting at you, Chris, he said. You don't have to tell me anything you don't want to. I was only wondering what this Mr Egglestone had to say to you that took so long.

With the index finger of her left hand Christine pulled down and let go, again and again, her lower lip. She did this when she was nervous or puzzled or both together. It was a bad habit, annoying to other people, and she had often been scolded for it by her mother as a little girl. He told me he's got leukaemia, she said. He said he's probably only got three weeks to live. And she looked at Jack as though he might know what to make of it. But Jack shook his head: Don't give me that. You don't phone a complete stranger to tell her you'll be dead in three weeks. I never said he was a complete stranger, she answered. I said I couldn't remember him. And if he's a stranger to me, he says I'm not to him. He says we were on that poetry course together in the Lake District. And I'm in his address book. – You're in his address book? – Well there's nothing very odd about that. Why shouldn't people on a course swap addresses at the end of it if they feel it has been a special time? The fact that I can't remember him is neither here nor there really. And, let's be clear about this, it's not just me he's phoning, he's phoning everyone in his address book, he told me that at once. So he's into the w's, said Jack. Not far to go. No, he's nowhere near the w's, Christine answered. He's only in the b's. – So why, may I ask, did he phone you? – Because on the course I used my maiden name. I don't mean I told people I wasn't married. I used my maiden name because I thought that's the name I'll use if I ever get anything published. You never told me that, said Jack. Didn't I? she answered. I'm sure I did. But it's no odds whether I did or I didn't. You didn't, said Jack. And he gave her another look and went very deliberately back into the house.

Christine stayed in the garden. It was pleasant out there, quite like the country really, for a suburban place. Foxes came with their cubs in the summer early mornings and you heard them, the dog and the vixen, barking and screaming in the winter nights. And owls too sometimes, in the hospital's big trees. She stayed out, fingering her lip. She stayed until around her shoulders she felt chilly.

Indoors, Jack was watching the news. There had been another massacre. I think I'll go to bed, Christine said. He switched the television off. I'm sorry for this Mr Egglestone, he said, of course I am. But I don't see why he has to tell everyone in his address book that he's going to die. Aren't his family and a few close friends enough? And how many strangers does he have to phone a day, I wonder. He'll hardly get through them, will he, if he's only got three weeks. In the Wakelin household, Christine had become the authority on the dying Egglestone. He does have a family, she said. Three girls, to be exact. But his wife left him and took them with her when they were still at school. She said he was selfish, apparently. So he hardly ever sees his family, and he hasn't told them what his condition is. And perhaps there aren't all that many people in his address book, perhaps half of them are crossed out dead, they are in ours, and perhaps it's the old address book that his wife left behind when she cleared off and she started another for her new life and most of the addresses in the old one, the one he's working his way through now, were her side of the family and her friends anyway, they are in ours, you must admit, there'd be nobody alive in ours if I waited for contributions from you. But how should I know? I've never met the man or if I have I can't remember what he looks like or anything about him. He told me he'd just been told he'd got three weeks to live and he was going through his address book in alphabetical order and he'd reached the b's and come to me. Now can we leave it at that?

In bed Christine reflected that you shouldn't let the sun go down on your wrath because one of you might be taken by death in the night and forgiveness be prevented. But it wasn't wrath, she decided, and really they had nothing to forgive. Anyway, Jack was already asleep. Christine lay awake trying hard to remember anything whatsoever about Alan Egglestone but nothing came back to her. Instead, with sudden emotion, she remembered somebody else on that poetry course in the Lake District, Steve somebody-or-other, quite a young man, a good deal younger than her at least, which he hadn't seemed to mind but had suggested they bunk off for a walk together one afternoon when there were no workshops and everyone was supposed to be getting on with their own poems quietly. He knew the way up from the old coffin road to Alcock Tarn and beyond into the dale that was known as Michael's Dale after Wordsworth's poem about an old man who was building a sheepfold up there but his son had gone to the bad and broken his old father's heart so some days he climbed into the dale and just sat still by the work in progress 'and never lifted up a single stone'. Tears came into Christine's eyes on that line of the famous poem, the poor father, the poor disappointing son, and the young man called Steve who had obviously found her attractive enough to suggest a walk with him to places she would never have gone to on her own.

Next morning Jack got the breakfast as he always did. Nothing much wrong then, Christine thought, and quickly googled Alan Egglestone, to see whether he had become known in the passing years, but nothing came up that could possibly have anything whatsoever to do with him.

After breakfast, in fact just as she was leaving home to do her morning in Oxfam, she told Jack that Google had never heard of Alan Egglestone. So it was a waste of money on him as well, said Jack. Christine saw that Jack knew at once that he should not have said such a thing. But she left the house with only a curt goodbye before he could apologise. On the street, walking quickly, she reflected that you should no more leave the house wrathful than you should turn aside to sleep wrathful because you might go under a bus and the wrong that needed righting would remain a wrong for ever. Then quite deliberately in the back of the shop with the other Tuesday Ladies sorting out the tons of stuff families send to Oxfam or Help the Aged when a loved one dies, she thought about Steve and Alcock Tarn and the steep climb beyond into Michael's Dale. It was early June and the shallows all around the banks of the tarn were entirely black and seething with quite big tadpoles and the word 'selvaged' had come back to her out of one of the poems Hardy wrote for his wife when she died and his dead love for her revived, the white-selvaged sea, the black-selvaged tarn. Steve said that in their density but every single one of them distinct, every one of them in the mass a separate possibility of further life, each driven separately into the next stage of its life, they resembled sperm, the selvage of the tarn was spermy. And she had thought that not in the least indecent or embarrassing. Her word and his were such as might occur to you if you suddenly saw something in a new light. And when they began the climb into Michael's Dale, out of the rock face there a rowan jutted, jutted out and at once rose up, out of rock, out of very little sustenance, out and at once upwards, as it desired to, and flowered densely, creamily, in its own peculiar scent, upwards into the air, out and up over nothing, over thin air, over a sheer fall, upwards. Steve insisted that before they began the climb itself, into the dale, they should get as close as possible to where the tree started horizontally out of the ferny rock and as soon as it could aimed for the sky. He took her hand and helped her, it was almost like rock-climbing, and when they got to the place itself, the very place of the tree's emergence out of the hill, he concentrated so hard on the sight, on the thing, on the exact nature of the phenomenon, she felt, in a nice way, quite forgotten, nice because she had the double pleasure of contemplating him, his self-and-her forgetting intense attention, and the rowan tree itself by which he was so rapt.

Back home, Jack had laid the table for lunch, which he never did. He looked very hang-dog and said at once, I'm sorry, Chris, I shouldn't have said what I said. I know very well your course wasn't a waste of money, you enjoyed it, didn't you, and that's all that matters. Yes, I did enjoy it, she replied, and it did me good. All my women friends noticed the change in me. I was well for nearly two years afterwards, if you remember. Jack cheered up. Now what are we going to do about this poor bugger Egglestone? he asked. Anything or nothing? Nothing, said Christine. What *can* we do? Nothing. – I mean, he didn't say he'd phone you again, to let you know how he was getting on? And you didn't say you'd phone him? No, said Christine. No he didn't and no I didn't.

So Jack and Christine Wakelin continued their own slower courses towards their separate ends. And the phone call meanwhile continued to work in them, separately. Christine had heard Alan Egglestone's voice and could not get it out of her head. Indeed, day by day it became more present there, more insistent. Helplessly she listened to its aftertones of terror and desperation. She recalled how little she had spoken, how he had scarcely given her chance to speak, and what could she have said anyway of any use or comfort? What did he want, except not to die? Did phoning alphabetically through the address book help him in the least? All she heard now was a man talking on his own to a person who did not

remember him. She pitied him, but the dominant feeling in
her on his account was horror. And she saw Jack watching her.
She understood, and it sickened her, that they had Alan
Egglestone in common. In bed or at meals or standing side by
side doing the washing-up, one or other of them without
preamble, as though it were the only possible subject of
reflection or conversation, might wonder aloud about him,
posing a question, rhetorically, not really expecting an answer.
Or from Jack or from Christine came a speculation. Perhaps,
said Jack, he was hoping for a miracle. That would be quite
understandable. Say there are fifty people in his address book,
well perhaps one of them had heard of somebody who
stopped a leukaemia dead in its tracks, halted it, by some
miraculous means, or held it up for a while at least and won
the dying person an extra five years, or a year, even six
months? You may be right, said Christine. Though he didn't
ask me did I know any such person. She saw this made Jack
wonder again why Alan Egglestone had phoned her at all.
Then a day or two later, quite suddenly, she said, It struck me
he was maybe going through in that methodical fashion to
check there was nobody in the book he owed an apology to
or who owed him an apology and he phoned to say there
wasn't much time left for making amends. At that, visibly,
Jack's suspicions really did return: Did he ask you that? – No,
he didn't. But it has occurred to me. And later that same day,
actually interrupting Jack who was talking about something
else, she said, It's very wrong of him not to tell his wife and
children about his condition. He must want them to feel bad
when they find out he's dead. But nobody should be vindictive
when they're near the end. Phone him and tell him, said Jack
rather crossly. – I don't know his number. – There's ways of
finding out. – I don't want to find out. I don't want to speak
to him again. I don't want to hear his voice. I hear it anyway,
Jack, all the time. I don't want him adding to it in the flesh.

Once or twice Jack said outright that her Mr Egglestone was a bloody nuisance. He'd no business phoning people up like that and spoiling their lives just because he was nearing the end of his. Everybody has to die, said Jack. Why is he so special? And he looked with even greater suspicion at Christine, so that she knew he believed there were things she hadn't told him about the damned poetry course. And in town one day, trailing along with her while she did the shopping, he asked in a false-casual sort of way whether she still had anything from that course, any old letters, poems, photographs, any souvenirs at all that might help her, and him too for that matter, understand why Mr Egglestone had phoned her to tell her he was dying. No, she replied, putting the liver and bacon in her bag, if you really want to know, I threw everything in the bin one morning about two years after it when I started to feel bad again. Everything I owned about that week – it was all in a folder with a ribbon round it – I threw the whole lot in the bin, I watched through the window till the bin men had reached next-door-but-three, then I went out and threw my folder in the bin so they would certainly take it and I couldn't change my mind. That's what I did with my souvenirs of the poetry course. You never told me that, said Jack. No, I never told you that, said Christine.

Day by day Christine saw Jack looking more worriedly at her. I know what he's thinking, she said to herself. Then three weeks after the phone call, to the day, another beautiful evening, down by the beans, he was watering them and she was standing oddly to one side, half watching, half not, and fingering her lower lip in the way he didn't like but had got used to over the years, he set down the empty can and said, Chris, you're not going funny on me again, are you?

What We Are Now

1

By then – his mid-fifties – Robert Taylor had become quite well known in his subject and would occasionally be invited to give talks at other universities. Sylvia had never gone with him: he never suggested it, she never asked, he was only ever away for one night, she had things of her own to do. But when he mentioned that he would be going north in late November, to her old university, at once, surprising herself, she said, Perhaps I'll come with you. Would you mind? Delighted, he said. I suppose they might run to a double room, they won't cover your travel, of course, but we can afford it, so why not? It will be cold, but you'll wrap up. Yes, she said, I'll wrap up. I'd quite like to see the place again. Do you know, he said, I'd forgotten you were there. How odd.

After that neither spoke a word about the trip until a fortnight before its date. Then Robert said, Still want to come? It's only a student society, you know. I expect we'll be on campus in the guest house. Sylvia said that would be perfectly acceptable and she would go and book their railway tickets. Better get open returns, he said. It's a bit dearer, but we might or might not want to look round next morning.

So that was that: all set up. Sylvia felt peculiarly excited, and at least Robert did not seem to mind.

Getting beyond the Midlands, Robert said what he always said: Can't think how we ended up in the South. And Sylvia said: We should move if you feel like that. And Robert: No jobs. And once you're settled… Then he went back to his talk, underlining a few things he should emphasise, and for a good long while all he said aloud was, At least the Quiet Coach is quiet today. Sylvia read *Martha Quest* till Derby, then closed the book and watched the fast passing of the landscape outside.

Arriving punctually, the day very still, sunless, cold, Robert left her and went to find out where the bus stopped for the campus. I shouldn't think they'd stretch to a taxi, he said. And we're in good time. I'm not on till 5. Sylvia stood in the coming and going of countless strangers. She had no definite memory of pausing there, years ago, on the threshold of her adult life, but much of the feeling of it woke in her again, the fear and confusion through which pulsed a quick curiosity, the desire to learn and seize what her life needed for its furtherance, for her happiness. So she stood there in that particular place in a body that had borne three children, and felt, it is tempting to say, younger than them. But 'younger' is wrong, there is no chronology in feelings; in thinking and feeling, for good or ill, the energy is present now, on the act or event of memory comes a new upsurge of pain or joy, dread or longing, in an unstable mix, and the aging body is invested willy-nilly.

Then out of the mêlée, where Sylvia stood waiting for her husband but forgetful of him in a throng of feelings that had nothing to do with him, a man came in absolute clarity towards her, a policeman's helmet, of pink plastic, on his head, a *Guardian* newspaper in his right hand and his left outstretched to her, begging. He wore a long army coat, frayed jeans, split shoes, no socks, his face was grizzled dirty white, he stepped closer and closer and not until she was in his aura, in the smell of him, did he halt and appraise her, familiarly, insolently, aslant, and with a light of glee and triumph in his clear blue eyes. Well, well, he said, Sylvia Smith, as I live and breathe. Effulgent moment! You have come back.

She knew him by his blue eyes and the slant of his head. The rest – the clownish helmet, the begging hand, all the dereliction – fell into place the way thunder follows on forked lightning. Full recognition, into the chasm of icy shock. She saw what he had become. But worse than that, she saw back down the perspective of twenty-five years to when she had known him, and the match was terrible. She saw the horror of likelihood, of strengthening probability, of foreknowing confirmed, worst possibility become, as it was bound to, fact. Oh Alfie, she said. And wept. Well, well, he said again. Tears from the marble virgin.

Over Alfie's shoulder, through her tears, Sylvia saw Robert. He had halted and was staring at her. Seeing her look, Alfie said, Your keeper has returned. Stepped back a pace, took off his helmet, bowed low, and in his eyes when he raised them she saw an unveiled desperation. 73 Stone Street, he muttered. It's the one with a few tiles missing. I sleep late. You'll have to shout. And be warned: the toilet's fucked. Then he shoved past her into the concourse, with his left hand making gestures of cringing obsequiousness and with his right holding out the helmet, for alms.

Friend of yours? said Robert. He looked more frightened than concerned. She shook her head, then nodded it, rummaged for a handkerchief and dried her eyes. Well? – I'll tell you. Where does the bus go from? – Robert turned and strode away, Sylvia hurried after him, the wheels of their cases made an insistently fussy, bickering sound. He said over his shoulder, I suppose he goes back to your social work days.

2

I'm so sorry, Rachel said, there's been a double-booking. We'll have to go to T 57 instead. Katie said she'd wait and redirect people. Robert, Sylvia, Rachel and four or five others trailed along the corridor and up two flights of stairs to T 57, which was locked. Oh I'm so sorry, Rachel said. I'll have to go to the lodge for the key. At first there was silence, Robert clutched his briefcase very tightly and stared at the floor. Sylvia did better. She pitied the ones left, who all looked much younger than her own two girls and a boy. She asked in a general way how they liked being at their university. I was here myself many moons ago, she said. I had a wonderful time. Katie arrived with three stragglers, then Rachel with the key. Inside, Sylvia helped move the chairs and tables. Robert stood at the window looking out at a leafless tree. He's not cross, Sylvia was thinking. He's disconsolate.

There were seats for thirty but only seven were needed. Robert asked might he have some water, in case he dried up. Katie found a bottle of Buxton Sparkling in her bag. It's not been opened, she said. Robert said thank you, he could manage without a glass. Numbers rose to nine while Rachel was reading out her introduction – Robert's publications – and welcoming Mrs Taylor as well. But when Robert stood up a very large boy wearing sunglasses hunched his way out of the room mumbling apologies. Hand-outs, said Robert. As usual he had over-catered. When all had their sheets, he began.

Sylvia, at the back, over by the window, watched. She had never heard one of his talks before. She was nervous for him. In the guest house, because of Alfie, he had come close to saying he wished she had stayed at home. She wished it too. So she sat to one side, her eyes fixed on him, willing him to do himself justice in his talk. But he glanced her way so often, as though for some corroboration, that she looked down at her hands instead, that were clasped as still as she could keep them on the unpleasant table. Only when he began to forget himself and her, for the subject, did she look up again. He had his script, but he was speaking over it, without it, he had an audience, they wanted to learn, they were attending. Now if he caught Sylvia's eye, she was one among the rest, listening, and from face to face he could check how he and the subject were faring and adjust the pace, the tone, the mix of progression, recapitulation and asides, accordingly.

I'm sure you don't, he was saying, but you really must *never* think of the English Romantics as weaklings. No one should follow Coleridge's route down from the summit of Scafell – certainly nobody alone and without ropes. And consider the distances – ten, fifteen, twenty mountainous miles – he and the Wordsworths thought nothing of, before breakfast. Keats, dead of tuberculosis aged twenty-five, little Keats, trekked a thousand miles through the Lakes, the Lowlands, Northern Ireland, the Highlands, six hundred of them on foot and the rest, by whatever means, anything but comfortably. With a bad sore throat finishing at Inverness, he took a boat back to Tower Bridge and went at once into the company of his Hampstead friends, astonishing them by the far-travelled radical oddity of his appearance. Then nursed his beloved younger brother Tom through to the end. As I said at the outset, my subject today is not Keats's poetry but his determined and consequential fashioning of a life he could call his own. That first quotation on your hand-out, from a letter to Benjamin Bailey, 22 November 1817: 'The first thing that strikes me on hearing a Misfortune having befalled another is this. "Well it cannot be helped. – he will have the pleasure of trying the resources of his spirit."' Does that sound harsh, unfeeling? With absolute rigour Keats applied it to himself. See what he wrote to Benjamin Robert Haydon in May that same year: 'I must think that difficulties nerve the Spirit of a Man.' And to Bailey again, 23 January 1818: 'The best of Men have but a portion of good in them – a kind of spiritual yeast in their frames which creates the ferment of existence – by which a Man is propell'd to act and strive and buffet with Circumstance.' And this, perhaps my favourite, to Mary-Ann Jeffery, 31 May 1819 – his brother dead by then and he himself, as we might say, *mortally* in love, knowing he would not live long: 'Now I find I must buffet it – I must take my stand upon some vantage ground and begin to fight – I must choose between despair & Energy – I choose the latter...'

Sylvia listened and watched. Robert had a very open face, she saw him revealed in an oblivious candour. As he spoke, as he came more and more confidently to life in the subject, his old accent and the tone of the North surfaced. His gestures were gauche, but he meant them, his earnestness was manifest. He wore a dark suit and a tie, his thick black hair, greying a little, was neat, nothing about him was at all unkempt. But she saw that in one respect at least he felt he had a right to think of himself as Keats's fellow-wayfarer. Loving her, he had said, being loved by her, he had for the first time in his life felt confirmed and marshalled kindly on the way he wished to go. Before that era in his existence it was all contrary, always willed and effortful and solitary. She felt suddenly and with sorrow that back then, before her, already steeped in Keats, in the poems, the letters, the biographies, he had known best what it feels like to take your life in your own hands and struggle to shape it against the circumstances of class, family, misfortune and poverty. And perhaps this now was only the after-sense of it, the reviving of the memory of it in a seminar room talking to young people, younger than Keats, who – it shone in their faces – were listening. Then, still watching, still listening, Sylvia let her thoughts wander to Alfie, his dereliction, the sorry wreck of him, and she wondered how it could ever, in truth, be said of any man or woman that they shaped their lives. Perhaps the only difference was how much or how little you 'buffeted'. And with a shock of sadness she thought she might never be able to discuss that question honestly with her husband Robert.

Only Rachel, Katie and one very silent boy called Sam trailed with Robert and Sylvia through a cold drizzle to the campus café afterwards. But everybody loved your talk, Katie said. Sylvia saw that they were worried about money and when Robert went to look for the toilets she gave Rachel £30. For my share, she said. And perhaps get a bottle of wine? Soon there was some conversation, with the girls at least. Sam kept silent but looked from speaker to speaker as though this were his chance, and he must seize it, to learn what matters. Sylvia saw that Robert liked him; at times he seemed with great tact to be answering questions the boy had not dared to ask. Then he was tired, the spirit, the faith, suddenly went out of him, he looked to Sylvia – who at once reached for her coat, to end the evening. The girls were profusely grateful; Sam shuffled, mumbled, shrugged, and bowing his head hurried away.

3

In the dark, lying in her bed, Sylvia said, Do you want to talk about it? No, I don't think I do, Robert answered. – Goodnight then. – Goodnight. But soon after came his voice again, in a strange key as though he were speaking in a dream. Did you sleep with him? Sylvia stared upwards into her own length of darkness. Yes, I did, she answered. But not in the way you mean. Quite often we were together in the same bed, and we did sleep, though not much, as I remember, but that was all, more or less, I saw him naked, he was very beautiful, he had a clear white skin, he was slim and strong, he had curly hair, he reminded me of a postcard someone sent me from Athens, of a statue of Hermes, the messenger-god, by Phidias, I think, or Praxiteles, truly Alfie looked like that. – Did he ever see you naked? – No, never. He asked me, but I wouldn't let him, I wore a nightdress, we slept together, he put his arm round me, but I would never let him do anything else. I was a mess, Robert, in those days, a real mess. A long silence followed, very long it seemed, and the two of them lying apart in separate beds. Then Robert said, Go on. – Yes, well it was when I was doing my social work, as you called it, not that you know anything about it, at the start of my second year, three of four of us went out at nights into derelict buildings, an empty school, ruinous back-to-backs, that sort of thing, we were looking for men sleeping rough, there was one I remember who slept in a graveyard, he couldn't bear any sort of roof over his head, we visited him too, with soup and bread and now and then a dry blanket. I didn't know Alfie when I started all that. He was a postgraduate. I met him one morning in the library in the first term of my final year. He said straightaway that he knew a lot about me, about the soup-run, for example, and would I talk to him, he was lonely. After that he waited for me outside classes and lectures. He came and sat in my room when I was working. Till long after midnight he would stay. Everybody knew. They said I should make him leave me alone. But I wouldn't, I didn't even want to, I liked him, he was the oddest and most likeable person I'd ever met. Two or three times we slept together in that funny way, in my single bed, when I was doing my finals. It didn't hurt me, if anything it helped me, and he said he'd never been so happy in his life before, even though I wouldn't let him see me naked or even kiss me properly. He knew all manner of things. He listened to the radio most of the night when he was on his own, as he mostly was. Strange stations. He knew all the world's music, all the world's politics and what seemed to me to be the private lives of any number of people in history or in the news. He listened, he remembered, he forgot nothing. What was he supposed to be working on? Robert asked. Rimbaud, Sylvia answered. He was horrified by the thought that you would stop doing something you were supremely good at. I can't see how you could make a thesis out of that, said Robert. Perhaps not, said Sylvia. His supervisor, who was quite a conservative man, wanted him to study the logic of Rimbaud's progression from the early poems to the *Illuminations* and then to nothing. But Alf would only ponder the last thing, the nothing. Why would you thwart yourself like that? For effectively that's what he did to himself. First he did it by not writing what he *could* write. He idolised his supervisor. He said he couldn't write anything good enough to show him. So he wrote nothing. Like self-harming really. One day he came to my room and showed me Baudelaire's 'L'Héautontimorouménos'. That's me, he said. I'm the man who wounds himself. But a week later he had another take on it. Why did Rimbaud stop? Because he was honest, he said, because he saw and admitted it had all been lies. *Je me suis nourri de mensonges*, he said. I've fed on lies. Nothing he had written was binding, it was inventions, only one man's inventions, not binding on any one else and not even on himself because he was very clever and could always come up with some other quite different inventions, more lies. After that Alf was worse than ever. Lies, lies, all lies, all of you every day telling nothing but lies, feeding on lies. He looked at me and he frightened me and every bit as much he frightened himself. And sometimes it seemed grand and terrible, a noble tragic thing, terrifying and beautiful like any real tragedy. But mostly, at least when I think about it now, it just seems perverse, a sort of petulance, by his truthfulness and contempt for the diet of lies he set people against him, wilfully, perversely, whenever they began to approach him and be kind to him. For he was attractive, like a child he was endearing, with children – I've seen him – he was lovely – but he wilfully made people dislike him who might have become his friends, he halted it, he spoiled it. Self-harmer, killer of the good in him, he put everyone off who might have helped him. – Except you. – Except me, said Sylvia. And in the end I didn't help him. Perhaps I was as perverse as him. I was a coward, I know that much. Suppose he had looked on my naked body and found it wanting? Suppose I had become his lover and a disappointment? As I said, Robert, I was a mess back then. After Finals I only went home for a day or two. Then I came back here. He wanted me with him. He had no home to go to. His father was long dead and he couldn't get on with his mother, I guess because she loved him too much – he was her only child – and he worried her sick. He got to university because a teacher, whom he worshipped, hauled him out of his dumbness, shyness, clumsiness, self-lacerating oafishness and made him listen, speak, work. Here it was the same. The tutor he adored, who became his supervisor, saw the gifts in him, made him work, and he got a First. And you have seen him now, Robert, what he has become. – From the back I saw him, in that silly hat and that filthy coat. – When we were young, Robert, he made me laugh. With him I laughed as never before or since. I owe him merriment, thanks to him I know what mirth is, day after day laughing, and remembering the occasions, alone or in company, laughing out loud over them again. That summer we hitched the length of Italy. He was as reckless as Shelley, he was heedless, he didn't care where we went, what we ate, what we saw or didn't see, where we slept. He clowned and nattered, he had excellent French and good Italian, only in a foreign tongue did he ever speak clearly, otherwise it was all thick Geordie, fluent long sentences, stream of consciousness eloquence, laced with Beckett, Joyce, and the poets, any number of lines and stanzas of poetry, in a thick Geordie mumble. He made me laugh, Robert, I rejoiced,

I was braver with him, I liked myself better when he and I were together. – And still you wouldn't fuck him. – No I wouldn't, no I didn't, and when you say it now, like that, in that voice, how I wish I had, oh how I wish I had, but I was a coward and deep down he terrified me. The men we took soup to, the derelict old men with the foist in their flesh, who housed among dead pigeons and broken glass, in the smell of soot and wet plaster, in the stench of their vomit and excrement, with mouths like the vents of hell, I squatted by them for hours, listening to their life-stories, I wanted to know how they got to be like that, and most often they had a reason, always a similar reason, they were doing fine, then came a blow, a misfortune, an injustice, an interference they could do nothing about, it flung them down, after it they were never the same again, they became what I saw by torchlight in the ruins, but there was a reason, an excuse, the life-excuse, there was a before and after, what might they not have done with their lives but for the dolorous stroke, they might have lived to be loved and respected in a house and home by a hearth with a loving wife, children, grandchildren, they were on course for all that, then came the thwarting that was not their fault. But Alfie terrified me because I saw he would not need any such interruption, he would make no excuse, he would go the way he was bound to go, year by year, almost imperceptibly, and become what this morning I saw him to be in his smell, no socks, pink policeman's helmet. Sylvia halted, tears halted her. I think you're wrong, said Robert. I bet he tells anyone who'll listen that he is the way he is because a girl wouldn't fuck him twenty-five years ago.

They lay apart, he listened to her crying. Now his wish to answer her back entirely left him. But nor could he comfort her. He lacked even the will or the desire to. Her grief annihilated him. At first he had felt resentment, as though in some insidious fashion she were wronging him; but then the sense of self-identity necessary to sustain that feeling deserted him. In ways he could not yet fathom he felt undone by her story, pushed aside by it into what he often feared himself to be: a person who lived by force of will alone, by hard work, without trust, fearful, incapable of any recklessness, debarred from insouciance, a man living meanly, by effort alone. It seemed to him certain that in this abominable upsurge of the past she would look again and with a colder eye on him and ask for honest answers to the questions, What is he now? How did he get like that? And then a worse thing occurred to him, worse and equally ineluctable. She would consider herself, her own self in her marriage to him, and ask how it had happened, how had she let it happen, how had she got to be where and who she now was? For it was axiomatic to Robert that all intelligent and attractive women might have married somebody else, they could all, he believed, recollect three or four other offers, they had all had several perfectly acceptable men in love with them and whenever they liked they could muse over different outcomes. Something fissures the routine and she asks herself, How did I get where I am? Must I stay there?

Robert listened to his wife sobbing herself to sleep. He lay at first in torment, then blankly, dumbly, dozing at last among rapid nightmares, until it was time to wake.

4

I'll go now, Robert said, if you don't mind. There's a train I'm allowed to catch at 9.35. So I'll go for that one. They stood together in the kitchen by the electric kettle and the makings of a breakfast but suddenly he wanted no breakfast nor even a cup of coffee. It's only 8 o' clock, Sylvia said. But he was fleeing. You come back when you like, he said. You'll surely want to look round. There's the Cathedral, of course, though nowadays you pay. I've got things I ought to finish by tomorrow, I can work on the train. You come back when you like. But do come back. She stared at him, aghast. I let you cry yourself to sleep, he said. Nobody should do that. It's wrong, it's unforgiveable. Robert, she said, don't be silly. But he would not look her in the eyes, he made no answer, he turned and hurried away.

Left alone, Sylvia decided she would have some breakfast in a sensible fashion, return the key to the lodge, order a taxi and surprise Robert waiting for the 9.35. But when the taxi came, astonishing herself, she asked to be taken to 73 Stone Street. The driver, a young man from Croatia, only a week in the job, set his sat-nav and got her there through bad traffic in twenty minutes. He looked uncertain when he saw the house, but Sylvia nodded and paid him off quickly.

She stood on the pavement, wrapped up against the cold, with her handbag and her case on its little wheels. It was a long terrace of small houses facing an identical terrace across a narrow street. No. 73 stood on the corner and still had the large downstairs windows of a shop. Just beyond, dwarfing all the houses, rose a defunct gasometer. There were indeed tiles missing from the roof of Alfie's house, quite a few; and a pane was broken – not just cracked, a triangle was missing – in the window of the room above the door; upstairs and down all the curtains were drawn. Sylvia tried the bell, but it made no sound. There was a knocker, so she knocked – and again, harder. She crouched down, pushed open the letter box, and with a rush of grief and excitement inhaled the smell of the nights of her social work, the lairs of men who sleep rough. The hall was cluttered with bicycles and pretty well carpeted with old post that had footprints on. She stood up, knocked again, waited. He had said she would have to shout. So again she crouched, held open the letter box and shouted, Alf! Alfie! It's me. But heard nothing, only smelled the damp and the disgrace.

Then behind her, from across the street, Sylvia heard: No point knocking and shouting. He's dead till noon and might just as well be after that. A fat woman in a soiled white dressing gown stood on her doorstep, arms folded. Sylvia interested her. You're not Health, she said. You're not Social Services. You're not his probation officer. You're not the police. You might be Jehovah's Witnesses, they sometimes have suitcases, but as a rule they come in pairs. I'm a friend of his, said Sylvia, from twenty-five years ago. God help you, said the woman. Take my advice and go now before you see him. I saw him yesterday, said Sylvia. More fool you then, said the woman and went indoors.

Again Sylvia crouched at the letter box and shouted through it, Alf! Alfie! On her left twenty yards away a man had halted on the pavement with his dog, to let it shit. Sylvia banged at the knocker. The man, whose face was grey and bloodshot, waited, watched. Fair enough, she said to herself, I'll visit the Cathedral. But then the curtain moved at the window above the door and through the hole in the glass Alf showed his face, ghastly as Lazarus. Don't go, he muttered. The dog had finished. Passing between Sylvia and Alf's door, its owner said, Come to take him away, have you? I wish to God you would.

Alf opened the door to Sylvia. He was wrapped in a blanket, of the sort the Salvation Army used to issue. His feet were bare, yellowish, the nails black. But from there to the hem of the blanket, though unclean, moved her with a memory of whiteness. You've come back, he said. His curls, thick on top and draggling down in ringlets, were filthy grey. Through a sordid grizzle his teeth looked mostly bad. But his lips, that she had never kissed but had loved for their eloquence in the tongues of comedy and tragedy, and his eyes, the bright intense clear blue, there the boy still lived who had entranced and troubled her. The boy stared out through a sort of palsy, fully conscious, he stared out through shades of senility, the wit, the lips, the eyes of him still in there living and knowing in what squalor they now housed.

Unbidden, Sylvia stepped over Alf's threshold and, advancing her foolish case among the bicycles, backed his door shut. The smell of him and his damp abode turned her stomach and afforced the past in her in its revolt against the present. Where shall I go? she asked. He put on a voice. This property, madam, once the corner shop in a thriving neighbourhood, would suit an upwardly mobile young couple looking to get a foot on the ladder and start a family. Downstairs and upstairs the accommodation is deceptively vile, deceptively poky, deceptively soiled by the habits of the present owner, much deteriorated, and crying out – the property, not the owner – for some loving improvement. Coffee? said Sylvia. Tea? Ah, said Alf, that would be the kitchen. Come this way. She followed him through the bicycles, over one of which lay his army coat and perched upon it the policeman's helmet. She followed him left through a smashed door half off its hinges into a lightless galley heaped with old take-aways and opened tins whose contents had been more or less eaten. On the encrusted stove stood an aluminium kettle, the kind you might buy for camping. No milk, I'm afraid, he said. Or none more recent than Midsummer Night, my birthday, you remember, and the teabag has been through the mill. But the water is as good as any on this street and coffee, yes, after a fashion I do have some, but God's bollocks, I know not where. Alfie, said Sylvia, can we just sit down somewhere? Ah, said Alf, that would be the sitting room. Upstairs I can show you later. I have a loft through a hole in the roof of which on clear nights you can see the stars. And it's there I lie with my little radio, listening, listening. But to the sitting room. Are you sure you don't want to use the toilet before we settle?

There was no furniture in the sitting room, only piles of old newspapers, and books, many open books, cd's, cassettes, a heap of coats and a black marble statue of a naked woman holding up a torch. She doesn't light up any more, Alfie said. She did once and she was good company for me to read by in the long winter evenings, but now she don't and she ain't and I am for the dark. Does your keeper think? Does he sit alone on the shore of the wide world and think? Well I do when it's too dark in here to read, as without my lady of the lamp it mostly is. Think, think, till life, liberty and the pursuit of happiness to nothingness do sink. Sit there will you, on the *Guardians*, and I'll sit here on the *Suns*. The balance, you know. Never let it be said he was unbalanced.

Sylvia sat, holding her handbag on her knees. Alf sat, wrapping the thin blanket tight around him. His face was suddenly vacated, the energy went out of him, she watched it fail and lapse, he began to tremble. She felt more horror than pity. It exceeded her. Their knees were almost touching but she watched him as across a gulf. Neither spoke, and their looks said to one another, We have nothing to say. Nothing is funny, not even blackly. The truth is abysmal, and that is that. She felt the cold and the damp, she could smell it in the air and on his breath and in his flesh, the foist, the Lazarus smell. He trembled, his eyes implored her. You need help, she said. Very slightly he shook his head, not to say, No, I don't, but as though still wondering over the fact of it and her saying it in his house. Then he bowed his face out of view, clutched the blanket into his armpits, and said nothing, only trembled. Soon she could not bear it, the silence, the trembling, the distinct smell and faint warmth of him in the fetid air. She stood up. I'll go and get help, she said. I'll fetch a doctor. That roused him. He raised his eyes, reached out for her hand, pulled her down onto the pile of damp newspapers, leaned forward, and his tongue resumed its life, faster now, its own self, the thick local muttering, closer to her, so close she breathed in the breath of it, youthful, tainted, sardonic, desperate and lyrical, the old tongue of their sorry love. You were let off, were you? He let you off, did he? I knew you were coming, I knew his name, I've known it for years, I've known for years you might come, I've been watching, listening, waiting. Till they sent me to jail, I got into English and read all the notices, and when I'd served my time I got in there again, once a week at least, and made my enquiries till the porters threw me out. If you'd come while I was in jail I'd have killed somebody. I knew he'd come here one day and I prayed to my last angel you'd tag along and so you did. I know all the trains, I guessed which one you'd be on and there I was and there you were and the last remaining angel who gives a shit for me sent him off looking for a bus so I could approach you in my best hat and speak to you and say my address. I knew you'd come. I was awake, I heard you banging, I heard you shouting my name, I wanted you to bang and shout again and again and again, nothing that good has happened to me for years. I heard the fat cow opposite speak against me and when I thought you were on the point of leaving, up I popped.

Alfie, said Sylvia, what's to be done? Marry me, he said. A hot bath, a shave, a trip to the dentist's, a new hat, I'd be as presentable as him and a lot more fun, I've still got my wits, I know all manner of things and that there under my blanket works OK or it would if a breath of hope ever breathed on it. All you've got to do, it's a small thing to ask, is marry me. I can't, Alf, said Sylvia. Why were you in jail? – Stalking, what else? She reminded me of you, she worked in the library, her name was Eleanor, still is perhaps, I was in love with her, still am perhaps, she reminds me of you, I was there when she came out of work, I followed her home, I stood all night at the bottom of her garden, I wanted to talk to her, only that, and I stood in her way just once, and said, Won't you talk to me? Leave me alone, she said, or I'll tell the police, but I couldn't so she did and still I couldn't and again she did and I went to jail. And before I came out they told me I was barred from the city centre, including the railway station, and when I came out they gave me a travel warrant to the railway station and arrested me, just about where I accosted you, and sent me back in again. But for thinking he might come and talk about Keats and you might tag along and I'd miss you, I quite liked being in jail, I was warm, I was clean, I ate three meals a day, they let me read many books and listen to the radio, they sent me to Education, for a while I was teacher's pet, I wrote little stories, very good, Alf, she said, you'll do well if you keep at it, but I fell in love with her, she reminded me of you, I wrote things that were inappropriate, she said this will have to stop, but it couldn't, I couldn't, I was in love with her, so she had me expelled. See what I'm like, Sylvia. There's good in me, much good, you won't regret it, cross my heart and hope to die if you ever regret it. I used to sit quietly in the libraries but they won't let me in now. I read all the newspapers, I knew all the news, I loved the reference section, I read articles on hamsters, bubonic plague, probability theory, Florence Nightingale, Dr Joseph Goebbels and much besides. I knew all things and haven't forgotten them either. Now I'm not allowed in the public libraries but − God is merciful − I *am* now allowed on the railway station and very often there's papers and paperbacks thrown away there. Would you like to see upstairs? Would you like to visit my mattress grave? Would you like to lie in my arms and view Orion, say, or Cassiopeia or Gemini, the loving twins? I thought not. Would you like to use the toilet before you go? Well you can't, it's fucked, I piss into bottles, I shit into plastic bags, I carry it out the back and the neighbours phone and phone, how they do phone, whom do they not phone? Parks and Gardens, they phone, the

Mortuary, Pest Control, Recycling, Health, Waterways, the Fitness Centre, you name it, they phone it and beg I be taken away. Sylvia, you saw me beautiful once, you said I was beautiful, I don't forget that, clean me up, Sylvia, bathe me in lovingkindness, I'll be like a little chimney sweep, weep, weep, clean as a water baby, if you bathe me.

Stop it, Alfie, she said. It won't do. You need help. Sylvia, he answered, Sylvie, *fille du feu*, loveliest of the amiable Gérard's daughters of fire, remember his ending, poor sod, remember I told you how he ended, by the rope, from a lamp-post, in the foulest alley in Paris, and only a crow for company. Sylvia, my love, I want someone to talk to, it's as cold as the polar star in my head, it's that cold in my heart, that cold in my balls, I'm as lonely as Christ, that's all there is to it, nothing more, nothing less. I'm Adam's nightmare: I awake and find I am true. It can't be, I cry, I cry to sleep again, I awake again, and again I find I am true. Fuck off now, leave me be, prick-teaser, marble virgin, you saw me naked, you said I was beautiful, you saw in my risen flesh that I knew your beauty, loved it sight unseen, never let, never allowed me, my hands, my lips, never allowed, not even my adoring eyes, of all its wreathèd pearls her hair she frees, not once, unclasps her warmèd jewels one by one, she never did, loosens her fragrant bodice, never, by degrees, her rich attire creeps rustling to her knees, it never did, for me, it never ever did. Why him not me, why his kids and not mine, do I not love little children, did they not come unto me and I made them laugh? But go on now, go your ways, go back to your lies, go back to your feasting on untruth three times a day. Fuck off now, if you run you'll catch the 12.35, it's straight through, that one, gets you in at 15.41, you'll be back with your keeper for tea, go back there, stay there, don't come this way again, stay where you belong, in the untruths, you missed your chance, I had a mother once, she loved me, I broke her heart, I bought this house with the

211

money she saved up for me, I've lived off her money, never claimed a penny, never burdened the state except when they jailed me and whose fault was that? Remember Florence, the market, Lerici, the beach, and that night on the hills in Calabria, ah bitter chill it was, you wanted my arms around you then, I wrapped you in my jacket, you lay on my heart on my body's warmth in my arms, so happy I was that night, like I was meant to be, you asleep on my heart and my eyes wide open on the big pulsating stars. Remember, you liar? I had an aunty once, she lived at the estuary, I cycled out to see her on one or other of my thirteen bicycles, on Sundays chiefly, she cooked me a Sunday dinner, sometimes I stayed a day or two, once I stayed a week, she did my bit of washing, mended things, I got cleaned up, she was my mother's sister, sister of mercy, widowed, childless, she looked after me, it was unconditional, she's dead now, cold in the earth, cold and mouldering in the wormy earth, you wouldn't let me see you, wouldn't let me kiss you and now after all that you won't even marry me, fuck off then, out of my house and home, go back to your keeper, go.

There was spittle, an old man's spittle, at his mouth, he wrapped the blanket tightly around him, bowed his face out of her view, she saw into his curls, they seemed to be seething, writhing. But she said to him, Robert is not my keeper, Alfie, nor do I believe you blame me, we were as we were, we are as we are, I loved you after my fashion which was cowardly, that I do concede, that I regret, who knows if I'm as I am because of that? He raised his face. Sweet love, he said, dear friend, go away now, it will pass, it always has, the fit was on me, forgive me, go now, I'll read and listen to the radio and know more things and think of you and sometimes you will even think of me. Go away now, thank you for coming, in truth I could not bear it, bless you for coming, though it is unbearable, go now.

Wrestling with the Devil
in the Run-up to Christmas

NEITHER THE WARDEN NOR his wife got to sleep very easily. They went to bed quite late; read a while; chatted a bit; then each side by side and alone tried to get to sleep. But that night, very exceptionally, they had both before too long sunk, pretty well together, deep down, when the phone rang on her side of the bed. Such alarms in that first depth of sleep, sometimes fatal, are always a thorough shock. You can't think who you are or where or why or what the devil is going on. Husband and wife *gibbered*, no other word will do to describe the sounds they made. Then she managed to say, It's for you.

Slowly coming wide awake, after a while the Warden's wife asked, Who on earth is it? That dickhead, Fox, said the Warden. He says he's locked himself in the toilet, the *women's* toilet. He says the knob came away in his hand, he couldn't fit it back on, or rather he could but it wouldn't engage with the spindle, he thinks the nut must have sheared off. Then with his fiddling around he pushed the whole thing through, he heard it fall on the other side of the door. He was left with a useless knob in his hand. Will I come over and let him out? He thinks if I come and insert the spindle I'll be able to turn the knob that side and the door will open and he'll be able to get out. And will you go? the Warden's wife asked. Why can't he phone the lodge?

Why does he have to bother you? Yes, I'll go, said the Warden. No sense bothering them in the lodge. To be honest with you, Elizabeth, I'll be glad to go and let Fox out of the ladies' toilet. Well, cover your head, said the Warden's wife. And take an umbrella and a torch. And watch your step. I will, Elizabeth, said the Warden. And you try and get back to sleep. You still there, Foxy? he said. Of course you are. I'll be right over. And he bowed and kissed his wife goodnight. She could have sworn she heard him chuckling.

In the vestibule the Warden put on a heavy mackintosh over his pyjamas and pulled a Santa Claus bonnet well down over his bald head. In the porch he swapped his slippers and bed-socks for a pair of fleece-lined wellington boots; reached the flashlight from its hook; selected the cheerfullest of his half dozen golfing umbrellas; and set off, humming something Christmassy, into the pouring rain.

The place of Arnold Fox's confinement was in the far north-eastern corner of the north (the remotest) quad. It had always been a toilet, but that amenity itself was reached through the far wall of quite a spacious, though airless, room which, in the days before there were any women, had served as a den for the college servants to go to for a smoke and to pick winners. A small effort had been made when the women arrived with their special requirements, but still its best friend would not have described that room as one you would wish to linger in. It attracted lumber, back copies of *The Angler* and *Costwold Life*, for example. Also, luckily for Arnold Fox, the larger room, though not the toilet itself, had a phone, almost never used, good for outgoing calls only and only within the College network.

The Warden rather liked the College in the dead days of the year. No students, no conferences, only a skeleton staff and the few stragglers, Fox being one of them, who seemed to have nowhere else to go and for whom the Warden had no sympathy whatsoever. They could go to Whitby, he said to Elizabeth. Why on earth not? In my day, people did. Whitby or Dungeness. A holiday, a boarding-house over Christmas, stiffened one's sinews for Hilary. Truth was, he would have liked the place for himself, all the lights turned off, to walk about in at night, from quad to quad and back again, through the little passages, with his excellent old lamp and cheery umbrella. Still, he was looking forward to rescuing Arnold Fox.

North Quad, Staircase XIII. Leaning backwards on the heavy door, the Warden shook out and folded his umbrella and left it standing just inside. The stairs were in total darkness. Of course, he might have switched on the electric lights – this is not the thirteenth century! – but it pleased him to climb by flash-lamp, smiling at the thought of Fox waiting ashamed and desperate in the Ladies' Powder Room four floors above. He took his time, paused on each landing, looked down through the big windows into the blackness of the quadrangle, and congratulated himself on his excellent health. A big man, a heavy man, but not the least breathlessness, everything working well. As Elizabeth says, I'm good for another ten years, maybe even twenty. And he felt something like gratitude to Arnold Fox for giving him this adventure, not just the exercise, testing his heart and lungs, but also the interruption of his normal life which a man needs now and then as much as he does a steady and healthy regime. Once in a while to see the world oddly, from a strange angle, this keeps a man's intelligence on its toes, as one might say. So, thank you, Foxy.

The top landing was in darkness too, but a line of light showed under the Retiring Room door. The Warden smiled. Had Fox sneaked up in the dark? Or in daylight? Either possibility amused the Warden; but the latter the more. Hours and hours, from daylight into twilight and long past midnight confined in that place and not daring, until thoroughly desperate, to phone for help!

Very quietly the Warden kneeled and applied his excellent right eye to the keyhole. Dear God, what a vision! Fox, clear as under a microscope, sat leaning against the women's toilet door. His legs stretched out and slightly apart, his hands by his sides, staring straight ahead, at the keyhole, at the Warden's eye, unseeingly, with an expression of mixed fear and sorrow that, so thought the Warden, quite exceeded his comical, but surely not tragical, plight. Enough of this, he muttered; rose to his feet, inserted the fallen spindle, turned the knob, and with some violence pushed open the room door. Fox gave a loud shout, clutched at his heart, stared but, so it seemed, could make no sense of what he saw, and put his hands over his eyes as a child might before something in the adult world quite beyond him to deal with. Oh, pull yourself together, man, said the Warden. It's me, not Beelzebub.

Fox peeped out. Oh, it's you, Warden. Oh, thank God for that! But the Warden had noticed that against the left-hand wall a pile of *Punch* and another of *Tatler* had fallen; that the drinks cupboard, hidden behind them, was revealed; and that its door, wallpapered to be inconspicuous, hung wide-open. Ah, he said. I did wonder. I almost said to Elizabeth, It was the drink he was taken short for. It was on the tip of my tongue to wonder aloud to Elizabeth whether it might not be our friend Foxy who's been imbibing and not signing this last quarter. It crossed my mind, Arnold, and the spirit moved me to the verge of sharing the suspicion with my dear wife. It's a long way to the women's toilet, I remarked, and a climb up four staircases. Plenty of such amenities are available, and far more accessible, to a man innocently walking the College in the dead of night. And I doubted, in your case, Fox, whether the *frisson* that might come of visiting a Ladies would have played much of a part.

So saying, the Warden went and kneeled among the tumbled magazines and took a close look inside the hiding-place. Not a secret sherry man, I see, nor a spirits man either. Between you, me and the doorknob, Foxy, I get Tombs to mark the levels in almost-invisible ink, and seeing any depletion, he checks if it's signed for. So not sherry, gin, whisky, brandy, ouzo, raki, poteen or meths. Claret, perhaps? Claret, said Fox in dying tones. A whole bottle? A whole bottle. Signed for? Not yet, Warden, not yet. I had been in there – he gestured over his shoulder – and coming out and heading for the cupboard and the honesty book, I fell into a sort of swoon and when I woke I found myself in utter darkness with the knob in my hand.

Tell me, Arnold Fox, said the Warden, hunkering down and bulking very close to him, this neck-tie you wear, is it some sort of statement? Any number of Fellows have asked me. Ask him yourself, I say. Am I Foxy's keeper? But now that I am in a sense your keeper – I can rejoin my beloved Elizabeth whenever I choose, taking this little chap (he held up the spindle) with me – being for a while in that sense your keeper, I ask you, Mr Fox, what exactly do you mean by your red neck-tie? And he thrust playfully at it with the bare end of the spindle. Some say you think you are Lenin, making straight the way of Our Lord Joe Stalin; others that you think you are – or wish you were – a powerful cardinal or a sex-slave of the Whore of Babylon. Which is it, Foxy? Any of them or none? Why in the name of all that's holy do you wear a red neck-tie?

In the beam of the Warden's gaze Arnold Fox's face showed the witless terror of an about-to-be-flattened rabbit. It's a long story, Warden, he squeaked. Let me let you into a secret, Foxy, said the Warden. I'm not called Warden. So call me what I'm really called! I'll tell you what, Arnold Fox: Guess my name! You can have three goes. And it has to be my real name. Not the one in the *Record* or Debrett's. And if you don't get it in three, I'll rip out the phone and lock you in here for the rest of your natural life or until Tombs or a lady or a desperate drunk breaks in, whichever is the sooner. First guess now, Foxy. Fox closed his eyes. The Warden stood up, pleased. Brian, said Fox. The Warden chortled. Oh, you're done for, Foxy. Sure as hell fire, you are done for. Brian! For pity's sake! You might as well have tried Alice.

Silence. Arnold Fox looked very down in the mouth. Another thing I keep getting asked by the Fellowship, said the Warden, is how far on are you with Habakkuk? And I'm no more able to answer that enquiry than I am the other concerning your neck-tie. It occurred to me the other night – and by the way, my wife and I have the devil of a job ever getting to sleep and quite unprecedentedly we had both together just managed it when you phoned, and that intrusion was very nearly the death of us – it occurred to me the other night while I was doing my damnedest to get to sleep that I had forgotten all I ever knew about Habakkuk. On the subject of Habakkuk nothing whatsoever came into my head except that for the past nineteen years or so he, or his book, has been what you call your 'research interest'. So the other night when my dear Elizabeth, God bless her, had got herself safely off into the Land of Nod, I *creeped* to my study and opened the Holy Bible. Not much of Habakkuk, is there, Foxy? Less even than there is of Nahum who, as I daresay you know, precedes him. In my large-print Authorised Version Habakkuk takes up not quite three pages out of a total of one thousand five hundred and sixty-six. Haggai is shorter, said Fox, in self-defence. True, said the Warden. Three quarters of a page shorter. But length isn't everything. I read the whole of Habakkuk in just under three minutes and to be honest, Foxy, I couldn't see what you have seen in it to detain you for nineteen years. Is it not much like Nahum? Or Haggai, Micah and Malachi, for that matter. I mean, the usual bloody tripe. Allahu Akbar, *avant la lettre*? Tell me, Arnold, what did I not see in Habakkuk that you have been seeing in him these nineteen years and more? But before you start, have another guess at my real name.

Fox closed his eyes. There was a deep silence, during which the Warden became aware of the trickling of a cistern behind the door Fox was leaning against. Must get that fixed, he thought. Lowers the tone. Fox opened his eyes. Your name is Jake, he said. It most certainly is not, said the Warden. Oh my, oh my, what a risible throw! And now you really are staring into the abyss. So tell me, Arnold Fox, as your time runs out, what your nineteen years of wrestling with the Book of Habakkuk have contributed to the sum of human knowledge.

Well, said Fox very glumly. There's 3:5 'Before him went the pestilence, and burning coals went forth at his feet.' True, said the Warden, but I struggle to see how that improves upon Nahum 3:3 'The horseman lifteth up both the bright sword and the glittering spear: and there is a multitude of slain, and a great number of carcases; and there is none end of their corpses; they stumble upon their corpses.' You may be right, said Fox, licking his dry lips, but, with respect, I do think Habbers 2:16 is very good value: 'Thou art filled with shame for glory: drink thou also, and let thy foreskin be uncovered: the cup of the Lord's right hand shall be turned unto thee, and shameful spewing shall be on thy glory.' Getting to the bottom of that might take a year or two, would you not agree? Pah! said the Warden. For that and this, Malachi 2:3 'Behold, I will corrupt your seed, and spread dung upon your faces, even the dung of your solemn feasts; and one shall take you away with it' – for the sweet pair of them five minutes would be more than enough. Warden, said Fox, ashen, shaking, near to tears, I have to confess I was two years, six months, one week and three days trying to make sense of my chap's 3:17-18 'Although the fig tree shall not blossom, neither shall fruit be in the vines; the labour of the olive shall fail, and the fields shall yield no meat; the flock shall be cut off from the fold, and there shall be no herd in the stalls: Yet I will rejoice in the Lord, I will joy in the God of my salvation.' And when I thought I'd got near to understanding it, a still small voice in the night told me I was as far off as Aldebaran is from our own little dead moon. Foxy, said the Warden, if that is the case, and who am I to doubt it, you would have needed, at the very least, all the years of Methuselah, which were nine hundred and sixty-nine, I believe, to have any grasp whatsoever of Haggai 2:17 'I smote you with blasting and with mildew and with hail in all the labours of your hands; yet ye turned not to me, saith the Lord.'

Arnold Fox had no answer. The Warden saw this, and said, I am reminded of a former Chaplain of this College, a willy-wet-leg by the name of Blem – or perhaps Blam, I had trouble with their vowels in those days. I came up in 1963 on a closed scholarship from a small grammar school in the parish of St Bees in the County of Cumberland, and within a week I suffered the first of a whole run of suicidally deep spiritual crises. I wrote to the aforementioned Reverend Blem, he invited me to his rooms for a cup of Camp Coffee, I told him I was sleepless on account of Matthew 18:7 'Woe unto the world because of offences! etc.' – I felt very sorry for Judas Iscariot – and Matthew 13:12 'For whosoever hath, to him shall be given, etc.' (repeated 25:29, in case we didn't get it the first time). The Rev Blem put his hand on my knee and told me he was sorry, he had no answer, he couldn't help. Matthew, he said, was not his period. And what might your period be, Chaplain? I asked. Second Temple, he replied. My specialism is the so-called Minor Prophets, Hosea to Malachi, but I omit Obadiah. Obadiah is *much* shorter than Habakkuk, said Fox miserably. So he is, said the Warden. But to return to me. I come in distress to the College Chaplain and he tells me he can't help because all he knows anything about are eleven of the twelve Minor Prophets. I'm very sorry, child, he said. On Matthew I can't help you. Who can? I asked. God knows, he answered. In this benighted place probably nobody. I tell you, Foxy, the iron entered my soul when I heard that.

The Warden sank deep into the memory of that first youthful encounter with the uselessness of a clerk in Holy Orders. Scarcely out of short trousers he had been ushered from home by his doting and wildly optimistic parents into the care of those who, far away in the South of England, *in loco parentis* were to supervise and encourage the healthy development of his body, intelligence and immortal soul. Dwelling in it all again and moving on, with a grim smile, to congratulate himself on his resistance and hard-won independence and success, he forgot all about Arnold Fox, in whom an extraordinary transformation was taking place. His trembling had ceased, his complexion was rosy, even fiery, his nostrils flaired, his feeble lank moustaches stood upright, spikey and black. His scarlet neck-tie stirred and fluttered as though too much new life-blood was pumping with great force from his heart into his face and into all his limbs. Almost as violently as from the sleep in which the encounter had begun, the Warden woke from his trance and saw Fox transformed. What the devil has got into you? he asked in alarm. I know your name, Fox cried. It has come to me out of the very cloud of unknowing that is your sinful levity. Oh bollocks, said the Warden. No, not Bollocks, said Arnold Fox, you are the Foul Fiend, your number is 666, you are the Beast, the mark of it, covered by that absurd Father Christmas cap, is on your brow, your names are many, they are legion, you toyed with Flibbertigibbet, Mahu, Modo and Smulkin, but settled in the end on Haberdicut. Haberdicut is your secret name. Proof that I have guessed right is our mutual transformation, I into youthful strength, you into feeble dotage. Give me the one-knobbed spindle. It is mine now and you are done for.

Fox, risen to his feet, in height and breadth now was quite the match of the Warden who minute by minute was visibly diminishing in energy and power to compel. Without a word he handed over the spindle and, feeling his legs giving under him, slumped into the posture of moral collapse against the toilet door. And now, Mr Haberdicut, said Fox, watch this! He strode to the phone – an ancient, black and heavy model – ripped it from its socket and dashed it to pieces on the floor. And one last thing, then I'll be off. Toppling more towers of back copies of the Senior Common Room's light reading, he knelt at the drinks cupboard and took bottle after bottle into his arms. I want you to be stinking when they find you, he said. And very slowly, with great solemnity, as though performing a sort of Black Sabbath christening, he emptied sherry, gin, whisky, brandy, vodka, raki, ouzo, poteen and meths over the Warden's red bonnet, hidden under which, he had said, was the Sign of the Beast. He went once more to the cupboard, selected a decent claret and slipped it and a fine silver corkscrew, 'for the journey', into an inside pocket of his overcoat.

Then it was over. In the open door, he said: Your dear wife, I am sure, will raise the alarm when she wakes from her blameless sleep and misses her bedfellow in his accustomed place. Tombs, I happen to know, is in Las Vegas but no doubt some other strong chap will be summoned to kick in the door. And there they will discover you, Haberdicut, fallen. By then, with a bit of deserved good luck, I shall be well on my way to I will not tell you where. Count it a blessing if you never clap eyes on me again. And live in the knowledge that I know your secret name and can harm you whenever I choose. Then Arnold Fox was gone. Through sluices of stinking drink the Warden saw the door close; faintly through the gurgling in his ears he heard the knob turn on the other side and the spindle being withdrawn. He licked his wet lips, he smiled.

Ashton and Elaine

1

ASHTON – NOT HIS REAL NAME, but even supposing he ever had a real name, nobody in this story knew it – Ashton was found behind Barmy Mick's stall late afternoon on a Saturday in the week before Christmas, as the market closed. Mick's son Kevin, a boy of eleven, found him. He went to fetch some sheets, boxes and sacking, to begin packing up, and when he lifted the tarpaulin, under which they were kept dry, there lay Ashton, shivering. Kevin covered him up again and went to tell Mick. Dad, he said, there's a coloured lad under the tarpaulin. Mick took a tilley lamp from a hook over the stall, and with it, drawing off the covering, illuminated Ashton, who lay on his back with his eyes wide open. Fetch your mam, said Mick. She was soon there. All three then, father, mother, child, stood looking down at Ashton in the light of the lamp. Day was ending in a drizzle. The lamp had a haze, a tremulous mist, of light around it.

Ashton wore a stained thin jersey, stained thin trousers that were too short for him, unfastened boots that were far too big. No socks, his bare ankles looked raw. He shivered, and stared upwards. The mother, Alice, bowed over him. What you doing there, love? she asked. Ashton, who was perhaps Kevin's age, said nothing. Mick handed the tilley to Alice and knelt down. What's your name, son? he asked. Again Ashton said nothing;

and it was not possible to tell, from his expression, whether he understood the question or not. He seemed to be clenching himself tight, as though trying not to shiver, and his face perhaps showed only that: the effort, and the failure. Mick stood up. I'd best go and fetch somebody, he said. Alice handed the lamp to Kevin, kneeled, drew one of the packing cloths over Ashton, up to his chin, and laid her hand on his forehead. Ashton closed his eyes, perhaps – who knows? – to safeguard a kindness behind his lids. But he could not stop shaking and his face, which, eyes shut, looked more exposed than ever, still manifested the struggle.

Mick came back with a policeman. Alice stood up. Kevin shone the light over Ashton. The policeman squatted down, removing his helmet and cradling it between his big hands in his lap. Ashton opened his eyes. Can you talk to us, sonny? the policeman asked. Can you tell us how you got here? The rain came on heavier. Ashton said nothing, only stared, and shook, the thin cover showed it, crumpling and twitching. Better get him moved, said the policeman, rising, putting on his helmet, turning aside, speaking into his walkie-talkie. Alice knelt again, rested her hand on Ashton's forehead. He closed his eyes.

The ambulance, first the siren then, in silence, the twirling blue light, drew attention to the scene behind Barmy Mick's stall. A score of people assembled, keeping their distance, in a half circle, all gazing, none speaking, two or three held lamps, in which the rain shone. The ambulance men, in their uniforms, were as imposing as the policeman. One knelt, Alice moved aside, he drew off the cover, and in a murmur asked questions, which got no answer, meanwhile feeling over the child's limbs and, very delicately, under his spine where it rested on the sacking. The other removed his loose boots – so bruised the feet – and with great care the two together slid him over on to the stretcher laid by. Then they lifted him and walked the ten paces to the ambulance's wide-open doors, Kevin following with the boots. The doors were closed. Slowly, quietly, the ambulance felt its way out of the market. At a distance the siren began to howl. Everyone dispersed. The last shoppers went home, the stallholders resumed their packing up.

2

The consultant on duty at the Infirmary that afternoon was Dr Fairfield, a paediatrician, a local man who, on the way to begin his shift, had called at the maternity hospital to see his daughter who had just given birth to her first child. The sister in charge undressed Ashton, still speechless, staring and shaking, and stood back, watching Dr Fairfield's face. Many times she had watched him assessing the state and the immediate needs of a child; and on the way home and sometimes in the night when she thought of her work, she saw the child in question, or perhaps a whole series of them, all hurt, all harmed, all distinct in *how* they suffered, but as the register of that, almost as the accumulating sum of it, she saw Dr Fairfield's face when he first kneeled to be at the same height as a child standing before him or looked down closely from above at a boy or a girl laid on a clean sheet on a trolley. And now, watching him as he contemplated Ashton, the sister saw something like puzzlement, like wonder, in his eyes. Many years in the job, he looked, to her, in the case of Ashton, to be being pushed to the edge of his knowledge and comprehension, to a sort of frontier, beyond which lay only a wasteland devoid of any human sense. Unspeakable, he muttered. The boy stared up at him and shook as though under the skin he was packed with raddling ice. And still his face looked tormented by the effort not to shake, as though if he shook it would be the worse for him, but to halt the shaking was beyond his strength. Among the marks on his body those on his wrists and ankles, of shackling, were perhaps, being intelligible, the easiest for the eyes and the mind to bear.

A trainee nurse came to the door. The sister kept her away and brought her message to Fairfield that the police were in reception. Tell them I'll come down when I can, he said. But it won't be soon. They'll want the clothes and the boots, I suppose. And could you ask her to find Dr Adegbie. Ask Dr Adegbie will she come up, please. Then he turned back to Ashton, spoke softly to him, rested a hand on his shoulder and began to study what had been done to him and what a doctor might be able to do to mend it.

3

Back then disappearing was a lot easier than it is now. You walked down a street, took a bus, sat among travellers at a railway station, unfilmed. Of course, children who were reported missing would be looked for by the police and sometimes also by the general public in organised search parties; but the unreported missing, why should anyone look for them? And a child who, as in Ashton's case, arrived from nowhere, speechless, unless he was on a list with a photograph or a description or sketch of what he might look like – and Ashton, the police ascertained, was not on any such list – how should a place of origin be found to return him to? The two scant bits of clothing and the cruel boots said nothing. The police labelled them and put them in a cupboard in a plastic bag. And at the Infirmary Ashton was given, first, pyjamas and later, when he could walk, clothes that fitted him comfortably so that in his outward appearance he did not look odd among the other children on the ward. He walked well enough, in a hunched and hesitant fashion, but he did not speak, though the doctors found his speech organs to be healthy. He had, moreover, keen hearing and very sharp eyes. But he would not speak. He watched. 'Watchful' was the word that came to mind whenever a doctor or a nurse remembered Ashton in the Infirmary. He was easily frightened, he had resources of terror in him that on unforeseeable occasions suddenly might be broached; but his usual state was watchful, his eyes looking out in a restless wariness.

4

The peat- and gritstone-country even today, crossed busily by trunk roads, motorways and flightpaths, surveyed unceasingly by satellites, if you once raise your eyes to it from the west side or the east, it will lie in your dreams and in the imagination high and level ever after, as a foreign zone, as a different dimension of the life of the earth. The cities for more than two centuries with blackening labour pushed up into it, climbing its streams, and the ruins are up there still. In the cities the moors feel very close. In the age of the smogs you might not often have noticed them, but the smogs are a thing of the past and from railway platforms now or from high office windows, look out east or west, you are bound to notice that the moors are there. You are very close to a zone and a form of life in the world which under the human traffic and the human litter goes down and down many thousands of feet, unimaginably dark, unimaginably old, and with not the least memory or presentiment of love or pity.

In 1850 a millowner by the name of Ferris did the usual thing and built himself a mansion outside town high above the dirt and the noise by a stream that had not been spoiled and with the open moor accessible from his garden through a small back gate. The house, which to please his wife Mr Ferris christened Astolat, was of the local stone whose appearance for a while was light and sparkling. But the smoke Mr Ferris had hoped to escape came up there on the wind, some days the very air had a bitter taste, and Astolat blackened in the look it gave to the world. Between the wars, when the mill was done for and the family went bankrupt, the Local Authority acquired it cheap, changed its name to Hollinside, and used it first as a convalescent home for men whose lungs had been ruined in the mines and the mills, and then, after the Clean Air Act, as a children's home. Quite soon the rhododendron leaves no longer dripped soot whenever it rained, the women no longer wiped the lines before they hung the washing out to dry, and the children, taken for hikes across the moor, no longer blackened their hands when they scrambled on the crags. The stone of the house stayed black, but upstairs and downstairs the many rooms let in the light through generous windows, the tiles and cladding of the conical towers reflected every weather, all indoors was brightly decorated, and the spacious sloping and terraced gardens received the southern and the western sun. The brook, steep-sided, was fenced in safely for its passage through the grounds; but the tones of voice of it, soft or ferocious as the weather dictated, lingered in the dreaming memory of the children long after they had grown up and gone elsewhere.

When Ashton came to Hollinside in the latter part of January 1963 the stream was utterly hushed in ice under feet of snow. That winter had begun in earnest on Christmas Eve, deep snow, a hardened ungiving earth, week after week, the birds dying in thousands. Hollinside, warm and cheerful indoors, stood in a scoop of frozen stillness, from where, tracking the stream, very soon you might have climbed on to England's backbone, three hundred miles of it, the long uplands, snow on snow on snow, under bright cold sunlight, bright chilling starlight, and the visitations of blizzards out of blackening skies on a wind that cut to the marrow of every living thing. Ashton, never speaking, looked enchanted by the snow. Warm and safe, the bustle and chatter of the room behind him, he was seen standing at the window, viewing a silence that perhaps, after its fashion, seemed to him kindred to his own. The wariness went out of his eyes when he contemplated the snow. He watched the frozen powder of it falling in sunny showers from the trees when the birds, small handfuls of imperilled warmth, swooped on the crumbs thrown out for them on the cleared flagstones.

Fuel and food, the doctor, the nurse, the workmen, the visiting teachers, came up to Hollinside after the snowploughs out of town. And twice a week, Mrs Edith Patterson was brought down early from Lee Farm on the moor, by her husband, Fred, in his truck, to help with the meals. She met Ashton on a Friday – he had been at Hollinside three days by then – and on the way home that evening she spoke about him in tones which caused Fred, driving very cautiously through the banks – almost a tunnel – of snow, to glance at her often. There was an excitement in her voice, and she seemed, as she talked, to be trying to understand why meeting Ashton was so important. He doesn't speak, she said. And it's not that he can't, it's that he won't. And when Fred asked how he made himself understood, she had to think about it. I don't rightly know, she answered. I don't recall that he smiled or nodded or shook his head. But he takes everything in. His teachers are sure he's learning. When he's upset, he starts shaking. But when he feels all right, he looks at you like you were a blessing on him.

Night cannot fully descend over fields of snow. It seems to hover, quivering, lit from below. The farm lights showed. The dwelling made a brave appearance, its barns and byres and useful sheds clustering round. Elaine stood watching at the big kitchen window, her gran, Edith's mother, holding her shoulders and also, above her, looking out. As the truck drew in and halted on the crunching snow, Elaine waved her right hand.

5

After the blizzard of 24 January the roads were impassable. Edith could not get to Hollinside, nor Elaine to school. The stillness around Hollinside deepened. Ashton stood at the window looking out. How immensely blurred all the outlines were! The ground fell away in soft undulations over terracing and steps. Mrs Owen, the Matron of the home, came and stood by him. He looked up at her. She saw that he was tranquil. She smiled at him, he looked away again at the vast soft forms of snow. Seeing him there, two or three other children came to the window, so that Ashton stood at the centre of a small group. And nobody spoke. Tranquilly the children and the Matron regarded the stillness which overnight, by a silent fury, had been enlarged and intensified. Thinking about Ashton later, when he and the snow had gone, the Matron felt a sort of gratitude, she felt gladdened and encouraged by him, because she was certain that in him then, in the hush after the snowstorm looking out, some hope had started in the life that he kept hidden.

Four days after the blizzard, Ashton's teacher, Miss McRae, rode in shotgun, as it were, on the first snowplough to get through to Hollinside. She noticed a change in him – nothing very concrete or easily describable, more like a shift of light over a surface of ice, snow or water. He did not speak; but a keener alertness and a more trusting openness had come into his face; and his movements, of his hands especially, were quicker and more expressive. She told him about her adventurous journey up to Hollinside, and seeing him so attentive, she chose her words very precisely. Soon after midday she was to ride down again, the snowplough in the meantime having pushed on to some of the outlying farms, Lee Farm among them, clearing a way. Leaving, Miss McRae did as she had often done before. She took a sheet of white paper and wrote in a clear hand: Goodbye, Ashton. I will see you again the day after tomorrow. Two things happened. First he nodded and smiled. And on that unprecedented sign Miss McRae would have ridden down between the ten-foot walls of snow on a high of happiness. But more happened. Ashton did more. He took the pen out of her hand and below her message, quickly and neatly, he wrote: Goodbye, Miss. I will see you on Friday. Then he gave her back the pen, bowed his head, clasped his thin shoulders and shook as though all the cold of the moors had suddenly entered him.

The big yellow snowplough came lurching up the drive. The children crowded to the windows to watch Miss McRae climb in and be carried off. Passing through the hall, she told the Matron what had happened. He can write, she said. And very fluently. It was his secret. And now he is terrified because he has given himself away. The Matron hurried to the schoolroom. Ashton was not there. Arlene, who hadn't wanted to see the snowplough, it frightened her, said that he had run off and Miss Roberts had gone after him. He was upset, Arlene said. He was making a funny noise. The Matron found him in his bed, Miss Roberts standing over him. He had drawn the blanket up over his face, gripping it very tightly. Nothing could be seen of him except his black knuckles. But the blanket itself, tugged and convulsing, gave the two women some idea of the thing possessing him.

Edith came in next morning, having missed her usual day because of the snow. They told her about Ashton's sudden writing and what it had done to him. Though he sat at the breakfast table with the other children, Edith saw that he had withdrawn into himself. He would not let anyone see into his eyes. Of course, he was by no means the only child ill at ease. Across from him sat Albert, continually making faces, but as though for himself, as though in some private place he were trying them out, all he could muster, until he might hit on one that would have the power to placate the world. And three places along from Ashton there was Barbara, who never stopped muttering, never stopped cocking her blonde head this way and that, listening, as it seemed, to arguments about herself, harsh judgements and harsher, and her in the middle, listening, defenceless. But all that day Edith watched Ashton. And when Fred came to fetch her and with infinite care very slowly drove home through ravines of snow, she said she had been thinking about it again, she felt so much better lately, and would he come in and see Mrs Owen with her tomorrow, and talk about Ashton.

Next morning early, Edith in her canteen apron and Fred in the dark suit he wore for all solemn occasions, talked to Mrs Owen about Ashton. It would be company for Elaine, Edith said; and remembered she had said this last time when they went through the whole procedure, all the forms, and pulled out when a boy might have come to them, her nerve failing. I'm better now, she said. And added, into the pause in which Mrs Owen considered them, Aren't I, Fred? Fred nodded, took her hand, and nodded again. When he's better, said Mrs Owen to Edith and Fred, why don't you take him up to the farm for a day? See how he likes it, see how you all get on.

They left it at that. But when Fred came back again in his work clothes to fetch Edith at 5, Ashton was standing in the big bay window, looking out. Their eyes met. Fred nodded, smiled, and raised his left hand in a greeting like that of an Indian chief who comes in peace. I'll swear he nearly smiled, he said to Edith, driving home.

6

Towards the end of February then, the freeze still looking set to last for ever, early on a Saturday Fred and Edith fetched Ashton out to Lee Farm, for a visit. Edith sat in the back with him and about half way home, as he stared in his silence into the climbing and winding narrows of packed snow, she told him in a few words, to prepare him, about Elaine. He faced her at once, very close, so that she felt abashed and almost fearful that by her tone of voice and her words, only a few quiet sentences, a child could be so instantly and wholly rapt into such attention. It was as though he could see her daughter in her eyes. She patted his arm, and pointed through the window at a sudden gap and a perspective over a vast tilt of snow on which showed traces of drystone walls and, far off, there stood a house, the limitless bare blue sky curving over it and behind it. That's where Elaine's dad was born, she said. He only moved to Lee Farm when he married me.

Elaine was watching for them at the window, with her gran. She waved in great excitement as the truck halted. Getting out, Ashton was hidden from her, and he kept between Edith and Fred coming into the house. Edith felt the silence deepening in him. She ushered him ahead into the big warm stone-flagged kitchen. And then it was as though the adults vanished, that is how they remembered it later, they stood back and aside and were not there, only the children were, Elaine in her best dress, a soft dark blue, short-sleeved, her left arm ending at the elbow in a bulbous flipper, her face, under black abundant curls, of startling beauty, hesitant, fearful what this newcomer would make of her, this stranger, the black boy from nowhere who would not speak – he stared, he widened his eyes looking into hers, for a long while, so it seemed, but not that he was considering her, weighing a verdict, rather that she was flooding into him, through his eyes, into his silence, and when, as it seemed, the look of her had filled him, then, very foreignly, as though this were the custom in a faraway long-lost other country, he closed his hands, crossed his arms against his breast, and bowed his face out of her sight.

You've been baking, Mother, said Fred. Edith undid Ashton's duffel-coat and hung it up. Elaine snatched hold of his left hand in her right. Come and see, she said. I know you don't talk, but Mam says I talk enough for two so we'll be all right. Come and look. And she dragged him out of the room.

7

A few days later, sitting in the schoolroom at a desk with Miss McRae, Ashton reached across her for a sheet of paper and a pen, and wrote: Elaine showed me through the window where she went sledging. Then her dad said he would come out with us if we liked. So the three of us went out. I wore my new wellingtons in the snow. Elaine's gran made a cake. Elaine's mam said I could come again if I liked. Elaine's dad said would I help him with the sheep? They are having a bad time in the snow. Here we feed the birds. – He wrote quickly and neatly but with a pause between each sentence during which, deep in his throat, he made a sound which at first was like the low insistent working of a small engine, and then more like a purring, a humming. The letters he made were not at all pinched, flattened or cramped. They were rounded, well-shaped, and making a word he joined them fluently. When I watched them forming, Miss McRae said to the Matron afterwards, it felt like watching him breathing. His letters are airy.

Anxious that, as on the first occasion, Ashton might fall into a horror at what (and now so much more) he had disclosed, Miss McRae hid her feelings under a brisk teacherly manner. Good, she said. Ashton, that is very good. And now I'll tell you what we'll do. She fetched a light blue folder from the cupboard and on it, in black capitals, she wrote: ASHTON'S WRITING. So all your work goes in here. He looked at her. His lips were pressed tight shut; but, beginning to be able to

234

read his eyes, she believed she saw triumph in them, a fierce and precarious triumph. She held open the folder, he laid that first sheet in it. I will see you again on Tuesday, she said. Perhaps you will have more to write about by then.

Driving back into town for her next pupil, Miss McRae recited the sounds that Ashton had made. Pace, pitch, rhythm and tone were all variable, which made for a great expressiveness. She improvised on a few of the possibilities. It pleased her best to begin quite high, in anxiety, move lower into exertion and concentration, settling then into contentment, a purring contentment, the lips tight shut, the tongue quite still, the humming and purring of contentment, in her throat.

8

Miss McRae could not reach Hollinside on the following Tuesday and nor, the next Saturday, could Ashton be fetched for his weekly visit to Lee Farm. Quite suddenly, in the first days of March, the thaw came and the sound of it, almost at once, was the roaring of flood. Under its carapace of ice and its muffling of snow the stream through Hollinside enlarged its bulk and soon became visible through fissures and abrupt collapses as a dark thing mottled grey and white, battering every impediment loose, ferrying all away, breaker and bearer in one, deeper, faster, more destructive and cluttered by the minute. From above, behind glass, adults and children, equally spellbound, watched.

The moor let go its dead. The trees that, tough as they were, could not withstand three months of ice, they died inside, they stood only as skeletons, gone in the roots, not holding, and the ice that had killed them, becoming water, broke them effortlessly and as mere flotsam, draggled with other life, delivered them downstream. Beasts came too, the bloated ewes, and the small stiff lambs evicted out of the womb into the snow, with bloody sockets, eyeless, they came down swirling any way round and any way up, and a long-legged colt, or somebody's dog or cat, and once, swelling monstrously, a cow, hastily the moor got rid of them. Half a shed came down, a ladder, fencing, a chicken coop, any one of which might clog a bridge so that things nobody wished to see lodged there publicly for days. The lanes themselves, as their packed snow dissolved, became fast tributaries into the bigger rivers, the Irwell, the Tame, the Etherow, the Goyt, that now, afforced, finally could heave their effluent and torpid sludge thirty, forty miles into the sea.

Ashton watched. Among others or alone if he was let, he stood at Hollinside's big windows, watching. And at nights, closing his eyes, still seeing what he had seen, he listened to its roaring, for nearly a week the melt roared near below him, by his side, with sudden particular cracks and poundings, a clatter at times, a grating and once a sustained long undulating shriek. When he slept it was the motor of his dreams, he surfaced out of sleep and still it roared, he sank again, dumbly comprehending it.

Then the fury was done with. The stream through Hollinside became its former self, a modest thing with a low and amiable voice, and over it, that first early morning of quietness, louder than it, the birdsong started up that had been held back for weeks, the first singing of birds after a winter that had killed their kind in thousands, they sang and sang on the threshold of spring in the echoing pearl-grey, silver-grey, rosy grey light. The stream made a pretty tinkling, running quickly and almost out of sight between its accustomed banks, and over it, early morning, early evening, the surviving birds made a triumphant din of song. Along the slope, under the big windows, ran tidemarks of the stream's few days and nights of violent aggrandisement, lines of leavings, some of them hideous, some ugly bits of junk, torn remnants of birds, little sodden cadavers, which the caretaker and his two sons cleared away in sacks into a skip so that the children shouldn't see them. But Ashton, the watcher, had.

9

Towards the end of April Ashton moved to Lee Farm. He had a room of his own next to Elaine's at the front of the house looking out miles over the moorland and down towards the valley and the vast conurbation. The room was light and neat and would have been their second child's, had he lived. Ashton still went down to Hollinside for lessons with Miss McRae on the days when Edith helped with the meals. But he slept all his nights at Lee Farm. On three further days Miss McRae or another teacher came to him there. That was where he lived.

After tea, Ashton and Elaine shut up the chickens for the night, and brought in the eggs. He helped Fred usher the cattle in through the muddy yard for the evening milking. He learned quickly, they were soon used to him, he flitted among them, watchful, settling them. Then he stood to one side, the cows snuffled and clattered, the machine hummed, Ashton attended. He takes it all in, Fred told Edith. I never saw a lad look like that. You'd think I'd let him into wonderland. And on Saturdays, warmly kitted out, he rode on the tractor with Fred into the top fields, to see to the sheep. Fred halted, Ashton jumped down and tugged a bale of fodder off the lifted pallet behind, leaving it where it fell. The sheep came running, they raised a great noise. Ashton climbed up again, to the next drop. When all that was done, Fred left the tractor and he and Ashton went together over a stile out of the green fields into the open moor. On the north slopes the snow still lay, very bright in the sun against the drab grass and heather. The wind felt chillier in the open. They found three dead lambs and left them lying. All their wool and flesh, the small body of them, would be gone soon. They'd be clean bones, disconnected, scattered. Fred strode off, Ashton keeping up the best he could, and halted, looking down into a snow-filled hollow. The snow had shrunk since his last visit, but still nothing showed that was any concern of his. Across the snow, from perches on the gritstone, two carrion crows regarded him and the boy. They're the ones, said Fred.

Elaine asked her mother, How old *is* Ashton? Nobody rightly knows, was her answer. About your age, I'd say – So he could be going to school like me? – Could be, said her mother, could be. Elaine did her homework at the big kitchen table while her gran and Edith got on with things. Ashton sat opposite her, drawing or writing. At first his humming and purring were a wonder to her. She didn't know what to think of it, so she had nothing to say about it either, only stared at him. But soon she got used to it, bowed her head over her work and sometimes, very quietly to herself, made a humming of her own.

Ashton drew a drystone wall with a hogg-hole through it, in great detail, all the clever fitting of the stones, and behind the wall rose the moor, and on the skyline, larger than life, sat two crows. And in his airy flowing script, with long pauses between each sentence, he wrote: Elaine's dad doesn't move his arms when he walks. He keeps them still by his sides. He stoops a bit. He goes up the hill at a steady pace. I have to run to keep up with him. He says when he was my age he was always out on the moors. He knew every rock and every stream. He says when it's a bit warmer he'll take me up there with Elaine. Then he'll teach me all the names.

Elaine looked at Ashton's writing upside down. It's better than mine, Ashton, she said. Whenever he saw Miss McRae she opened the sky-blue folder and he put his new work into it.

Once Elaine's homework was to learn a poem by heart. It's quite a sad poem, she said. But Mrs Entwhistle says it has compassion. Elaine read two lines silently, then looked away from the book and said them aloud. Ashton watched and listened. You could test me, she said, if – Unbidden, he came and sat next to her, on her left side, so close their bare arms touched. With the index finger of her right hand she pointed along the lines of verse. Their heads inclined together over the words. Then, unbidden, he covered the poem with his left hand. She looked up and in a poetry voice said:

> When I sailed out of Baltimore,
> With twice a thousand head of sheep,
> They would not eat, they would not drink,
> But bleated o'er the deep.
>
> Into the pens we crawled each day,
> To sort the living from the dead;
> And when we reached the Mersey's mouth,
> Had lost five hundred head.
>
> Yet every day and night one sheep,
> That had no fear of men or sea,
> Stuck through the bars its pleading face,
> And it was stroked by me.[3]

Ashton shook his head, disclosed the text, she studied it, he covered it, she tried again. In that way she got the poem by heart and recited it to the company over tea. Ashton helped me, she said.

After that, some evenings when she had done her homework, she fetched one of her old reading books, sat Ashton by her on her left side, and pointing along the lines read aloud to him in a clear and school-mistressy voice. Well? she said. He nodded solemnly. It's hard to tell with Ashton, she said to her mother. He's a quick learner, her mother answered. But perhaps he knows it already, said

Elaine. Best assume he doesn't, said her mother. Besides, it won't hurt to learn it again.

Elaine's class were given a project: Memories. They had to ask one or two grown-ups, the older the better, to remember things, happy or sad, childhood, going to school, getting a job, getting married, good times and bad, and you had to write them out in your English book, perhaps with photographs; or better still, if you could, make a recording of the person remembering aloud. Fred bought Elaine a small tape-recorder and said she should ask her gran to talk about growing up in the city when Queen Victoria was the Queen.

Elaine practised on her mother, to get used to pressing the right buttons and saying, Recording now! This was at the kitchen table. Ashton watched and listened. Where did you and Dad meet? she asked, in a professional sort of voice. At the British Railways Club in Gorton, Edith answered. At a dance. Then there was a silence. Ashton and Elaine looked at Edith. Go on, Mam, said Elaine. You have to say more than that. You have to talk. He came down off the moor, said Edith, looking for a wife. And he found me. Was it love at first sight? Elaine asked. Edith leaned over and pressed Stop. Mam, you're blushing, said Elaine. Go and ask your gran things, said Edith. She's a better talker than me.

A couple of evenings later Elaine called Ashton into her room. She was sitting on the bed. Listen, she said. She pressed Play. Her gran's voice started, the accent very pronounced, it was her somehow brought closer, the tone of her, almost too clearly her, and only her. She was saying, Your mam had no father growing up. She was only eighteen months when he was killed. She only knew him in photographs and what I told her about him which wasn't much. My father looked after her quite a bit. He'd come to our house for tea every Friday. Gramp, she called him. He always went through the market on his way and she'd be waiting for him on her scooter at the bus stop. He bought her oranges. They were in a brown paper bag in a shopping bag and she hung them on the handlebars of her scooter. Then she went on ahead of him. She come in round the side, shouting, Mam, he's here! Mam, he bought me some oranges! Elaine pressed Stop. She looked up at Ashton. His eyes were very wide, his lips were pressed tight shut.

10

Every year on the Sunday nearest to 12 July, weather permitting, the family went for a picnic on the moor, for Fred's birthday. That year the sky was a cloudless blue. Fred, as always, invited Edith's mother. You coming, Mother? he said. Fine day, you'll enjoy it. And she always said, It's your day, Fred. You three go. I'll stay home, thank you very much. But she baked a cake which they took with them as part of the picnic. So the day had its ritual. But that year there was Ashton. You four go, she said.

They parked in the usual place just past the Boggart Stones, mid-morning, hardly any traffic, no one else on the moor. First things first, said Fred. And he took out the spade and the sack. Back then nobody thought you shouldn't help yourself to a bit of peat if you wanted to, for the garden, for potting. Still Fred didn't like to be seen doing it, which made Edith laugh. He strode off up into the moor, into a black rift he thought of as his own, where the peat was thick and firm and where from the road he was invisible. Edith stood by the truck getting everything ready. Sunhats, she said. One each, snow white. Elaine grabbed Ashton's left hand and hauled him away, past Fred, digging, his sack already beginning to be bodied into shape by the rich black after-life of plants, the layered seasons, the compacted goodness. The children ran off. You know where we'll be, he shouted. He watched them climbing away, his surviving child and the foundling, dwindling away and above him over the rough terrain. He saw, and then faintly heard, a lark rising over them. He wished they would turn and wave, but they were intent on the climb, so small already and diminishing further, the girl a dot of skyblue, the boy a dot of red. Once he saw her stumble. Ashton was on her left side then. Fred saw her reach for him – she must have seized the sleeve of his shirt with her flipper fingers, steadied herself – and they went on, until, in the hillside, a soft ravine of peat took them out of sight. He knew the ground, every character and variation of it, as well as he did every syllable of every word of the language of his daughter's body, the growth of that vocabulary year upon year as she shaped herself to live with, and become ever more dextrous, agile and expressive despite, the born deformity. But not till they reappeared, scampering higher, did he resume his digging.

On the rocky knoll the children turned and waved down to the truck, Fred heaving in his sack of peat and the spade, Edith standing by with the hamper till he should be ready to help her with it up to the picnic place. She waved and Fred did, and the children, on cloudless blue, waved back again, semaphore of love across the sunny slope, its textures of black and brown and many greens, its vigorous yearly renewal through the blonde dead grass, the bracken unfurling, the scent-dizzy bees in the heather, the black groughs, gold gorse, soft white cotton grass and, from where the children stood, the untold acres of ripening bilberries. Looking west from up there you can see the trig point on Broadstone Hill, turn south over the reservoirs to Featherbed Moss, east gives you Wessenden and the brooks that flow into it: so you might triangulate the Pattison family's happiness that sunny day. And north, over Broadhead, Rocher and Black, over Butterly,

Warcock and Pule, by moss and hill, on and on, to the north you might open it more and more and for ever.

That night Elaine was woken by Ashton crying out. It was sounds, not words, but sounds such as she had never heard from him before, terrifying, utterly confusing her, so that for a while – too long – she did not know where she was or even who she was that she should be hearing cries of that kind. She jumped out of bed, ran from her room and was hurrying to fetch her mother – but saw that his door was open and, in the light from the landing, that he was sitting up and covering his face with his hands. Seeing that, to be an immediate help, she went in. Ashton, she said, it's all right. There's nothing the matter. You're all right. She stood by him, leaned over, he uncovered his face and she saw the depths of terror that had been in hiding behind his hands. You're all right, she said again. I'll fetch Mam and Dad. But he closed his two hands on her hand that barely emerged from the left sleeve of her nightdress, enfolded the bulb and the slewed fingers in his warm grasp, shook his head, again and again shook his head, shook through and through, she sat by him on the bed and could feel him shaking as though all the cold of all the long winters of earth had taken possession of him. He would not let her go to bring help from a grown-up person. She sat with him, old as him, till his shaking lessened, his eyes in hers, her eyes in his, he watched himself better out of hers, she saw it happening, his terror being evicted. Sat, watched, till he was quiet and he let go her hand. Then abruptly he lay down, closed his eyes, slept.

Next morning he gave her a sheet of paper on which in his airy and flowing script he had written: It was only a bad dream. Even when you are happy you can have bad dreams. Please don't tell your mam and dad. Elaine read it, nodded. OK, she said. Then she added, Ashton, why won't you talk? It'd be more fun if you talked.

11

Six weeks later Edith was ironing in the kitchen. She had her back to Ashton. He sat at the big table, drawing. In summer Edith liked to iron by the window, for the light. And she was watching for Fred coming home with her mother and Elaine. Silence, but for Ashton's humming and purring as he worked; and that was an accustomed sound, like the crackle, sighing, sudden collapses of the fire in winter, or the chickens scratting around in the yard, accustomed, one ingredient, only occasionally singled out for particular thanks, in her own reassurance. Then suddenly, from behind her: Mam? She stiffened at the shock of it, but held steady, looking out through the window at a row of geraniums in pots along the south-facing shed. She *would not* look round. Well? she said, taking another of Ashton's shirts from the basket and laying it out on the board. Mam, he said again, in an accent as though he were flesh of her flesh, Mam, our Elaine says if I start talking I could go to proper school and you and Dad would let me go in on the bus with her. – Elaine doesn't know everything, Edith answered, over her shoulder, ironing his shirt. It's not up to us to say if you'll go to proper school or not. – But if I start talking? – Well it certainly won't happen without you start talking. So the sooner you start the better, in my opinion. She reached for the next thing, a pair of his shorts. Our Elaine says you and Dad'll take us bilberrying this Sunday, he said. Very likely we will, she answered. – I can read, you know. All the books Elaine gave me, I can read, he said. I should hope you can, said Edith.

The truck pulled into the drive. They're back, Edith said. Only then did she turn to him. She saw how he questioned her face. Don't shut up now, love, she said. Not now you've made a start. Then your dad and I will ask about school.

12

On Saturday 23 November Edith took her mother to the market I called Ashton after, where he was found. Many Friday evenings Edith's grandfather, coming round for tea, had brought her oranges from there; and many Saturdays, as a child and until her marriage, she had gone there with her mother. It was the best market on that side of town, worth the trip. So two or three times a year, for a treat, mother and daughter drove down from the moor.

Barmy Mick – the third (at least) of that name – was the star of Ashton Market. His wife backed him up with teas on the row behind, and his son – a Kevin, a Jack, a Keith, a boy of eleven or twelve as he always seemed to be – helped out at the front until he grew sick of it, till he really did think his dad was barmy, till it embarrassed him scurrying among the women with their purchases; and then he vanished and was replaced by another son who looked much like him. Going back two or three times a year to Barmy Mick's, however old you got, you might well feel some good things last for ever and will never change.

Mick's customers were all women. He faced them over his trestle tables, over mounds of ladies' wear, in the sun when there was any sun, under the awning and lit by tilley lamps in the seasons of rain and cold. In frocks or macs, in hats that might be as fancy as Easter bonnets or nothing but thin plastic bags, they stood there wanting him to make them laugh.

Edith and her mother stood on the fringes, but were soon enfolded into the midst as other women came and went. Barmy by name, he was shouting, barmy by nature, and as my missus tells me twenty times a week, You get much barmier, they'll take you away. So buy 'em while you can, ladies, not three, not five, not ten, it's fifteen pairs I'm offering and the socks to match, any colour you like so long as it's red, black,

245

yellow, purple, puce, limegreen or orange, and all fluorescent, and I'm not asking ten quid, I'm not asking five, God help me, mother, I'm not even asking two pound ten, call the yellow van now, I'm asking one pound seventeen and six, for the fifteen pairs and the socks to go with 'em, match 'em how you like or go for the contrast, each foot different, suit yourself, give the old bugger a treat, it's Saturday night. That lady over there, son, that lady who looks like Audrey Hepburn, fifteen is it, madam, and the socks just as they come? And Alma Cogan, just behind you, thirty, did you say? Take that lady thirty, Kevin, and here's the socks, it's Saturday night, give the old bugger a heart attack and off you go out and find yourself something younger.

Audrey Hepburn was standing near Edith. She had a friend with her, more a Diana Dors. It's his last chance, she was saying. If this doesn't perk him up I'm off with the butcher. Kevin pushed forward with her purchase in a paper bag. One pound seventeen and six, missus, he said. – You're sure they're all in there, sonny Jim? – Kevin shrugged. Count 'em if you want, he said. Audrey Hepburn did, holding them up. Kevin waited patiently. Puce goes nicely with black, he observed. Edith was watching him. That must be the lad who found our Ashton, she said. Her mother nodded. Very like, she said. Kevin moved on to the blackly bouffant Alma Cogan, and already Mick was calling him back. Leave them ladies alone, he shouted. Thirty pairs over here, another fifteen over here, Brigitte Bardots, both of 'em.

Edith drew her mother away, out of the crowd. It was starting to drizzle. You wanted some of your ointment, Mother, she said. And I thought I'd get some chrysanths. And then we'll have a cup of tea. But she halted on the outskirts, watching the boy dash in and out of the pack of raucous women, his father's patter accompanying and directing him. He ran to and fro, quick as a ferret, bringing the purchases, taking the money, giving change out of a soft wallet on his hip, a nifty boy, shrewd and grinning, self-possessed too, with a sort of reserve in himself, as though he were thinking this won't last for ever, one day I'll be off. Still Edith hesitated. Should I not tell him who we are? she asked. Tell him our Ashton is doing well and say thank you for finding him? And Mick, and his wife who does the teas, should we not go and say thank you for looking after him and fetching the policeman and the ambulance so that he got seen to quickly and came to us? Edith's mother shook her head. Best not, I'd say, she said. The less we go back there, the better, in my opinion. Have a cup of tea, if you like, then you'll have seen all three of them, where it started. But don't go introducing yourself. That would be my advice. The less talk about our Ashton, the better.

Raining again, ladies, Mick was saying, and twenty-six shopping days to Christmas. Kit yourselves out now for the festive season. Fifteen pairs for one pound seventeen and six and the socks to match. Look very nice indeed under the mistletoe in a paper hat. Mick's your man for the Christmas spirit. All good stuff, all hand-made, all guaranteed to give lasting satisfaction. One pound seventeen and six! As my better half never tires of saying, They lock 'em up when they get like you, our Mick. Nowhere cheaper in the whole North West, except maybe Liverpool, and what woman in her right mind goes traipsing off to Liverpool?

Kevin dashed again through the crowd of women, towards Edith and her mother on the fringes. Edith looked hard, to remember him, she took in his intentness, his sharp canny eyes, the quickness and confidence of all his movements. When he was close, he caught her looking at him. She smiled at him, Thank you, Kevin, she said under her breath. And with her mother she turned and left the market.

Notes

1. Matthew 18:1-6:

   1 At the same time came the disciples unto Jesus, saying, Who is the greatest in the kingdom of heaven?

   2 And Jesus called a little child unto him, and set him in the midst of them,

   3 And said, Verily I say unto you, Except ye be converted, and become as little children, ye shall not enter into the kingdom of heaven.

   4 Whosoever therefore shall humble himself as this little child, the same is greatest in the kingdom of heaven.

   5 And whoso shall receive one such little child in my name receiveth me.

   6 But whoso shall offend one of these little ones which believe in me, it were better for him that a millstone were hanged about his neck, and that he were drowned in the depth of the sea.

2. From the French children's song 'Aux marches du palais' ('By the steps of the Palace'):

   At the four corners of the bed.
   At the four corners of the bed.
   A bouquet of periwinkles, Lonla.
   A bouquet of periwinkles.

3. From 'A Child's Pet' by W.H. Davies. Elaine makes two or three small mistakes.